TEXAS CRUEL

TEXAS CRUEL

A PSYCHEDELIC SCI-FI WESTERN

REGINA WATTS

PAINTED BLIND
PUBLISHING
LITERARY ALCHEMY

Texas Cruel
© 2023 Regina Watts
ISBN: 978-1-957469-04-1

Text: Regina Watts
Book & Cover Design: M. F. Sullivan

Regina Watts Online: hrhdegenetrix.com
Painted Blind Publishing: paintedblindpublishing.com
Join Regina's mailing list for three free stories!

For my grandfathers,
John Charles & John Henry;
and, as always, for Duane.

August 1874
Western Texas
Hot as Hell

1

SHERIFF LORENZO BLAIZE snapped open his Colt .45.

All loaded. Six bullets. Two per, if required.

Sure hoped not. Wouldn't look good come next election.

When McLintock stuck his head in the room, Lorenzo clicked the cylinder back into place.

"Bout time Feel like I been sittin here ten thousand years."

"Sorry, sir—they's here now. Were busy admirin the ladies."

"Well, what kin I expect…if Mama hadn't civilized me, I'd be liable to stare, too."

"My Mama civilized me all the time, Sheriff… sometimes she civilized me so damn hard I couldn't sit in a chair fer three days."

Laughing, his bright white teeth flashing in a peripheral mirror amid the incongruously sensual décor of his nighttime office, Lorenzo said, "Ain't that the truth. Brings back memories. Git em in."

The deputy disappeared. The sheriff remained in the stillness, the weight of his cool revolver hefty in his hand. He raised it to the light of the many lamps burning low amid the velvet drapes and fancy French wallpaper, tilting the barrel this way and that.

A fine gleam along the surface of the metal. Needed buffing.

With a quick whip, Lorenzo drew a kerchief from his pocket. He had just begun to rub out the excess oil when the Natives filed in.

Well…"Indians" was Lorenzo's first thought, but it wann't right to call em that. Folk knew damn well by now it wann't India where everybody delighted in shootin and killin and robbin each other these days.

"Presentin the, uh—the Tribe, sir."

Lorenzo narrowed his eyes at McLintock, who waved the Natives in and evaded his boss's hard stare. Dumbass. Had to do one thing to seem respectful. Just get what the hell they called themselves!

The sheriff had not planned on standing, but now he did so just to counter his employee's stupidity. He even put the gun back into its holster to promote the courtesy his bad cop had failed to provide.

And boy howdy, he was glad he did.

Comanche? Tonkawa? Lorenzo smiled amid his assessment of the tall, broad-shouldered Natives who strode into the room in a line of three. Two younger, one older. One wore nothing over his torso to show he was tattooed up to the neck in an intricate pattern of many dots that meant nothing to Lorenzo; the other wore a garment and seemed not marked at all, except for a series of bite marks scarring his forearms and neck. Some animal attack.

The older one, their ambassador and medicine man going by his grasp of English, was obscured by a kind of cloak that seemed to Lorenzo a mite too hot for the season. Made him suspicious. Armed? Likely.

"Good evening, Sheriff," began the medicine man, nodding in a very modern fashion and taking a slow seat at the sheriff's gesture. "Thank you for seeing us tonight."

"I will admit, I was not particularly excited to be roused at such an hour." The Sheriff checked his pocket watch with a quick, familiar gesture that made the warriors flinch; still smiling, he tucked it back into his waistcoat and said, "Half past midnight."

"We have traveled very far looking for help and at last were directed to you. After all our trouble, we are most eager to present you with our petition."

"Petitioned many people?"

"No. We require a specific intersection of will and ability that we have not yet perceived."

"You got a very fine way of speaking English, my Native friend."

"You should hear me in my language."

"Which is?"

The old man smiled. His tattooed Brave, who evidently understood, made a noise like a small snort. The scarred one did not react.

"With all due respect, Sheriff…teaching the White Men the names of our Peoples has only given you power over us. You must never ask our name."

Lorenzo arched a blonde brow and exchanged a look with McLintock.

"Now, uh, friend…"

Facing the Natives totally again, Lorenzo folded his hands upon the desk and regarded all three visitors at once.

"I understand that things are different between you folks, but fer…*us*, fer folks livin in towns and cities and so on, we gotta know a fella's name before we kin do business."

"Then you may do business with me. Call me 'White Serpent.'"

With a glance at the man's fading hair, Lorenzo nodded. "Well, Serpent, it's good to meet you. I'm Sheriff Lorenzo Blaize. Welcome to my little town of Sandspur. Now…what exactly is it you reckon I kin help with?"

"Horses."

Was that all?

"Well"—Lorenzo contorted his mouth in a favorable, casual way as he leaned back in his seat, his hands folding over his black waistcoat with his sigh—"yeah, I reckon that might be somethin I kin help you folks with, dependin on the payment and the purpose. Ain't plannin nothin a fella like me wouldn't care t'hear nothin about, is yeh?"

"We wish only to defend what little is still ours from the Comanche people."

Lorenzo sucked a tooth. "Comanche! Now there's a tribe name I wish I *didn't* know these days."

"They are an erratic and dangerous band who have recently come to believe they have a specific reason to attack us. Our people are nomadic, but we are not horsemen as talented as the Comanche people and need far more horses if we are going to survive their interest in us."

Stroking his jaw, Lorenzo nodded in consideration of White Serpent's plea. Sounded likely enough. "These Comanche are more—what'd you call em—'erratic' all the time, fer sure."

"Unfortunately, as more land is lost and more buffalo are slaughtered, they only fight harder; and because we have actively dissuaded the Tonkawa People from assisting in their fight, we are viewed as enemies. We are gifted only that the particular medicine man who is leading his people against us is not supported by most Comanche—not after he permitted so many of his people to die in the battle at the trading post near Adobe Walls a few months ago."

"Ah, hell! I heard all about that—I know the sonnabitch y'er talkin about. What the hell's his name?"

White Serpent looked thoughtful for a few seconds. "He was called something else once, but my people were brought news of his name change around the time we were warned of his intention to strike against us. His medicine having proved less mighty than he claimed, his People are now calling him 'Isa-tai.' I am not sure how to say it in English. Something like…'the hindquarters of a she-wolf.'"

Choking with surprise, Lorenzo laughed and exchanged a glance with McLintock. The deputy's moustache quivered as the sheriff exclaimed, "'Wolf Cunt!' That's what you mean, I think—'Wolf Cunt.'" Still laughing, Lorenzo shook his head. "Y'all sure do have some sense'a humor. Made a lotta folk mad to earn a name like that."

The medicine man did not laugh.

"Yes. Most of his followers have abandoned him, but he still has a band of several hundred who believe his lies. So long as he lives, he will not stop fighting. Not until he has been completely abandoned and forced onto a reservation."

Damn. Old boy may have lost a bad battle to lose, but with a name like 'Wolf Cunt,' Sheriff Blaize couldn't help thinkin this here Tribe was dealin with a real sonnabitch. Gonna have to be worth his while if he was gonna get involved.

"I'd like t'help you, Serpent, but what kin you offer me? You know I'm happy to send any number of horses t'any man who'd buy them…but they ain't cheap horses."

White Serpent nodded. "I did not believe any horses would be cheap, and it is true that my People produce little that would intrigue most White Men. However…I believe that a wise man might see what I have to offer, and understand what it is."

"And what is it you have t'offer me?"

"A business opportunity," said the medicine man, revealing his arm to draw a cigar box from the depths of the furs.

Now, Lorenzo had thought that the fella in the back of the room had been bitten up fierce. But the medicine man, this old White Serpent? Sweet Jesus swingin in the breeze, that bastard's arms were *gnarled* with scars!

One could not help but stare. The arm Serpent extended to rest the box on Lorenzo's desk looked like an old tree branch that'd been struck by lightnin. Scars covered scars, an elaborate network of them working their way from the back of his hand and up along the bicep that disappeared back into his cloak.

Only when the arm disappeared did Lorenzo snap out of his trance and regard the cigar box.

The box itself was not noteworthy; but, if he were not mistaken, it was…making some kind of noise.

A scratching.

Looking curiously up at the Natives, Lorenzo lifted the lid with both hands.

The scorpions hissed from within, their spiked tails stabbing the air a few inches from his thumbs.

Lorenzo flew up from the desk and the cigar box and his toppling chair with a sharp, "Oh, Jesus!" that made McLintock unholster his six-shooter. The Braves leapt to respond, springing between the deputy and their shaman with knives already in hand.

"What the hell is *this* supposed to be," demanded the affronted sheriff, his pride wounded. Lorenzo wiped his sweaty palms over the front of his waistcoat and stared into the writhing black mass. "Some kind of joke?"

"No joke, Sheriff. This is our trade offering. For three hundred head of horses, we will offer you six hundred head of scorpions—a fine start to any breeding operation, and infinitely more valuable to you than three hundred horses will ever be to me in my remaining lifetime."

"And what in the hell am I supposed to do with six hundred heada scorpions? The ten in this box is already too many!"

"You have not yet seen what the scorpions can do, my brother."

Mouth firm, Lorenzo awaited an explanation.

White Serpent slapped the scarred Brave on the arm and got his attention for a few short words in their native tongue.

Nodding, a certain light of eagerness in his eyes, the Brave stepped up to the desk. Catching the sheriff's eye meaningfully, he then lowered his head, settled on a scorpion, and reached into the writhing box.

The nasty little bastards hissed and pinched, nine tails darting reflexively as the Brave abducted one of their number. He shut the lid with one hand while holding the chosen scorpion by its tail with the other.

Then, turning his hand palm-up, the scarred Brave lowered himself into the seat that White Serpent vacated for him.

The scorpion's tail lashed into his wrist so quick that Lorenzo barely saw the sting before the Brave cried out.

A certain sense of ignorant smugness washed over Lorenzo. Now what the hell else had he expected to happen?

But while the falling scorpion was caught and replaced in the box by the medicine man, a change came over the stung Brave's face. All his panting contortions of sharp pain melted abruptly into broad, smooth-browed relief. His eyes grew dim with the lowering of his eyelids and his mouth sagged open as though in astonishment.

While the muscles of the Brave relaxed into the cradle of his chair, Serpent looked at Lorenzo.

"This is the scorpion my tribe calls the World-Maker. They are sacred to my People; to our rites of passage; to the construction of the very universe. It is only with great reluctance that we ask you for help, and with greater reluctance that we would offer them—but the time has come for the creature that created us to also defend us in this hostile new world."

The Brave made a noise of wonder, his mouth unmoving but his throat and tongue working. As though in a dream. Was this stuff like opium? Interesting.

White Serpent studied the dreamer. "The World-Maker offers visions of a place that has no name, from which all life flows. It brings a man's soul down to Earth. Perhaps the scorpions have asked us to offer them to you now because they intend to help the White Men as they have helped us; and, in so doing, they will give us the tools to flee the Comanche."

While the Brave twitched in his seat, Lorenzo lowered slowly into his own. He folded his hands between him and the box.

"So it's jes some kind of spiritual thing? I don't know if I kin do much with that."

"The scorpion is used for far more than communication with ancestors in the no-space. My people turn to the scorpion for many matters. The abatement of pain; the incitement of pleasure."

The sheriff tapped his foot.

If it were some kinda routine he was observing, it was damn convincing. Lorenzo was liable to suspect they very well believed it themselves. Any man that let himself get stung up by a scorpion musta had a damn good reason fer it.

And if it did turn out that these scorpions—their venom, at least—was worth good money, Lorenzo would be the only distributor in the United States. Hell: the world.

Ain't harm nothin to give't some thought.

"Where yeh fellas say yeh needed them horses delivered?"

"Just north of the New Mexico Territory border. My son will help you chart a course. He knows the scorpions and the land, both. He will help you navigate the horses to us, and will also return with the scorpions to stay with you a time and guide your people in their care."

"That yer son?"

Nodding to the tattooed English-speaker, White Serpent said, "Roaring Bear will take my place when my time has come. Trading with and educating you will be a good experience for him."

Lorenzo placed a hand on the box before him, his fingers drumming.

"Well, I do have a great respect fer the intellect of the Native Peoples, and yer business advice is certainly worth thinkin about. And, hell…these days, to me? Three hundred horses, I don't find that too painful to see go at the right price. Question is, kin I make these here scorpions fetch me the right price."

"I have been led to understand that you are a man with far-reaching arms and a great many interests."

"Whoo-wee, my ears *have* been burnin lately, at that…you have been led t'understand correctly, my friend. Remember who told yehs that?"

"Your deputy recommended you highly when we encountered him north of here. So?" As the drugged Brave at his elbow stirred enough to turn his head a few degrees, White Serpent looked the sheriff in the eye. "Do we have a deal?"

The box beneath Lorenzo's hand shivered in lurid promise.

"What say you fellas stay with us awhiles and give me a little time t'think?"

"There is not much time left."

"I ain't fixinta make you folks wait here all month, now…jes a couplea days. Time to ruminate. Research the merchandise."

After a few long heartbeats of consideration, White Serpent nodded. "We may be able to stay on for as much as a week; but if, at the end of seven days, you have still not come to a decision, we must withdraw our offer."

Lorenzo nodded. "That's perfectly reasonable, my friend. Jes give me a little time to turn it over in my head…I'm sure, if nothin else, we kin find someone else to help yehs."

"I fear, Sheriff, that if you cannot assist me, we will have few reasonable options remaining. Please—think sincerely about the matter."

"I will. I swear I will. But!" Slapping his desk and putting on the charm again, Blaize rose. "I heard you fellas had yer eyes on the merchandise! Jes so happens I know the proprietress of this fine establish quite well…how about we have a chat with her about what we kin do to make yer time in Sandspur second to none."

2

THE FINAL MEMBER of the posse to be killed by the Needless Man openly wept, his empty hands held high.

"Please—please, I ain't ready to die!"

"Then when the warden woke yeh up fer yer funeral, yeh shoulda told him 'Go to hell.'"

With the gun he had taken off the body of the second lawman, the Needless Man put the last one down. The corpse flopped back, stone-eyed and mouth hangin wide.

He lowered the empty gun.

Fronds of desert grass shifted somewheres behind him.

The hammer of whichever gun Jimmy'd grabbed clicked down.

"You and I both know you kain't reload that gun faster'n I kin shoot this one, Rhodes."

The Needless Man said nothing. Jimmy stepped from the gramas with his gun leading the way.

"Now, here's the score. Ain't fixinta hurtcha, but I gotta git on and, frankly, I ain't none too keen on the thoughta yeh comin by my sister's home with me. She ain't liable to treat me kindly fer it, neither."

"Y'er makin a mistake, Felder."

Jimmy spat into the dirt, shoving the gun into the Man's back when he moved. "Don't turn around."

"Don't point a gun at me."

His empty Schofield swinging like a blackjack, the Man dropped from outta Jimmy's way and let him spend a round in thin air. When he came back up he grabbed holda the hot revolver and twisted Jimmy's arm hard at the elbow.

Somehow, the weaselly bastard rolled with it. All the posse lay dead—and there they were, two prisoners busted out and fightin over not a damn thing. The gun discharged once in the air and Jimmy ducked away from the sound.

His back to the ridge dropping sharply off behind them, the Man bared his teeth and very nearly had the weapon out of his former cellmate's wily hand.

Then the snake lunged forward, knocking the Needless Man back to the edge of the ridge.

Next thing the Man knew, he was flat on his back with Jim Felder's grubby fingers still in his open mouth.

Suspended in that half-second before Jim realized the gold tooth was loose.

But even with his eyes fresh open from having his bell rung cold out the blue, the Needless Man knew the tooth was out of place.

Only one thing for it. Bite down, and hard: like an animal, a demon.

"Son of a whore!"

The Man's jaw tensed until skin split. Lean muscle tore. Jim's efforts to extricate his digits only served to hasten one's severance as the Needless Man's front teeth caught down at the joint and slid sharply between two fragments of spurting bone.

It had not been very long since he had tasted blood, but the taste of blood in the free air had a different signification. The copper tang gladdened his heart such that he did not even wince when his fellow escapee stomped him in the throat to free himself. The Needless man kept on biting, snapping his teeth shut like that bastard snapping turtle back in Louisiana.

A finger gave.

The wrong one.

With a third of his middle finger having slipped down into the back of the Man's throat, Jim somehow managed to contort the remainder of his hand out of harm's way—thumb and forefinger, and one bloody gold tooth that receded into the darkness along with the gasping, scrambling, cursing traitor. Up he leapt, to the back of the edgy horse that was off and runnin afore he'd done more than lay an arm along its back.

Still, Jimmy made it up.

Too bad. Guessed he really was the stage-robber he'd bragged to be.

The Man sat up and spat the mouthful of Jim's blood onto the dirt.

Underbrush cracked in the distance. Jimmy getting farther all the time. Make enough noise, and he'd end up bumping into somebody liable to do something about him… if word of the escape had traveled fast enough.

Some men would enjoy the thought of that; of being Wanted with a big, hard, capital fuck-off letter 'W,' and a fella's likeness sketched at every street corner or saloon.

And if that were the case, and Jimmy got sent back up, the Man'd never get his tooth back.

The Needless Man stared off into the darkness. No question of where Jim'd show up sooner or later. Could the Man get there first? Probably not—didn't know the way.

However, being aware that he had not the least shot of getting there first, the Needless Man could now reprioritize.

There was little doubt that Jimmy's scream as he disappeared into the brush was likely to attract the attention of the law, assumin there were any lawmen left, but God had yet to craft a figure of authority who meant anything more to the Needless Man than a temporary and forgettable obstacle. Nor was he concerned about findin his way in the night, or clothin himself proper, or how he'd git to where he needed gittin. Jes so happened the law was kind enough to provide all that fer'im, the posse havin been armed and ready to shoot the very instant they set eyes on the prisoners.

Took'im twenty minutes to climb back to the top of the ridge down which he had evidently plunged. In that time, a body woulda expected to be descended upon by a fella with a gun, if there were any left interested in playin the bad odds.

Unhurried, the Needless Man picked through the corpses for the least bloodstained of their clothes. He dressed, savoring the crispness of the fresh air near the Pecos. When he really listened through the silence of night it rushed in the distance, laughter in its voice and his heart.

Dressed, with a plundered gun belt and the Schofield in its holster, the Needless Man looked for any one of the several horses left alive after he and Jimmy laid their ambush. He finally found one nervously grazing, and it did not discriminate much between its master and the Man what killed'im so long as whatever human what approached it did it slow and quiet. Jes glad the shootin was done.

He and the horse made their way down the ridge together, takin their sweet, safe time.

Then, on the plain, they traveled south.

Horse was tired already and more tired still when they'd been movin south an hour. Lucky fer it, the Man was tired, too. They rested together in the protection offered by a sumptuous muhly patch and set out again when the sun had risen. The Pecos marked the path, and the mountains developin to greater effect told him how many miles they'd already traveled since the breakout. Ain't much in the way of food save the horse, but there was a little jerky in the saddlebag. He did not feel particular urgency and did not think it would come to eatin his means of transportation.

Texas was vast and hotter than the devil's dick. Maybe he mighta been more eager to get a move-on if he and the horse were not able to watch the riverbanks reduce toward a more sufferable ford with every mile farther south. With all that foliage and these mountains and even plentiful timber upon 'em, seemed to the Man that there'd be good game if'n he really need it.

But he had somethin else to hunt. Ain't interested in takin no time chasin down bighorns.

And, sure enough, his focus was rewarded come nightfall.

He had not anticipated he would find a church of any denomination sittin alongside what musta been one of the more commonly used routes to Sandspur, but he supposed the itchy fingers of the men who said they loved Jesus had a way of creepin and crawlin into whatever corners might provide them even the scent of gold. Why travel about like most preachers when it was easier to sit in the middle of a web and let 'em come to you?

The horse strained away from him when he dismounted, its eyes still black with the terrors of what it had witnessed before it was stolen. Maybe it did discriminate after all. He tied it up and went inside, banging the door heavily open and peering within.

Empty still. Preacher musta been asleep in the back. Probably on top of the money box.

Dark wood boards creaked beneath the Man's feet, all the house of God straining away from him as had the horse.

Jesus was nowhere to be found around the altar. Protestant. Least they didn't pretend their religion had much of a damn thing to do with the sad sonnabitch, though they'd try to have you whipped for claiming it didn't.

What good things Jesus had brought into the world! Damn good thing the Man had been so acquainted with the good news, because it very clearly had served to make him a good, upstanding individual.

A door in the back of the building implied a rectory attachment, which he opened with a sneer for the missing lock.

Three rooms: a small office, a squat little kitchen that stood off of it, and one last room with one last shut door.

His gun in his hand, his black hat pushed back upon his head, the Man rifled through the office desk to get a little attention.

He had opened two drawers when the final door burst open. A youngish preacher, wide-eyed and disheveled in his long underwear, emerged with a shaking six-shooter in his hands.

"Now hold on a minute! Jes what the hell you think you're doin?"

"Lookin."

"I can plainly see *that*. I mean, what are you *doin*, lookin in my desk at all hours? Turn on that lamp!"

He did, mostly to keep the preacher's eyes on his free hand.

The scrawny man of God narrowed his eyes.

"Do I know you? I don't think I've seen you here before."

"You ain't. Never will agin, neither. Hopin mebbe yeh kin help me."

"I cannot help you while you stand holding a gun in my office, sir."

"Never know when a preacher's gonna pop out the bedroom with one of his own."

The Man lowered his gun to the desk and sat slowly in the chair. The preacher did not fully relax, but his shoulders lowered. His breathing might have changed, too. At the very least, the young man's cheekbones were no longer quite so taut.

"I reckon that's not an unreasonable point," said the preacher, still pointing the gun and still obviously wary. "How about you put that gun away proper, and I'll do away with mine? We can talk."

"Don't want t'encourage yeh to change yer mind about speaking civilly to me. Know a family by the name Felder?"

Taken aback by the question and its banal nature, the preacher's tongue darted across his cracked lips. "There's a dead fella by that name, buried in the cemetery out back. Son's in prison fer puttin him there, last I heard."

"That's *last* you heard. Now, you heard different. He got a sister?"

Preacher-man found his footing again. His face tightened up and so did his shoulders and hand.

"I think you oughta leave, Mister. I don't have the information you're looking for."

"Oh…I think you do."

"I don't. But you know who might? Deputy McLintock."

"McLintock…that does sound familiar."

"Reckon Jimmy musta had a few choice words to say about the fellow criminal what cozied up to Sheriff Blaize down in Sandspur right at election time. Human nature. So, you knew Jimmy? What'd they put you in the jug for?"

"That's a rude question t'ask a fella."

"The Lord knows all already," cautioned the preacher. "I think He has sent you here tonight so I may give you an opportunity to change your ways. It is time to learn the moral path—the paven one, rather than the one of mud and stones."

"If you will excuse me, Preacher, I prefer horseback anyway. Lookin forward to these trains goin farther and farther across the continent, too…but, I digress. Where's the Felder woman living these days?"

"I told you. I don't know the answer to your—"

The Man's fast hand snatched the revolver from the desk while he ducked his large body from the chair to the floor.

Just as soon as the preacher blew a round into the wall, the Man sprang up and shot the gun out of a hand left bright red with a bloody little stigmata.

"Ah! Oh, Jesus—"

While the preacher collapsed, the Man rose from the desk with the revolver still trained.

"He ain't here, Preacher. You forgot to put'im on yer cross."

Another shot shrieked through the air and pinged against the preacher's abandoned revolver, which whirled wildly off into a corner of the office.

"I won't repeat myself."

His lips tight, his beady eyes darting between his far-off gun and the one pointed directly at him, the preacher listened to the voice of God.

"She and her husband—their ranch is south of Sandspur, on the other side of the Pecos. A day's ride from here, maybe. Oh, ah—" His voice rose to an effeminate height on the pain. The preacher gripped his bloody hand, the wound pulsing more blood against his fingers with every heartbeat. "Ah, they have—they have *many* cowhands employed. If you're thinking of trying something—"

"How many?"

Sweat dripped down the preacher's face as he talked. The Man listened, the gun fixed on him all the while. He took advice on everything from the layout of the ranch and its approximate number of buildings to the measure of the family's cattle. He got everything he could.

When it was over, he nodded.

"This is all very innerestin, preacher, and I thank you fer recoverin yer memory fer my sake."

"Now please," hissed the preacher, his eyes blazing with hatred for the man who had, truth be told, lightly interrogated his prisoner. "Please, go."

"Don't worry. I ain't got no more business with yeh… assumin that's all true."

"It is."

Nodding, the Needless Man slid away his gun.

Eyes bright with the chance, the preacher lunged for the lost weapon in the corner.

Neither the Man nor the Schofield hesitated.

3

ORLENA'S BOWELS WERE all twisted up while, upon the outhouse seat, she sweated and sobbed and gnashed her teeth.

The cramps had woken her up a night earlier than expected. When they came early, they came bad. Every clot's passage was a knife in her uterus. And the effects upon her digestion?

Unladylike, to say the least.

No, ma'am. There weren't nothing ladylike about being a lady, and that was the brutal truth. Once you mixed motherhood into it? Then you were dealing with disgusting things all the time.

Not that most women weren't already.

She was in that cold little outhouse long enough to doze off, the blood splattering her thighs and the stench of menstrual excrement having lost all meaning to her. It was damn depressing waking up like that....more damn depressing to know she was gonna have to wash herself with perfectly good water, which seemed capable of drying up any day in this heat.

Worst of all, she'd been so surprised by the blood that she hadn't filled the bottle serving as her manual bidet. Now, still slick, she had to gingerly limp to fill it from the pump.

On the way, she paused to listen.

Nothing.

Not a thing.

Just the wind.

Orlena tried not to worry about what it meant, that empty sound of the wind. She cleaned herself off without thinking too deeply and got a pair of britches she could line with a wood pulp bandage.

Inside the house, she thought about getting back into bed, but the sheets on her side were wet with new stains and there was just no point in it.

After shuffling about in her dressing closet for her housedress, she lit a lamp in the parlor and sat down with the latest entry of some dime novel she generally pretended to be for the boy's bedtime stories.

Damn. God damn. Good God, Christ-whipping damn! It was bad tonight. Her heart raced, the breath panting from her mouth as she tried to focus on the text. Normally she loved reading these tales of adventure in the West, but sometimes they had a way of incensing her suffering.

For instance, not a one of them ever captured the baseline of profound suffering that one endured in simply *being* a woman. Hell, look at Orlena! She had to stop after a column of text and put the magazine down because her hands were sweating so fiercely against the pain that all she accomplished was smudging the damn ink. Groaning, pressing her stained hand to her forehead, she curled into herself in the corner of the sofa.

If Bert's balls felt the way her uterus did, you can rest assured his pretty little ass wouldn't do a damn thing. One of these mornings, she'd tell them to get their own damn breakfast.

The clenching of her teeth and occasional moans that seemed to release some of the pain into the air almost kept her from perceiving the bird call. It flew in from the winda and into her ear, through her brain, then out the other ear just before she realized birds had no more business being up at two in the morning than she did. No birds but owls, anyway.

And that weren't no owl calling to her outside.

Gasping slightly, the pain an echo of itself at once, Orlena stumbled up and rushed through the house on stocking-feet. The lamp trembling back and forth in her uneasy hand bathed her in a halo too small to be of comfort as she slipped out to the porch.

"Jimmy," she whispered, straining through the darkness for a sign of motion. "Jimmy?"

"Down here, Orlena."

She had hoped, but had somehow not *really* expected it to be him—to be his voice, ringing out to her through the dark. Now her heart sped differently. She rushed down from the porch, dashing through the dark to the splashing water that formed the background of her brother's voice.

Soon, it was more than a voice. Soon, it was a darker silhouette than the darkness; then, it was a man, stooped with his face under the water he pumped as quietly as she'd ever seen a man manage the task. As though the water hushed itself to cooperate with him.

The world had always seemed like that around Jimmy, though. Least, it had until he went to prison—but, when he did, she had known in her heart somehow that circumstances would contrive to permit his release. Fate could not be so cruel! He had never done anything wrong. Never done nothin but help his sister.

Finally seeing his face after three damn years made her cry out in love-pain and yield to the cramps she could not ignore. Orlena collapsed to her knees before him, illuminating his pretty face as he caught her in his arms.

"Careful, baby, careful—"

"Oh, Jimmy!"

Sobbing, Orlena kissed his unshaven cheek a few rapid times before remembering to put her lantern beside them. Thus liberated, she threw her arms around his shoulders and wept into his neck as quietly as she could. The stubble of his beard hurt her tender skin, but she did not care one whit.

"I never thought they'd do it," she told him when at last he peeled her soggy face away from him and admired it in the life. "Jimmy, oh, Jesus—"

"Well I thank you fer yer vote of confidence," he said with a wry laugh, releasing her to resume taking some relief from the grit of the Texas countryside.

"I believed in *you*, Jim. It was jes—when those boys came round talkin about gettin you out a few days ago, I didn't believe it."

"And you shouldn't have. I got my own damn self out—and Rhodes, but I reckon the law's got him by now…if'n he kin even walk after his fall."

"Rhodes?"

"Fella I did time with. Big, mean Black bastard. Real nuts. Figured if I broke loose with him, they wouldn't even think twice about me. So far, I don't think they have."

Her eyes, adjusting to the darkness, revealed a horse pawing the dirt twenty yards or so away from the house. "That ain't yer horse, Jimmy, and I know that fer a fact. They leave it fer you along with whatever the hell they slipped you to manage this?"

"How about you let me impart the information you require as you require it, so as not to burden yer clearly anxious mind with more concerns. I don't suppose, Orlena—"

Jimmy rested back on his haunches, his big, blue eyes turning to her from beneath a slightly cocked brow that mirrored the dark lock against his forehead.

"—that you could sneak a hungry man a bite t'eat?"

She had been planning to. The Stone Hill Gang had sent a pair of emissaries by to inform Orlena of their intention to free her brother, and to ask her if she might act as a temporary safe haven if he got diverted while making his way back to them. As she had told Jimmy, it seemed like a fantasy that she did not expect to take root in reality—but, reality has a way of surprising a woman.

While his horse took water of its own, Orlena parked her brother in the barn and crept into her house like a thief in her own kitchen. In a way, she was. Quiet, so quiet, she lit the stove and asked herself just what she was going to feed him.

Before she knew it, she was making cornbread at three in the morning and consulting the options for more substantial fare. She had been thinking of using the meat for a stew, but after taking it from the ice box and considering the size of the portion, sausage would be just the thing.

Of course, the metallic groan of the meat grinder was noise enough that she was braced to defend herself. Any moment, the man or the boy would walk in and criticize her for burning lamps in the kitchen outbuilding and kicking up a ruckus at such an early hour...but, to her surprise, there was nothing.

She got through grinding and was even halfway through cooking breakfast before she began to get suspicious.

Mouth firm-set, Orlena flipped the contents of the skillet, then turned with a brisk wipe of her hands along her apron.

Through the winda, a small silhouette stood in the barn door.

Explained the quiet.

This damn night was longer all the time.

Exhausted, wanting nothing more than to go back to bed with a hot water bottle, she stormed out to the barn with her brother's plate of cornbread, eggs, peppers, and sausage.

The boy was out there with him, having heard noises outside—or been awoken by his mother's earlier rising. The mere idea made her sour even before she heard their laughter.

"How about that! I love those, too. You ever—"

Orlena strode smartly into the barn, clearing her throat and earning an alarmed glance from the boy.

"You know damn well you're supposed to be in bed right now."

"But Mama—"

"Git on in that house this instant."

The boy turned pleading eyes toward Jimmy. His uncle dropped a big hand upon the back of his head and ruffled his hair, saying, "Aw, now, 'sall right. I'll see yeh agin real soon!"

Heartened, glancing one more time at his mother, the boy darted into the house. Jimmy watched him go with a smile that fell when he saw his sister's face.

"What?"

"Don't you 'what' me, James Cornelius Felder, you know damn well 'what.'"

"Well *hell*, Orlena, kain't a man out of prison see his—his nephew?"

Orlena looked away from him to step out of the barn and slap the eavesdropping child over his ear, hissing the command, "Git," as he hurried off with a whine and a hiccupped little sob.

Jimmy's tone soured when she stepped back in.

"Now what the hell you gotta do a thing like that to'im fer?"

"So he don't grow up and turn out a criminal like *you*." Arms folded tight, Orlena inhaled sharply and perched upon a bale of hay. "How's the food?"

"Good, damn good…sure do miss yer cookin', Orlena." Using a bit of cornbread to mop up the sausage grease, Jimmy looked thoughtfully at his plate, then up at his sister. His blue eye had that mischievous brightness.

"You oughta come with me."

"What? *No*, Jimmy, to where?"

"Gonna go meet up with the fellas and go on a job, and then—"

Orlena looked sharply at him, her jaw falling open. "A job?"

"Yeah! The hell you think? They ain't busted me out from the kindnessa their hearts."

"You mean you got broken out of prison jes to be put right back *in*? Jimmy, what—"

"Nah, Orlena, you don't understand. This is an open-and-shut thing, easy as hell. Some kinda big score once it's sold to the right buyer—enough to let a man settle down even when split thirteen ways, properly invested and managed."

"What the hell kind of score could do *that*?" With an urgent look toward the house and then back to her brother, she whispered, "You ain't fixinta do something the Federal government might come after you fer, are yeh?"

"What? No, Orlena, and don't you worry if I ever do… nah, it ain't nothin like that. You know, uh, that Italian fella runnin Sandspur? You know, that sonnabitch that stole our election."

"Lorenzo Blaize? He's half Italian, at best."

"Half Italian's half more'n anybody needs, if you ask me. Anyway, his boys are anticipatin a delivery of certain goods, and I have every intention of assistin in the acquisition of those goods out from under their noses. Then, it's on with my life. Oh, that was good!"

Having inhaled his food in record time, Jimmy cast the metal plate aside and wiped his greasy fingers on his trousers. Orlena regarded this affectation grimly while he said, "Hate to say I'm in a hurry, since that horse carried my sorry rear end fer what I may only imagine was the longest twenty-four hours it has yet to live, but is there any chance I could trouble yeh fer a little whiskey, a bowl of water, a razor and some soap as fast as you kin deliver 'em?"

"I thought you said you was in a hurry."

"I am, I am at that…but mebbe, if you see me lookin a little more civilized, you'll have second thoughts about refusin my offer to come along."

Repressing a smile, Orlena strode over to pick up the plate. "That'll never happen, no matter how damn close yeh shave…"

Her hand was on the plate. One hand. The other was braced lightly against her thigh.

That braced one was the hand he touched. His fingers slid around hers and her heart quickened. Orlena studied the plate, frozen in motion.

"I missed you."

His words ringing like a slap, she stepped away and withdrew her hand.

"I'll be back in a few minutes. Don't go anywhere."

Inside the house, her husband's heavy breathing echoed through each room. She treaded softly along the wall, slipping into their bedroom where the boy had likewise fallen into more silent slumber in his cot.

Soundless, every board cooperating with her, she crossed to the dressing table and removed the leather shaving kit she'd ordered for her husband's birthday.

His snore ended abruptly.

Orlena froze, her hands tight around the edges of the leather case.

Her ears buzzing with pressure that outfitted her limbs with a fine impulse to urgency, Orlena's body prepared to spring into motion at the lightest sign.

Her husband's snore renewed itself.

Orlena exhaled softly and took the shaving kit from the bedroom.

With a flask a whiskey, a mirror, and a bowl of water she heated on a kettle whose contents went partially into her water bottle, she made her careful way back out through the kitchen door and across the long way to the barn.

The sky was still dark, and the hour was surely not yet four, but the day already seemed to be coming upon them somehow.

Orlena asked herself each step of the way if this would be the last day that she ever saw her brother.

Would she feel anything about it, this moment, looking back on it from some obscure future? Would she feel good that she helped him? Bad that she didn't stop him? If something went wrong, and he died out there on that job, or was shot by the law, or finally got himself hanged, she had to reckon she'd feel awful about this day.

But Jimmy was unflappable, and when his smile lit to see her step into the barn, she realized it was not her responsibility to stop him. He could have just as easily done all this without being diverted, and then she would have never seen him at all. Never could have had a chance to stop him.

Instead, here was an opportunity to enjoy a sliver of him. Her brother. A moment in time that, in all likelihood, would form the final moment of an era upon which she would someday reminisce.

"What an angel you are…say, you havin yer monthlies? And waitin on me hand and foot!" While his sister put down his shaving equipment and retreated with the hot water bottle, Jimmy shook his head and said, "Y'er too good to me, Orlena."

"That's one thing you got right. What was it like in prison?"

"Ah, not much different than I wrote yeh in my letters. Stand here, walk there, stand here, show me yer hands, blah, blah, blah…Rhodes was an all right sorta guy to git stuck with, at least."

"The man you escaped with?"

"Uh-huh, the very same. Mean bastard, but good to his word…that didn't stop me from leavin him behind when the time was right, of course. Thought I had one up on him, but he's a hell of a fighter! He was about to smash my head open until I got lucky and tripped him down this ridge…"

While Jimmy spoke, he slowly unwrapped a hand that Orlena had, at best, half-noticed to be covered by a sleeve too long for his wrist.

It was not a sleeve at all, but a dirty bandage.

Orlena gasped when it was removed to reveal an angry red digit that was missing from the second joint.

"*Jimmy!*"

"I thought he was dead, so I says to myself, 'Well, hell, I know he's got a gold tooth back in there, I seen it the one or two times he's opened his mouth to speak. Waste not.' And next thing I know, he's clampin down. Hah!"

Jimmy reserved the worst profanity, being as he was in a lady's presence, but he still let slip a soft "Damn" while splashing whiskey on the quivering stump.

"That's awful, Jimmy! What if it's infected? Oh, James— don't go on with it like that, turn yerself in and see a doctor."

"Then I *will* git hanged. No ma'am, Orlena, I'm fully intendin on livin out the resta my natural years ownin a pretty bita property. Same as you and yer husband here."

"There are better ways to do it. Take a job with us!"

"And waste my ridin skills on movin yer cattle out t'Arizony or somewhere, only to come right back agin? I am afraid I do not find the lifestyle particularly allurin."

"How kin you be any good to the gang if you end up with an infection?"

"I ain't goingta. Anyway, one of the boys is used to diggin out bullets—he did some amputations in the war, I think. Worst case scenario, I'll have him cut the little bastard down to size when I git there."

"It ain't a *haircut*, Jimmy."

While he laughed at her, Jimmy splashed a little water on his face and took to lathering the round bar of Pears'.

"Nah, I reckon it's more like a shave…glad to know y'er as impatient as ever, Orlena."

"And good to know you're as much of a fool." Sighing, Orlena set aside her water bottle and briskly stood. She took up the razor before he grabbed it, telling him firmly, "You got no business shavin yerself missin a finger, else you're liable t'end up missin an ear, too. Jes let me."

He did, tipping back his head with bright eyes that were nonetheless somehow still suggestive of something unspeakable. She did not encourage or discourage the hope with words.

"It would be easy fer us to start a life somewheres, Orlena."

"I like my life here."

"Do yeh?"

"You shouldn't talk," she admonished him, wiping the razor off on her apron and skipping the strop.

When he obeyed her, she commenced to shave him and said after the first stroke down his lathered cheek, "I like the basic *structure* of my life here. I enjoy the security of a ranch and feel that the concept of a family, perhaps differently applied, could make me happy as well."

"But it don't, yet."

"You're gonna end up gettin cut, Jimmy…anyway, no. I reckon it doesn't make me happy. And you know why."

"You say that like it's my fault," he said as she wiped the blade.

Her face remained away from his. "Ain't it? At least a little."

"I do not recall discouragement."

"What was I supposed to say, Jimmy? What else did I know?"

"I understand."

"No one kin understand. I don't even understand. But consequences is consequences and, even though nobody knows but you and me and the Good Lord—and sometimes, I think, Bert—it makes things feel…more difficult than they need to be."

"They ain't gotta be difficult. Sure wish you were a little nicer to him."

"Well hell, ain't like I'm whippin him with this damn strap. I am plenty nice to him, especially on Sundays… but—I don't know. I feel badly about it. Him. All of it."

"I don't."

Orlena sighed and finished her task in silence, setting an example for the loquacious convict. When he was at last dried off, his cheeks and jaw smooth, he looked ten years younger than his true age and twenty years younger than he had with the beard.

Made her so damn sad.

After clipping his hair and giving it a rinse, she presented him a spare set of her husband's clothes that were left on the line overnight. All Jimmy lacked was a hat, which he assured her he could do without until Sandspur.

"Worse things than the sun on my face fer a day. I ain't enjoyed it more than an hour in three years. But is there any way"—his tone was that roguishly smooth one that was all too familiar and somehow boyish in her ears—"that you might be willin to trade onea yer ponies fer that horsea mine?"

Her head swam with the force of her sudden inhalation. "Somebody's gonna find it and know it, Jim!"

"Out here? It's miles off from where that posse lost it. We rode all day and night. Ain't nobody gonna know this horse; and, if they do, I'd like to see em prove it."

"My *husband* will notice it."

"Then make up somethin about a neighbor or some such. When was the last time yeh even saw one of em? He won't remember t'ask nothin from nobody."

Running her hand over her face, wondering how Jimmy

always managed to get whatever he wanted from her, Orlena said after a few seconds, "Take Saffron."

"Bless you, Orlena Felder."

"Orlena *Mayfield*, now. Go get that tired old thing in here, we'll trade em out…"

It was a shame to lose Saffron. She was a beautiful horse with a beautiful coat and a swift gait, but if there was one rider worthy of her, it was certainly Jimmy. Soon Saffron was saddled up; the sun rolled across the prairie; her brother, thinner than he used to be, squinted toward the light before embracing her.

"Wish you'd change yer mind, Orlena."

"I wish I could."

"Do yeh, really?"

She didn't say anything.

He jostled her, half-teasing, "How bout I jes kidnap you?"

"I don't want anybody to worry after me."

"Well…if ever you change yer mind, come lookin in them beautiful hills northa Sandspur. I'm fixinta meet them in there a ways, so mebbe yeh could find yer way t'us. I sure would like yer company…especially once this is all over."

"Please be safe, Jimmy."

"Oh, it ain't safe…but I'll live through it, don't you worry."

Smiling at her, Jimmy mounted Saffron and took up the reins. "I'll send some money fer yer generous consideration tonight. Let's go!"

With a brilliant neigh, the golden horse leapt off. Its hooves echoed north, the thunder and the figure growing smaller and smaller.

A cowhand emerged from a far distant outbuilding to stretch and shuffle to his outhouse.

At long last, Orlena realized she stood alone in the open door of the barn.

Drained, in less pain than when she awoke but still deeply uncomfortable, Orlena packed up the shaving kit and returned to the house. She undressed in silence, the gown noiseless as it fell around her feet. Her eyes grew heavier by the second.

As she lay beside her husband, he turned in her direction.

"Should I even bother t'ask what the hell you been doin all night?"

"Female problems," she said, turning over. "Fix yerself some breakfast if you want it today…I'm going back to sleep."

4

HORSES PAWED THE earth, the murmur of their hooves en masse more pleasant than their odor was foul. His own horse beneath him muted that somewhat, he suspected.

All the same, Lorenzo removed his hat and waved it to circulate the air before his face as he spoke.

"How fast you think you boys kin git three hundreda these mustang up to New Mexico Territory?"

Stroking his beard while consulting the docile ungulates roaming the vast acreage, the ranchero estimated, "Month and a half, bout. Two months if somethin goes wrong."

"And what would go wrong when I'm payin you to make sure nothin goes wrong?"

Laughing dryly, the ranchero looked at his employer with the telegraphed condescension of the experienced worker for his less experienced investor. "The hell couldn't go wrong? Rattlesnakes and dysentery aside, you got everythin from banditos to Comanche ridin up on yer ass."

"Those all sound like standard risks of the job to me." Lorenzo patted his horse's neck in response to an impatient fidget. "Basic things I pay you boys t'overcome."

"Sure enough, but the hazards git worse all the time. Them Comanche is unpredictable these days—how'd Preacher Taft's fire sort out?"

Lorenzo looked sharply at the ranchero. "What fire?"

"Ain't nobody told you yet? Ah, reckon cause the boys what woulda touldya went out there to fight it…I only heard about it myself after smellin smoke and seein a few young fellas pilin int'a stagecoach to go help, God bless em. Might still be there, for all I know."

They were…though where the hell Deputy McLintock was, Lorenzo had not the damnedest idea. Half-expected him to be at the scene, way he was always goin up north to consult with the preacher these days.

After an hour's ride toward the preacher's country church, the sting of old smoke crept into the sheriff's nostrils. His mouth contorting in displeasure, he hurried the horse that had not long ago been begging for a run and now seemed to regret its own desires. It panted, sweating even before they saw the smoldering remains of the little church and the fires that still burned around the prairie to counter the more treacherous one smoking at the edges of the building.

Sure enough, a few young fellas from Sandspur worked to make sure it was out. Some of them moved dirt to kill embers, some of them hustled water from the Pecos on horseback, others rested supine for a few well-earned minutes after a long night of fighting a fire that had left all of them smudged head to foot with black soot.

"Sheriff," said one of the diggers with surprise, dropping his load of dirt into its intended spot before greeting Lorenzo with a tip of his hat. "Glad somebody managed to tell you what was what."

"Not soon enough—then agin, I admit I have not been the most accessible this morning. What you fellas think happen here? Preacher make it?"

The boy's already solemn expression grew all the grimmer. He shook his head, removing his hat to mop a brow that proved sun-beaten beneath the soot removed with his sweat. "Nossir, he ain't made it. He's in the back. Least, I think he is—I saw through onea the old windas. Real quick. Didn't wanna look too long, you know."

"You did the right thing. You all did. Let me take a look around here and then I'll ride back to town, send a few volunteers up here to finish the job fer you. Mebbe bring a little food, huh? That's an idea…come on by the Pearl tonight. We'll gitcha all fixed up with a good warm meal and a nice rounda whiskey courtesy the Sheriff's office."

The fellas in earshot cheered. Lorenzo spared a faint smile for the one whose hand he shook, exchanging nods of respect before he released the kid to let him pick the shovel back up. Without another word, he returned to the hard task of keeping the fire from spreading across the prairie.

Workin with McLintock to haul in the Stone Hill Gang on bounty—the two or three they did manage to capture, anyway—was what got him the election. Gestures like free food for first responders or leasing out an impounded saloon to a hard-working entrepreneuse were the sorts of things that made Lorenzo well-loved.

Interest in crimes like the evident murder of Preacher Taft was what kept him from being what so many outlaw sheriffs were—thinly-veiled criminals holding whole towns hostage to an unjust regime.

That was not to say that Lorenzo Blaize did not have his own sense of the law…but a man's peculiar relationship with the law did not preclude understandin of right and wrong. Some things were just plain wrong.

Killin a preacher and burnin his church by slittin open his belly, then fillin the torso cavity with hot coals, was one of those plain wrong things.

How could the human mind begin to conceive of tortures so creative? This was precisely why Blaize liked the gun. It was plain and simple: straightforward. You got shot, or you didn't; you died, or you didn't. Only an especially sick sort of mind could envision this tableau of depravity, wherein the skeletal remains were almost as charred as the gray coals amid them. Their ashes were piled in the burned ribs Lorenzo revealed upon pushing away a segment of ceiling. The skull the boy had seen was open in an obvious scream, but he could not decide if it was the scream of a dying man or the scream of a man dead before the fire began.

Blaize inhaled sharply into the kerchief tied around his face, his eyes burning with an excess of dust kicked up by the disturbance of the crime scene.

This torture was a hallmark of the Comanche. Scalping was certainly the classic path down which the mind hastened when considering the unique forms of torture the People had used against one another and the White Man alike, but Lorenzo had seen and heard of many more. This was one that had reached him by hearsay only until now, and he looked upon the body of the preacher with a certain unhappy comprehension for what it meant.

"Looks like it's war fer more than jes our new Native friends if we don't git em outta here," he said to himself, picking his careful way around the cinders of the office.

The week was damn well nearly up, and Lorenzo had been indecisive when it came to humoring their Native ambassadors. He'd only just now gotten around to considering the logistics. The Brave's show of intoxication at the hands of the offered scorpions had wowed the sheriff no more than would any tincture of opium. Lorenzo assumed the venom experience resembled nothing more than the thoughts impressed upon the mind when medicated, sick, or drunk. Or poisoned.

But here was a problem on his land. A problem that he did not want to be his problem. Though he could not find arrows in this wreckage, much as he found none in the area surrounding the dead posse members, he could not help but think this bore some correlation with the presence of the Tribe.

A message from the Comanche? A warning to show reluctance to help those who had come all the way from New Mexico with open hands and a box of ten scorpions?

Or something else?

Sheriff Blaize coughed through his kerchief as he slid open the gnarled ruins of a desk drawer that jerked out on his most violent yank, partially disintegrating in the process. Scowling, he dusted off his gloved hands and studied the remainder of the furnishing.

He was no great lover of the protestant church, or the Catholic one for that matter. Wann't the churches' faults necessarily, though they did prescribe a heavier hand than they ought in matters of discipline if you asked him.

It was just a hellofa thing to believe in a kind God when you led the sorta life Lorenzo had led, and had watched others lead; and he was not particularly interested in paying homage to an unkind God.

Yet there he was, in that unkind God's House, an enemy of the mean-ass Virgin Motherfucker so far as he could see…and the old bastard had sent him a sign of one kind or another.

If nothin else, helpin the Natives was a charitable gesture that would drive Comanche interest away from Sandspur and back to the Tribe.

And if innerestin things still continued to happen in Lorenzo's town?

Well…then he'd have a pretty good idea of who was behind it.

5

ORLENA WOKE UP.

Cramps again? A little. They were there in the background, gnawing at her insides at a low level always around about that time.

Her husband turned over. The boy was, as usual, poised to remain comatose until the most inconvenient second. She slid out of bed and pulled on her housecoat, relieved that the pain was tolerable that night.

Lantern in-hand, its light down low as she could stand, Orlena picked her way across the yard to the outhouse.

Where was Jimmy tonight? Already back with his boys? If he pushed his horse, it was possible. The one he'd left behind was a docile, kindly creature that Orlena took to thinkin might be sad. She was sorry to think of the death of the lawman who rode it, but glad that her brother had made it through alive.

Yes, by God! At least somebody did. Somebody in their goddamn family made it out alive. Alive and *free*. Truly free. Not heavy with long days in isolation between a husband and child one did not particularly cherish through no faults of their own.

Orlena did not kid herself. She had not been equipped to survive in the world to which her family released her on her father's death. She had been lucky to woo any man, and to convince him that the baby was his. She had been especially lucky to woo a man who could give her and that child a comfortable existence—as comfortable as comfort could get in a world of lice-infested garments and the constant, suffocatin pressure presented by the possibility that any day Death would come a-knockin.

At least that night it did not come for her.

Upon rinsing herself and hands with the remaining water in the bottle, reminding herself she would have to get more in the morning or else stumble through the dark to the pump like the prior night, Orlena emerged from the stall.

The cold wind cracked through her bones seconds before the hammer of the revolver.

"Don't move."

Orlena stood very still. Stiller than she'd ever stood, that was as still as she grew. Before the war, when things weren't so bad with Pops, she'd gone out shootin with him and bagged a deer, and that deer saw her and stood just as still as she stood now.

Somethin about guns, she guessed.

"We ain't got no money in the house, mister," she said, amending swiftly when she realized the bald-faced nature of the lie, "well, maybe a little. I kin—"

"Shut up. I don't want money. I already killed sixa yer cowhands comin through yer property on accounta they was too responsible lookin after the cattle. Know why?"

Orlena was so taken aback—so busy processing the

notion that six (which six? the ones she liked?) of their cowhands (six!) had been shot (murdered—dead!) that she did not think to answer the low voice's question.

It answered for her.

"They thought I came tonight to rustle cattle. Ma'am, I assure yeh I did not."

Her tongue darted across her dry lips. The light trembled around her at the quiver of her hand. "Mister—"

"And now that you hear I ain't here to steal no money or rustle no cattle, you think I'm here fer somethin else. Some ass, right? Well, I ain't. Least not yers; not in the way yeh mean."

Just a little, the pressure around her ribs unclenched.

"Then why are yeh here?"

"You Orlena Felder, aintcha? Brother by the namea Jimmy?"

"I—"

"Think carefully, please."

Her fist tightened around the handle of the lantern.

"Yessir," she answered. "Yes, I am Jimmy Felder's sister."

"Thought so when I saw yeh. Just like he described; and livin just where that preacher said."

"What preacher? You mean—"

"Never mind nothin about that now. Where'd Jimmy run off to after he visited you?"

"I didn't—"

"Don't go lyin to me, please, Orlena. Where's Jimmy?"

Head low to avoid telegraphing her intent, Orlena kept silent.

"I asked you a question."

Her silence was her only answer.

Brush snapped beneath his approaching stride, the gun between them. She didn't have to look to know.

"You want to make this real ugly, ma'am, it kin git real ugly. Uglier than you ever seen."

The statement was so audacious she would have laughed if it were anybody—anywhere—else. "You think you'd be the only man who's given me an ugly night? Who are yeh, anyway? A bounty hunter? Some posse member what was runnin after him from the prison?"

"I'm the man who's gonna kill yer brother," was his answer just as, swinging the lantern in a wide arc, Orlena flung the heavy, glass-enclosed fireball back over her shoulder at the source of the voice.

For half a second, the man's rock-hewn features were flooded by the light. Then, the crack of the pistol and the explosion of glass signaled the coming of darkness while Orlena hitched her housedress up her ankles to sprint for the house with a scream—her husband's name.

"Bert! Help! Bert! Help! Help! Jesus, oh—murderer! Wake up! Get the gun!"

He already had and stood before the bedroom, a rifle in his hands and the sleep slapped from his eyes by the time she slammed the front door behind her.

White terror flooded her to look at him, her mind whirling with awful thoughts. What kind of clothes were these to die in? When would they be found? What would happen to the ranch, their possessions? Who would take care of the cattle? How long would it take to die?

What would happen?

What would happen tonight?

"What's going on?"

"Go back to sleep!"

Both parents whirled on the boy at his innocent question, their cries matched for urgency while Orlena dragged a chair before the front door of the house and jammed it beneath the knob. Her husband pushed the boy back into their bedroom and shut the door, scanning the rooms of the house that he passed on his way to his wife's hyperventilating side.

"What happened, Orlena?"

"A man—I's comin outta the outhouse and a man, huge, with a gun! He was lookin fer Jimmy."

Her husband's face screwed up in a combination of fury and derision that sparked some of her own. This was not the time, but he went to it anyway.

"I told you nothing good would come of keeping in contact with that outlaw brother of yers."

"*Please*—"

"What's he want Jimmy fer? To hang him?"

"I reckon so."

"Then he's the law?"

"*No!* Ain't no lawman holdin up decent ladies comin outta the *outhouse*, Bert! Land's sakes—"

A window shattered somewhere in the house and Orlena's husband shoved her into the hall coat closet, refusing to engage in a single word of further discussion.

Gasping, Orlena wrapped her hands around the knob and began to open the door—but the shout of her husband and the report of gunfire kept her hidden in the dark. Suppressing a cry of fear, Orlena braced herself and listened.

She did not listen long.

Six shots were exchanged in all. Of them, she could not help but count that five of them were her husband's. On the sixth, from the stranger's revolver, a cry arose from Bert and something clattered to the floor.

Only then did Orlena, with a shout of her own, throw herself from the closet while crying her husband's name.

"Not one more step."

The stranger stood in the doorway of the parlor, his revolver trained upon her.

Orlena obeyed, stopping in the middle of the hallway where her husband, out of breath, pressed a heavy palm against his bleeding shoulder.

Behind the gun, the man spoke coldly to her.

"Let's see if you'll wise up. Where's Jimmy, Orlena?"

"I told you, I don't know."

"Mebbe yer husband does. How about it?"

His focus—and that of his gun—slid back to Orlena's husband.

Bert ground his teeth and stared the stranger down. "I kain't care fer Jimmy Felder as far as I could throw him, and you kin figure if I knew I'd tell you and let you do with him whatche wanted. But I got no idea where he is, and the Missus don't, neither."

"No. She knows."

The man fired the revolver into Bert's kneecap. Orlena screamed as her husband collapsed, writhing in pain and cursing the day he was born.

Maybe just the day he married her.

"That jog yer memory?"

"Please," Orlena sobbed, her hands clasped before her, "please, I don't know!"

"I know a liar when I listen to one."

A floorboard's creak kept him from firing his next round, which Orlena thought might have been meant for her. The stranger whirled toward the unexpected noise and fired instead into the door.

Bert took his turn to scream. Orlena jumped, exclaiming the boy's name, her frozen hand hovering before her mouth.

The waiting.

The wondering.

The uncertainty wasn't nearly as awful as this faint flutter of thrill in her diaphragm.

A thought that had never before occurred to her in any distinct capacity now settled upon her shoulder, like a moth looking for a midnight snack from the lining of her housecoat.

What if?

What if it all…went away?

Then the stranger strode over and threw open the

door to reveal the boy cowering in the far corner, alive and well. Parental relief swept over Orlena to chide her for her monumentally hideous thought.

"Don't hurt him," she pleaded, a gasp on her lips as the man strode in and grabbed the boy by the arm.

"This yers?"

While the boy struggled, the stranger tossed him toward the hall and let him run to his parents. Though he made for his father at first, he noted the blood with a solemn little gasp and ran instead to mother's arms. She stooped to hold him, her arms wrapping around the back of his shoulders and the dark crown of hair behind the face vanishing against her waist.

"Now, are we all together?"

Orlena's eyes blazed with wet fury through the dark. "Everybody except the one yeh came for. Jimmy ain't here now, and I ain't got a clue where he's headed."

"The horse in the barn there says otherwise. White and spotted—I myself killed the lawman that rode it, and I would have taken it fer my own use had yer brother not evidently met with it once he kicked me down that ridge. Or did he not tell you about that when he came through?"

Orlena gritted her teeth, ignoring her husband's sharp look of contempt.

"I ain't sayin he didn't come by," she said, staring the man hard in the face, "but he didn't make it known where he'd be stayin."

"Hm."

Lowering the gun, the stranger looked carefully at Orlena.

Her tongue darted across her lower lip. "You're the fella he escaped with, aintcha?"

Hard to tell. If so, she was not sure she agreed with her brother's assessment that the man was Black. This stranger had no more race than a tornado had a race, and somehow this inability to comfortably slide him into a mental category left Orlena especially ill at ease.

"I know yer name, if y'er the fella I'm thinkin of. But if you go now—if you go, I swear I'll never tell it t'anybody. I won't breathe a word of what happened here. I kin keep a secret like you wouldn't believe, mister, I promise."

"Yeah," he said, regarding her with equally contemplative derision. "I kin see that."

After studying Orlena for another few seconds, the stranger raised his revolver and shot her husband in the head.

Blood splattered across Orlena's screaming face; across the wall behind her husband's slumping body; all along the back of the boy's head, which burrowed against her diaphragm as though he endeavored to clamber back into the safety of her shedding womb.

"Mama," screamed the boy, far away from her somehow.

"Where's Jimmy?"

Orlena stared at the corpse. At the glistening black-red brains visible through the back of a cranium shattered open by a bullet.

For some reason, all she could think about was having to clean it all up.

The stranger strode over and pulled the boy from her paralyzed arms.

"Tell me where yer brother is," said the man, pressing his revolver to the boy's skull. "Five seconds."

"Please."

"Four."

"Mama—"

"Mister—"

"Thre—"

"Okay!"

Orlena's shriek echoed through the ranch house. It silenced the boy's weeping along with the stranger's counting. Struggling for breath through her panic, her eyes flicking from the pool of blood crawling toward her feet to the helpless terror of the boy, Orlena looked the man in the eye.

"Okay," she said, her hand raising to wipe a streak of tears from one cheek. "I know where Jimmy is."

"Like I said."

"I know where he is—but I kain't *tell* you." The stranger uttered a quick snort of annoyance and she raised her hand flat out between them, saying, "I jes gotta show you. It's north of Sandspur, but you'll never find it without me to help you. Never find him. Please—give me a chance to show you."

"Okay," said the stranger.

His grip of the boy relaxed, as did the boy's face.

The stranger raised the revolver.

Orlena's mouth opened, the scene somehow detached from the sound of the gunfire.

The boy fell down with her husband. He lay immobile in the scarlet flood that had soaked through her slippers.

The stranger put his revolver away and removed the rifle from the puddle, shaking it off before bending it to wipe it on the dead man's long underwear.

"Git some clothes and put us together some food t'eat fer the next day. I'm in a rush to git some rest but I ain't in a rush to git Jimmy, not particularly…when it's his time, I'll be there. And now you know I ain't got no compunctions about bein there fer yer time, too, if I needta be."

Stunned, her eyes fixed to the dead bodies, Orlena said nothing.

The stranger wiped off the strap of the rifle and slung it around his shoulder, asking, "Whose son was that, anyway?"

Like a small child, Orlena burst into tears.

6

THE MAN HAD expected more fussin.

Night still had a lotta hours. She cried for about thirty minutes of it, mostly while darting back and forth between her rooms to collect fistfuls of garbage she wanted to bring. Then she wept once again, on the road, when watching the ranch recede. Refused to take her own horse and went with the dead lawman's horse Jimmy'd brought to her homestead.

Fine by him. Horse got recognized, sister of Jimmy Felder on it, easy to see how a sheriff would consider her complicit.

Some sheriffs would, anyway.

Felder had complained almost endlessly about the lawmen of Sandspur while they were sharing the cell. The Needless Man did not do much speaking and Felder got nervous in silence. His chattering filled the air from waking till sleep some days. Even then he mumbled through his dreams, muttering under his breath to distorted versions of his sister and dead father.

And sometimes Deputy McLintock or Sheriff Lorenzo Blaize; the latter of whom, so far as the Man had come to understand, did Felder a favor back in Lorenzo's bounty hunter days by waya bringin Felder in alive insteada shootin him dead and takin the money without any future headache. Certainly the decision had not been a kindness for the world, or for the Man; and not for Blaize himself, whom Felder would have liked to shoot in spitea the favor he owed.

Difficult to relate with the notion. The Man didn't *want* to kill Felder. He *would* kill Felder, not because he desired to do so but because it was just what was going to happen. It was the counterweight and consequence of the gold tooth that Felder had better pray still sat somewheres on his person.

Tempting to interrogate Orlena on the matter, but he did not want her all riled up again. She'd settled down once the ranch and all her possessions had disappeared into the darkness of night. Their horses picked carefully through the landscape, aided in their navigation by little more than a lantern from Orlena's home. When two hours had passed and, the hills south of Sandspur in sight, his horse swayed with signs of exhaustion from its already long day, he permitted the beast to stop and told Felder's sister to get down from her mount.

"Where are we?"

"Where we're sleepin."

She looked around with a grim expression, pulling tighter around herself the fur she'd brought to fend off the brutal desert night. Nothin for her or nobody else to see. Mountain-laurels and blue grama. Horses out of sight between a mimosa grove and a boulder.

"And I thought *you* were frightening, Mr. Rhodes. It's awful out here."

Here she went, already headin where he knew she'd try to git. "Best git used t'it," he told her, dismounting and pushing the lantern into her hand.

"What if something comes at night to take our provisions? A bear, or a cougar."

"Tie the food up in that tree."

"With the rope? How—"

Dropping his saddle upon the dirt, the Man regarded her through the steady lantern glow. Already more light than he cared to risk for very long.

"I lived with yer brother a year and a half in one cell, with a damn courtyard fer exercise. In that time, I got t'know him reasonably well. One look in yer eyes tells me yeh ain't the stupidera the two."

Her mouth tightened, those smart eyes narrowing.

As he said.

While she set to her task without direction, he picked himself a comfortable enough dirt patch. "I am bringin you with me to streamline the matter of reachin Jim. If I find yer presence is more trouble than it's worth, I will not hesitate to kill you and accept that finding him will be slightly more inconvenient than previously anticipated."

"There's no need fer that," she said, her tone somewhat shrill. "I ain't no trouble. And I kin make it easy fer you to find Jimmy."

"Uh-huh. And?"

"What do you mean?"

"There was somethin waitin in the next room there."

Glancing over her shoulder at him, her nostrils flaring, Orlena said, "It's jes—I don't...know *exactly* where he's stayin."

The Man exhaled slowly.

His eyes slid shut.

He pushed back his duster and set his hand against the Schofield while Orlena cried out, her hands extended before her.

"Wait! Nono, wait sir, please—"

"What'd I say?"

The barrel was out of the holster.

She fell to her knees, saying, "Call! Call! It's a call!"

The gun had leveled with her head by the time of her final utterance.

It lowered.

"What's a call?"

The more frantic she was, the more evident grew the twang in her voice. "How we'll find him. A birdcall—he'll find me if he hears it, or at the very least he'll call me to him. We jes need to figure a little more…*specifically* where the Stone Hill Gang is spendin its time these days. I got some idea, I jes—I gotta figure the precise whereabouts. Iw's thinkin maybe we might stop by Sandspur! I could ask a fella Jimmy used to know. Wilt McLintock. He used to run with the Stone Hill Gang but spent a lotta time round town, too. If I kin have a word with him, I might learn somethin worth tellin."

"Make the call."

Without hesitation, she did. A twittering lark song whistled from her lips. He did not anticipate that twenty years of practice would have let his own face contort to replicate the noise.

The twittering ended in an uneasy whistling that breezed from her lips. Her eyebrows lifted in a hopeful plea, her hands still between them.

He holstered the gun and resumed making camp, arranging dried brush outside their cover to serve as a kind of alarm.

"Then we'll stop in Sandspur," he told her. "And talk to Jimmy's friend together."

Orlena shivered dramatically in her fur without a fire. The Man did not sleep heavily but did close his eyes, his ears tuned to Orlena's uneasy respiration as they lay on opposite sides of the camp.

Apparently, she could tell he was awake.

"What's yer real name, anyways?"

"Go to sleep."

"It don't matter to me none. Just wonderin."

"Then you ain't need to know it. My name is whatever I tell you it is. Now, sleep. Might be yer last opportunity fer a while."

"The last opportunity *you* give me, you mean."

He did not deign to respond. The female Felder's stewing was audible until she said in an obnoxiously plaintive voice, "It's amazin how cold it gets out here."

"That tree y'er fixinta climb ain't no good t'you, Miss Felder."

"Mrs—well. Well."

"Yeah. Well. It is in my experience, Miss Felder, that females is somethin to be avoided in all situations. They ain't no good, present company included."

Scoffing, Orlena said, "Now hold on a minute! You kain't say a thing like that! You don't even know a damn thing about me."

"I know plenty about you, Orlena Felder. More than that dead husbanda years did, I reckon."

She did not reply.

"Like I said. Women make trouble wherever they go. Mighta been an altogether different life if yer husband ain't married, fer one."

"More like if you ain't come around."

"Nah…I ain't the one held accountable here. My comin through yer life ain't nothin but the natural consequencea the decisions you and Jimmy made yer whole lives up till now."

"Jes what is it you got against Jimmy? He busted you outta prison, ain't he?"

"I'da got myself out soon enough. It's easy. You jes tell em you love Jesus now, and put on a big showa reformin and prayin. Soon enough they ease up on this or that and they let yeh slip out through the cracks. Gone, like dust."

The slight huff of her breath served as an acknowledgement. "But that don't explain why it is you hate Jimmy so damn much."

"He's took somethina mine that I ain't care to give. I aim to git it back and fix his hide fer what he thought he could do to me."

"What's he got that's yers?"

The Man sat up to find she had already propped herself on the elbow. With one broad finger, he pulled wide the corner of his mouth and showed her the missing molar tucked in the back of his cheek.

"Yer *tooth*," exclaimed Felder's sister in shock, an unpleasant laugh warbling the edges of her voice. "Why, that's all!"

He removed his finger from his mouth and lay back upon the bedroll pilfered from the ranch house.

"Miss Felder," he said, fixing his hat once more over his face, "I do not reckon you could begin t'understand."

"Because it's nonsense?"

"Because yeh got so much you think you need that you ain't got no *person* in there under all yer property."

"Jes how the hell kin you say that about me?"

Now it was her turn to sit up.

Didn't move his hat. Didn't care.

"You mighta talked to my brother, but you ain't never talked to me. You don't know a damn thing about me."

"I know you ain't actin the way a woman oughta act when her family's got shot in fronta her."

"And who are *you* to say how a woman should act, exactly? You jes said you steer clear of us."

"I try to…but then they show up anyway."

With an inarticulate noise of disgust, Felder's sister flopped back down into her bedding. "God willing, you'll be rid'a me soon enough."

Ain't God's business when a man finally shakes off a

harpy like Orlena Felder, but the Man kept that to himself so's to have a little peace.

As per usual, he did not dream but dozed in and out of time. His hat shifted back upon his head. Colors flickered between his shut-eye gaps. Sky black, sky dark blue, sky hazy orange.

Sky interrupted by Henry rifle extending from his nose to the hands of the ranchero over him.

"Good morning, bright eyes," said the smug sonnabitch.

The female Felder stirred with a gasp, crying out beneath the shaking of the other ranch hand on the hunt for the last of his employers.

"Wake up, ma'am! It's Silas—"

"Oh, Silas! Yes, thank God—shoot him, shoot him now—"

Taken aback by the woman's command, the fella with the rifle could not process the statement and began to say, "Right now? But—"

The Man caught hold of the repeating rifle's barrel. By the time the ranchero's head whipped back, the weapon was already torn from his grip and slamming hard into his diaphragm.

The ranchero fell into a genuflection with a sharp wheeze, his arms folded over his gut. Flipping the rifle around into his nondominant hand, the Man yanked his revolver from his side and cocked the hammer.

Ol Silas was quick on the draw, but the Man was quicker. While the rifle blasted into his face, its barrel braced up against the man's knee, his usual shootin hand twitched with muscle memory to send one, two, three rounds from the Schofield quick into the fella scrambling up from where the Man had knocked him down to a knee.

"Bennett!"

Her cry of the ranchero's name a high sob, the female Felder pulled her fur over her face to let it absorb most of the blood splatter. When she lifted her head a few flecks remained visible about her hairline.

Bennett gagged in a shocked, wet death-rattle. He twitched while the icy fingers of death crawled over his limbs. Then he was still.

Fella what took the rifle shot was still alive but barely, face half-gone and pourin blood down his front.

The Man grabbed Silas up by the shirt and looked in his minced features.

"Anybody else out lookin fer her?"

"P—p—"

"Tell me and I'll end it fer yeh."

"Five—five more."

"Then we best git on to Sandspur directly, without more attention."

He shot Silas through the remainder of his skull. When the body's head dropped back, the Man lowered it to the earth and went to work breaking down camp.

Felder's sister hyperventilated, her eyes wild with the evaporation of hope.

"Don't look so troubled, Miss Felder…I git my tooth back and Jim winds up dead, I reckon you still got many happy, healthy yearsa life left to live—and a homestead all yer own. No wonder you ain't cried much when I thinka't now. Seems like I sorta did yeh a favor back there, didn't I?"

This time, Orlena didn't argue.

$$7$$

THE DEVIL HAD taken Orlena from her home. Ain't no human being as mean and empty-eyed as the one that killed Bert (and the boy) and took her in the night like she were a goddamn stolen horse. Then to turn around and imply *she* was the wicked one! Why? Because she was shocked? Too shocked to cry or fight back or do anything but hope there would be a means of escape in Sandspur?

Most importantly…why the hell did it bother her so much just what this man's opinion of her was? She did not care for or respect him one whit, obviously; but to have her soul called ugly by someone so vile was a moral reproachment that nagged her while she rode alongside her captor.

"We'll sell these horses when we git into town and use the money to pay board fer the night, if we gotta. You git the information you need from McLintock, and we kin go up t'yer brother and be done with it."

"How can I know you won't go back on yer word and shoot me when y'er through?"

"I reckon you kain't, except that I'm tellin you I ain't got no particular issue with yeh personally."

"Then why the hell'd you kill my husband and son that way?"

"To show you I ain't playin around."

She gritted her teeth, glancing over her shoulder at the horses—her *own* horses, mind—once ridden by the now-dead rancheros.

Dead. So many dead! Oh, Jesus. What was that now—eight? Eight rancheros and Bert.

And the boy.

A breeze still cool with the memory of the night passed through her frayed hair. She shifted back upon the saddle, suddenly aware of the soaked medical bandage. Her cramps were not so vicious that morning as they had been over the past two days.

Never again would she cook breakfast for them when she did not feel like it. She would not have to get up from her own bed to put the boy back to his; would not have to entertain her husband's sexual advances when such activities were furthest from her weary mind. There was not a damn thing she would ever have to do for them again except pay for a couplea caskets and burial spots in Preacher Taft's cemetery so she wouldn't have to see their stones all the time when she got back to the property.

Assuming, of course, she survived all this.

What was most unnerving about this Rhodes fella was not just the pure lack of anything mortal in his eyes or carriage. It was that she found herself almost *believing* him. When he told her she would be allowed to live if she traded the life of her brother, she heard the truth in his voice…and the other, unspoken truth. Hovering above all his words.

The promise that, if she fled him and ran far as she could, she would be the next one he looked for when Jimmy had been dealt with.

She had a lot of questions to ask herself.

Namely:

Was it not very tempting to yield her brother's actual location?

To *actually* consult McLintock for the precise whereabouts of the Stone Hill Gang, in order to return to her life as quickly and safely as possible?

It certainly was.

And that was why this strange Man's comments about her moral compass had stung.

He was right. Orlena Mayfield was a mask that fell away from Orlena Felder. Now, without need for pretense or performance for any onlookers, she found herself in a vacuum with a stranger who was sicker and eviler than she could ever hope to be.

Maybe.

The ride to Sandspur seemed especially long, as they went in a wide arc through less-traversed hillsides and shunned the least possibility of people. He had affixed the plundered horses to the back of hers, ensuring that if she got wise and tried to ride away she'da been damn easy to run down and kill.

It would not do to try to flee directly.

Whatever she ended up doing, however she would get out of this situation, the answer would come to her so long as she bided her time. She just had to stay alive until Sandspur and then, however she could, find someone to help her. She would have to do it discretely. Rhodes had a draw as quick as a rattlesnake's lunge, or quicker. Pulling a gun was an action he'd performed his whole damn life, so far as Orlena could tell. One arrant word to the wrong person in hopes of securing help and he could shoot her dead, mount his horse with but a few more casualties littering the way, and be gone before the life had faded from her body.

And, having been forced to watch the murder of her husband and son along with two rancheros, it would have been an abysmal waste for her to let herself die.

So, the long ride to Sandspur, she stewed. The environment was tragically gorgeous, the prairies around her ranch yielding to these craggy hills and valleys of somewhat more exotic cacti and grasses than she usually clapped eyes upon. Aside from the overbearing sun and the vultures that looked on with anticipation, flying sometimes in broad circles overhead, they rode in the solitude of their thoughts. Her husband's hat kept the sun from her eyes.

Her dead husband's hat.

Her mind kept circling around that one thought. Back, over and over again, to how man and boy looked when they fell dead to the floor; how unbound from constant worry her chest now was for the first time in over five years; what it meant to be free, absolutely free, and how desperately she wanted to keep that free life. To enjoy a taste of liberty before whatever more natural death awaited her could be enacted by the hand of Fate.

She did not want to die.

And she did not want to give up Jimmy.

But...but.

Then it was a question of killing this Rhodes fella; or seeing him killed, at any rate. How? With any luck, there'd be a manhunt on for him and Jimmy. A wanted poster or two, and it'd all sort itself out when they finally found themselves in the town that operated like an anthill down in the valley beneath them. Their horses had come to a stop at the crest of a hill and stood with lashing tails while their humans assessed the activity.

"It's bigger than I remember," she commented, her voice rough with disuse after a day of arduous riding with a mere four breaks to speak of. His hands balanced naturally upon the saddle's pommel, the Man lowered his head in agreement.

"It *is* bigger. Bigger than it was when I got turned in. Easier to fade into the people than I thought it would be."

Unfortunately, he was right. Sandspur had grown substantially since she had last been. Several more houses were even in various states of construction along the outskirts. Beautiful men, five or six years her juniors, labored beneath a vanishing sun that made their bronze flesh sparkle with sweat.

She could have any man she wanted. Yes! It occurred to her now for the first time. Hot damn! What did being an older woman (in her twenties, already so ancient) matter when you owned a homestead like hers? Live through this, and she could enjoy a life as free as any man's. A few liberties! Now that would make her appreciate the world again.

The young men were packing up for the day and smiled boldly up at her while, upon the Man's instruction, she asked for directions to a saloon where they could eat and rest—and, hopefully, find McLintock.

At her question, the helpful boy's brow furrowed.

"Well, truth be told there ain't too many. Mebbe only one what's suitable fer a—fer a nice lady like yerself."

"You ain't know she a nice lady, son," said the Man, squinting out across the town rather than at the boy he addressed. "Jes tell us where men in this town head for a drink and a good time."

Hesitating, then looking at Orlena in a somewhat different, more thorough way that she didn't like, the boy said, "You might wanna stop by the Pearl. They's a little expensive, but it's the liquor license does that. Least you know the whiskey ain't gonna strike you blind, and that they's got plentya clean—rooms."

He glanced at the Man significantly on this last word. The Man nodded, then said with a gesture over his shoulder, "Where yeh think my friend here kin sell these horses a'hers?"

After receiving a few suggestions, the Man tipped

them with money taken from the dead rancheros' bodies. He departed with Orlena and her horses reluctantly riding alongside him. The boys' directions made short work of it and soon they had their remaining mounts hitched at the stables in the back of the parlor house.

Two stories. Big as a ballroom. With the coming of night, all the building's lights glowed. Men poured in.

The Man known as Rhodes addressed her.

"Gonna behave yerself? Yeh done well so far; better than I anticipated."

"I ain't fixinta get shot by nobody, leasta'll you." Rapidly brushing her dusty hair into order enough to be seen in impolite society, she added, "And anyway, I'm ready t'wash my face and sleep in a *bed* tonight. Will you extend me that liberty, at least?"

"Let's see how well you do findin this McLintock fella… then we'll have a talk."

As busy as the traffic into the Pearl was, the interior seemed bursting at the seams by the time the Man shepherded her into the building.

At first glance, the parlor house was no different from any saloon she'd happened past or taken Communion in before marrying a protestant. Nicer, for damn sure. No sawdust under her boots—even a sign that said 'NO SPITTING ON THE FLOOR, PLEASE' in carefully painted cursive, albeit situated in an easily ignored spot above the bar. The gambling gleamed with fastidious attention to detail and from one wall to the other, men circulated with their fellows to laugh and drink and throw dice and cards for cash.

And, among them, women moved from group to group until they found a client they could work with.

It was all a little startling somehow. So—*open*. Had this place even been here when last she'd visited Sandspur? Orlena hesitated after taking her first step in and glanced up at the Man, but he was already making his way through the crowd. Looking back to see that she followed.

The bordello was not the only thing that seemed new. Sandspur had grown so homogenous! Mexicans milled about, and there gambled some Black cowhands taking a night off, and she detected the alien voices of a few Frenchmen. The town was small compared to a true city like El Paso, but it was well on its way…and it was obvious the Pearl was the center.

In such centers, gentlemen were used to existing in a particular way. She understood the mistake, really. They saw a lady evidently alone and, though her head was covered and her look skittish, they made an improper assumption.

"She's a sweetheart! Say, cutie, whazzyer name? Talk t'us a little while. We don't bite. Shoot, angel, why yeh lettin that dress hide those nice legsa yers? Hey honey I gotta room fer the next two nights upstairs, come on up, I got a couplea yer girlfriends waitin. Jesus, she looks like a virgin! Blow on these dice fer me, wouldya sugar?"

The saloon floor of the parlor house was vast and humiliating to cross, the chorus of commodification coming from all angles. She evaded at least one hand, but most minded their personal space…though a lot was left to be said for where they put their eyes.

For every man who did show her attention, however, there were twenty more packed in the uproarious leisure hall. There had to be at least ten men to every woman, and that was a meager estimate made through a stinging veneer of cigar smoke and shifting bodies and a singer going on in captivating Spanish that kept Orlena's ear straining before she bumped into the Man's back.

"Anybody gives you trouble," he said firmly as she came around to stand beside him at the bar, "address it to me."

The old guy runnin the bar blew right past the vaguely ethnic Man and spoke to Orlena first. "This ain't normally a place fer a woman by herself, miss."

"Miss Felder," she answered reflexively, glancing toward the second floor. "So I've gathered. Reckon we'll find elsewhere to stay fer the night, if you could recommend a place; but we were directed here by a couplea young fellas and—you know a man by the namea McLintock?"

The barkeep, who had turned his eyes away to some work cleaning something beneath the bar, looked at her for a second, more cautious time.

"Yeah," he said, his moustache giving a peculiar sort of twitch. Eyes lowering again, he continued, "Deputy McLintock comes in pretty frequently."

Deputy! Guessed she'd find him after all…and if he didn't know where the Stone Hill boys were hiding these days, maybe he could help her in some other way. With a sigh of relief, Orlena leaned against the bar. "He's an old family frienda mine."

"That so."

At the barkeep's skeptical tone, Orlena doubled down into what was technically not a lie.

"Yessir, he's a frienda my brother's."

"And yer brother is?"

"Not important," answered the Man for her, earning his first actual acknowledgement from the bartender.

Orlena continued pressing, "You ain't seen him around lately? Tonight?"

"Oh, maybe. He comes in and out all the time to see the sheriff."

For the first time in their bloody acquaintance, the Man made a small huff from his throat. Almost like a laugh. "What is this, the sheriff's office?"

"You'd think just about, way he does business outta the upstairs till all hours somenights…but, between you and me, it ain't the law's business."

Orlena looked at him curiously. "What do you mean?"

"Ah, I shouldn't gossip. I'm an old hen! You jes remind me a littlea my wife when we was young, and—"

The Man was slammed back out of her periphery and somebody with a "hard 'r'" kinda accent fresh outta dead-ass Dixie slid up to twang, "Glassa whiskey, Meyer."

The barkeeper looked perturbed. "We're havin a conversation here, Chrysler."

Having regained his balance, the Man grabbed the hick by the back of his shirt and slammed his face hard into the bar.

People gasped. The bartender stepped back, much as did Orlena.

"Beggin yer pardon," said the Man gruffly, shoving the bellrung interloper away from the bar. "You were sayin, sir."

"Oh, uh—"

The bartender was not allowed to stutter further. His teeth bared, Chrysler shook his head like an animal and snatched for his gun.

The Man had his ready to shoot.

The interloper froze, his eyes slightly bugged with fear.

The Man nodded his head. "Put it back."

"You first."

"You don't wanna find out how quick I am." The Man kept his gun trained on the youth even as others in the room could be heard quietly sliding weapons from their holsters. "Let's take our turns with Meyer nice and easy here, so's we kin both walk away with our lives."

"Ain't seem like y'er gettin what I'd expect from a bar, let alone the Pearl. Leastways, I come in to drink; not ask questions. Mebbe y'all should do the same…specially if'n you two're gonna be walkin round civilized society *together*."

"Then how about you and me head outta this fine establishment and settle our disagreement in the street."

"Fine by me," said Chrysler with a haughty look from the Man to Orlena. He lowered his gun only once sure the Man was doing the same. Conversation resumed one group at a time, but the subject had no doubt changed.

And Orlena's plans, somehow, had also changed.

The outcome of this all depended on whether she was willing to wipe away her existing morals and enter a new dimension of existence. She had been realizing that on the ride in. When following the traditional values of keeping up the family and normalcy and docility had all brought her nothing but a kind of physical and even spiritual imprisonment, how could she deny the appealing temptation behind embracing her urges toward evil?

Especially since it was only a survival mechanism. Evil. She knew that already.

After all…legally, she *was* complicit in facilitating her brother's flight. She had absolutely seen to his escape and made only the lightest of attempts to dissuade him from his intended path. She was the unwilling recipient of great wealth and land as a matter of inheritance, but a recipient nonetheless; and that, combined with Jimmy's flight, made the deaths of her family and the rancheros particularly suspicious. In the eyes of the law, she was already immoral.

And in the eyes of the Needless Man, if she did not help him, she was already dead.

Therefore, when the Man warned Chrysler before they left the bar, "I shoot to kill," and Chrysler's response was, "So do I," Orlena cried out.

"*Wait*," she urged, gripping the Man's bicep as she appealed to Chrysler. "Wait, please—you kain't kill him."

The Man glanced at her for perhaps one half a second but did not engage beyond that. Chrysler sneered a little.

"On accounta he's some kinda—"

"On account," she said, her voice authoritative as she stared the idiot down, "of the fact that this man's helpin me find my brother and shoot him dead for what he did to my family."

Chrysler's eyes widened in somewhat vapid shock that was echoed more intelligently by the barkeep.

"This man is—he's a bounty hunter. My employee. Please—you kain't shoot him. Without him, I won't be safe…and my family won't be avenged."

Something shifted inside of her. A decision was made. Going along with him was the only way of ensuring her security not just from death but from the law.

Jimmy had to die.

"Well…damn."

Turning his head to spit with annoyance into spittoon that nonetheless earned a displeased look from the bartender, Chrysler said with a roll of the tobacco under his lip, "That may be so, but ain't nobody kin sucker punch me and go about they business without learnin a valuable lesson."

"Then settle it without shootin each other. Hell— you wanna use yer guns?" Orlena's eyes shone bright with mischief that made her feel alive for the first time in twenty-four hours. "I got a good suggestion fer yeh both."

8

LORENZO PACED FROM his desk to his winda three times while waiting for the Tribesmen to make it to his office above the noisy bordello's main floor. Night had not yet fallen and already it sounded like a madhouse…least the madame'd be able to make her lease payments fer the resta the year.

"Here they are, sir," said McLintock with a gesture, a look of obvious exhaustion written across his features.

"Thank you kindly, McLintock. Hang on a few minutes more and I'll let you go fer the night…hopefully, this'll be short."

White Serpent took the seat across the desk, his expression grim in the expectation of refusal after near a week of waiting. Leaning back against the slightly cluttered top upon which he perched with his arms folded, Lorenzo said with consideration for the medicine man, "Havin had a few days to consider yer proposal, Serpent, I have decided t'eagerly accept yer offer of trade."

The shaman's eyes brightened in extraordinary joy. Roaring Bear, the Brave who knew a little English, smiled and translated his relief to his friend. The scarred man exclaimed something in their native tongue and shook Roaring Bear happily around the shoulders.

"This is welcome news," said the medicine man, containing himself so as not to tip his hand and in some way lose the bargain before it had been struck. "When can the delivery be made? I understand it will take some time for the horses to reach our lands."

"Yeah, well, I talked to a fella. Said we're lookin at a month and a halfa transit there…I kin only hope not quite as long will be spent comin back."

White Serpent nodded in understanding. "We know it is a very long wait for your end of the trade, and we are truly—"

"Now, you don't need to thank me agin. I'm gettin plenty outta my end."

Pushing himself up from the desk and striding around its perimeter, Lorenzo reclined in his chair to fish a cigar box out of his desk drawer.

"My only question," he said, offering cigars to the medicine man and his fellows, "is how I'm gonna git all three hundreda them horses from here to there without the very Comanche who so concern you swoopin in to do what they do best…that is, stealin horses and killin the men what are with em."

White Serpent nodded grimly as he leaned forward to accept a light. "The trip will no doubt be arduous. We understand that you will likely lose horses in transit and have already ordered more than we anticipate being able to use in the immediate future. Hopefully, if they survive, we will make good use of them in later trade."

"This day and age, that's wise plannin…well, let me think about it jes one more day. How about I send a stagecoach and a few crates along with y'all—you kin transport the cargo back that way."

"A fine idea," agreed Roaring Bear, saving his cigar for later. "And I will return with them, as agreed."

"Well, gentlemen! This is turnin into what I anticipate to be quite a favorable arrangement…I do love an agreement wherein all parties come out ahead."

If he could just make it work.

Alone in his office, with McLintock turned in for the night and the Pearl really rumbling his floor, Lorenzo rotated the cigar and puffed on his thoughts with his eyes muggily fixed across his reflection in the winda.

What Lorenzo needed was somebody who knew his way around a gun. Preferably somebody expendable. Not one of his deputies, in other words, or anybody else whom he held in personal esteem. No doubt the rancheros were used to dangerous situations of all kinds, but it would make Lorenzo feel better to know somebody with a deadeye was overseein the operation.

And to make damn sure it weren't some kinda put-on.

After all…say it really were a trick. Say the horses got there and the cowhands were killed. Wouldn't be the first time in the history of their great nation that such a thing had occurred, but Lorenzo would nonetheless look like a real ass. Goodbye, re-election, no matter whom he paid.

Hell! He hadn't even tried the scorpions' venom himself. All he'd done was watched that Brave hallucinate in his office awhiles. If he wanted to know with absolute certainty that it was all they said it was cracked up to be, Lorenzo needed to sample the merchandise.

It was just, well…

He was not eager to let a scorpion sting him, which was of course the major factor to overcome in matters of marketing.

Better be damn worth it.

In his room down the hall from his office, the whispering cigar box sat atop his bureau.

Careful as he could, he lifted its lid and had a silent conversation with himself about the wisdom of this experiment. Wished he hadn't sent McLintock home.

One of the scorpions quivered as though in anticipation, its tail raising into the air.

Every thought was launched from Lorenzo's head when a gunshot cracked through the street outside.

His own revolver in his hand, Blaize pressed himself to the frame of the winda and peered through the unreflecting pane into the street below.

A man he did not recognize shot two glass bottles out of the air through which they were uneasily arced by a particularly drunken throw.

Blaize released his held breath, laughing a little at himself. Revolver back in its holster, he studied the scene and thought to himself he was beginning to change somehow. Once upon a time, it would've been him out there showin off. Once upon a time, dressin up as sheriff felt like a costume. Less so all the time.

Old Lorenzo, after all, woulda ignored the shootin match completely and ended the night by crawlin into bed with onea the girls.

They just hadn't been doing it for him lately, truth be told. Oh, he still slept in the parlor house on accounta he owned it and had a good room with real good service, and when he did business at night it was more convenient, but the idea of hiring one of the women drained his energy. The sameness of it all made the power of his position lose its zest.

These days, what he wanted was not a suppliant paid gal but one of them women that was like a wild horse. You could ride em around and teach em how to eat outta yer hand, but their hearts yearned for something more than a rider could ever simulate. With one like that, whether horse or woman, you had to be firm when they showed signs of wanting the wild life. Had to remind em why it was better to be tamed.

Could have just been his own feelings on it, of course.

Lorenzo chuckled to himself as he pushed through the gamblin, drinkin, partyin guests of the Pearl to get to the match that had, by the looks of the full street, emptied out about half the men and an eighth of the women. Chrysler Holmes was in the middle of hittin two and missin one when the sheriff stepped onto the walkway and fired his revolver into the air.

All heads turned. Blaize holstered the gun with a brisk assessment of the crowd.

Brisk, because it ended on her.

Her exhausted face was so startlingly beautiful beneath all the dirt that it tugged at his heart somehow. Untamed brows were her only flaw that he could see, and they only served to draw further attention to a pair of glamorous blue eyes so sharp that they reminded him of diamonds. There was more there than even the shrewdness he saw in the mirror.

Sometimes he spoke rough with em…but Blaize loved women. A strong woman was seventy times as strong as the strongest men, only they didn't show it because they were smarter, too. Frankly, that was *why* Lorenzo spoke rough with em. It was a man's only defense against a woman like this one, whose features were so statuesque and solemn but whose flashing eyes revealed a mind on fire.

Lorenzo smiled at her and addressed the crowd.

9

THE NEEDLESS MAN'S first impression of Sheriff Blaize was: teeth. Straight white teeth too straight and white for a man livin in Shithole, Nowhere. Too straight and white even for the man runnin it.

"Well heck," the sheriff said in a jocular way, his smile fixed on the female Felder before it bounded back to Chrysler and the Man. "I heard all this gunfire and got a little worried! I am awful glad to know we're all havin a good time tonight."

Striding off the walkway, (a few murmuring men turned their faces down while shuffling back into the bordello or up the street to avoid the sheriff), Lorenzo navigated through the remaining spectators. Soon he stood before the Man.

"Now, fellas, I ain't mean to put a damper on a good time, but y'all very well know you kinnot be shootin all up and down the street outside the Pearl. Or—mebbe yeh don't."

Now the sheriff *really* saw the Man, which the Man did not like. Being seen was inconvenient.

He stared emptily back. Waited for Lorenzo to turn his eyes.

After a few long seconds, he did.

"Regardless, if'n you fellas wanna take a walk fer some fresh air and have yer shootin match outside town, I'd be happy to supervise. Make sure things are conducted fair… and safe."

Felder's sister, who was more Orlena to the Man all the time, hovered at a distance of five yards. Animal-fear eyes darted toward dark alleys. The night. The coyotes. The men.

The devil she knew.

Her arms folded over her bosom and her eyes lowered to the ground while Chrysler said with a sneer, "Mebbe instead you oughta have a talk with this here stranger and make sure he knows it's rude to go askin after Deputy McLintock without explainin why."

"I did explain," said Orlena sharply, her eyes flickering up and hanging on the Sheriff's as they seized the chance to turn on her. "I—I don't wanna have t'explain it agin. I want to speak with Deputy McLintock to get a little information."

"Pertaining to?"

"I believe I would prefer to speak to the deputy, Sheriff."

Teeth again. Broad, fine smile. Alligators, sharks.

"Well, you never know! I am sure I know jes about everythin that he does…mebbe more."

Her nostrils flared. A look toward the Man.

At his nod, back toward the Sheriff.

"You know a Jimmy Felder, Sheriff?"

Yes he did. Beneath an arched brow, the sheriff said, "I am familiar with the name."

"You was the bounty hunter what brought him in afore yeh was sheriff," said Orlena, clearly an expert in acting; as were all professional, thriving, free criminals. "Maybe you're right. Maybe you know precisely where he's at these days."

"Last I heard he was still sittin pretty in that prison.

What business you got with Jimmy Felder exactly, Miss?"

"That'd be between him and me, sir."

Orlena stared the lawman down. Parental sternness in her eyes. Hate to be her kid.

"Well," said the Sheriff, "perhaps when Deputy McLintock is at work tomorra I kin ask if'n he knows what Jimmy's up to these days…and why he ain't in prison servin his judge-appointed sentence no more."

"I would also like to know that," said Orlena stiffly, adding with a glance from the Man to Chrysler and then to her feet, "and a few other things."

Now free to regard her with abandon, the thirsty Sheriff drank Orlena Felder up. He righted his rude stare after a second or two; only to look at the men and suggest, "Well how about us four take a coach out to the edgea town and do a little shootin?"

Avoiding the law was the general idea upon breaking out of prison. Lorenzo Blaize was not the law. He was the kinda fella what dressed himself up in the law without knowing the first real thing about it; the kinda fella what used the law only as long as it made him wealthy and famous. Too many bastards like him were running towns into the ground; at least Sandspur was ascending with him.

For now.

Orlena was wisely quiet in the ride. Her decisions, so far, were smart. At least, the Man had more respect for her than he had for Jimmy. She did not see herself accurately but nobody really did. Even the Man must have had some delusions of which he could not divest himself. An undeniable sense of righteousness in anti-morality. But he was just as much slave to the moral structure by way of operating against it. Every man operated in or out of the framework and was thus beholden to it.

All he could do was be aware of his delusions, his blind spots. Men like Lorenzo Blaize were never aware of it. Not really. Thought they were sometimes; smarter ones. Blaize was a smarter one.

But there were some hypocrisies that could not be overcome. Ran too deep. Rooted too firmly into the base of the personality.

And when it came to personalities, Blaize had that kinda slick-crafted one what ain't seem real in a man even though he got no other to replace it with.

The lady was taken in an open coach along with the sheriff and the Man, who did not await an invitation prior to joining them. Chrysler looked resentfully up and said, "I'll take my horse."

"See yeh there," said Lorenzo, tapping the driver on the shoulder before turning back to his guests.

Teeth. Teeth teeth teeth.

"So where the twoa yeh from? Kain't say I recognize either onea yeh."

"My name's Orlena Mayfield. I don't think I ever made yer acquaintance while I'ws livin closer to here, Sheriff."

"Oh, y'er from around here!"

"I lived in spittin distance a long time, yessir. Still do, really, if you kin spit over the mountains. Hardly recognized it comin over the hill today! Sandspur's changed a lot in the time I've been married and stuck at home."

Fewer teeth; a stiffening of the features. Casually: "Married? Here I thought you looked too young!"

"Lands, stop." Orlena laughed in genuine gaiety and waved a hand, pressing it to her cheek as she said with a quickly fading smile and a glance at the Man, "Ain't too young to marry, ain't too young to be a mother, ain't too young to be a widow with a dead son."

The sheriff's mouth opened. Genuine shock; not forced. "A widow?"

"Yessir."

His eyes flashed from Orlena to the man. The Man looked at Orlena, waitin for her to say somethin stupid.

She didn't.

"Comanche?"

The sheriff's question was levelled to the woman only after the Man proved unforthcoming.

"My brother," she told him. "Jimmy."

It was a good story. Damn good story. Quick as a whip, Orlena Felder. He had not had faith in her until she lay that tale down on the bar. Lady made the right choice to lie by the man who shot her husband and son, rather than to got shot fer tellin the truth on him at the wrong place and time. Still had to be watched, Orlena Felder. He would not be lulled into trusting her. Still: respect was there.

The sheriff's eyes widened at the answer, then narrowed along with his face.

"Why the hell would yer brother kill yer family?"

"I aim to find that out with the helpa my friend here, Sheriff."

"And yer friend's name?"

"It's J—"

"Jack Allen," said the Man.

"You a bounty hunter, Mr. Allen?"

"Reckon I am now. Got my own issue with Felder… followed him through Orlena's ranch and run him off, though now I wish I'd caught him."

"Well, Miss Felder—I jes kinnot *believe* you are Jimmy Felder's sister, Lord have mercy on my soul!" Blaize seemed so distracted by that apparently astonishing fact that he momentarily forgot about the homicide of her husband and son; then, shaking himself from some rumination spurred on by her face, he said, "Well, suffice it to say that the Sheriff's Office of Sandspur would like to have a word of our own with Felder. When was this?"

"Last night," said Orlena, her gaze distant across the red sky cooling purple in the unilluminated East.

"Last night," answered Blaize in shock. She nodded, unspeaking.

The sheriff's serious expression tensed as the coach rocked around them.

Outside of town, Blaize took pains to help Miss Felder down from her seat. The Man rested his foot on the step of the coach once getting out of it, his eye on Chrysler as he dismounted his horse. With the crate of empty bottles donated by Meyer, the went out a ways from the coach so as not to bother the horses.

Then that flirtatious tone came oozin out the sheriff in spite—or perhaps because—of the fact that he'd just learned she was a fresh widow.

"What say you fellas let a third join yer shootin match? Miss Orlena, would you deign to sully yer lovely hands by throwin a few bottles fer us to shoot down?"

"Long as none of y'all get confused as to *where* yeh should be shootin," she answered wryly, tossing a glance at the Man before turning back to the crate. "I ain't no great throw, now."

"You'll learn with practice," said the sheriff, eyes glued to her figure.

Orlena removed the first one from the crate and looked back at the men. "Ready? Who's first?"

"Whoever's quickest," answered the sheriff, reaching for his gun.

Orlena smiled a little, stepping back a few skips. Lobbed the bottle with a strong arm.

Gunshot cracked through the air.

Sheriff's gun in his hand still cold; Chrysler's not out of the holster yet.

The Needless Man lowered his revolver while the shattered glass rained upon the earth.

"Hot damn," said Blaize with a whistle for the Man. "Now that's a quickdraw! Think you kin do that agin?"

He did. First one bullet shattered one bottle from Orlena; then Orlena threw two and the sheriff threw one and the man had all three destroyed before the broken shards of the first had hit the ground.

Chrysler fumed and insisted, "That's nothin."

Orlena flung a bottle for him and he shot it, but two was too many. One fell to the ground in a single piece and shattered on impact.

Blaize chuckled as though to himself. "Everybody has bad shootin days, Chrysler…better to git em out in practice than realize yer havin one when you got a guy standin a hundred paces in fronta yeh."

Without warning, Orlena lobbed a bottle through the air. Now it was the sheriff's turn to show off, whipping his gun up and whirling around to shoot it from the air soon as set eyes on it.

"Good shot, Sheriff," said the Man appreciatively.

"Praise from Caesar. Ain't no amateur yerself, Jack. Care fer a little one-on-one?"

"Hey," said Chrysler, "what the hell I come out here fer, anyway?"

"Ta waste some bullets from the looksa't," said Orlena.

"All right," said the ranchero sourly, adding a doubly sour look at the sheriff stifling his laughter. "I know when I ain't wanted."

"Hey, Chrysler, don't be so sore—come by my office tomorry and lemme throw some work atcha. I got a job fer you…"

When the sullen ranch hand was out of the picture, the Man and the Sheriff stood ten feet away from one another shoulder to shoulder. Fifty feet out from them, Orlena hurled the first bottle into the air.

The gun and the Man were the same. A metal organ outside the body but part of the body. Shot cracked through the air and snap went the bottle, falling back down to the earth.

"Where'd you learn to shoot, brother? Good God damn but you got some speed t'yeh!"

"Ain't nothin t'it."

"What's yer secret?"

"Anything I'm meant to shoot, I do."

Sheriff Blaize laughed and got one of two bottles flung through the air. The Man got the other, both their shots coming at once.

"Well I ain't no slacker myself, but it's clear you got some yearsa practice. You in the war at all?"

"Lotsa ways a man kin learn to shoot."

One, two, three bottles. The Man took two and let Blaize have the third to be polite.

"I reckon that's true," agreed Blaize, squinting through the densely falling night and then, upon adjusting his cigarette in his mouth, bending his head to peer through the smoke at the revolver he commenced to reload. "Every time a man fires a gun fer any reason, that's practice aplenty."

"It is at that," agreed the Man, taking his own chance to reload.

"You know, Jack, it happens I been keepin an eye out fer jes such a sharpshooter as yerself. Pull, darlin."

One, two-three. The Man took all three bottles before Blaize had his reloaded gun out of his holster.

His face struck by a momentary twist of jealousy, Blaize lowered his unshot Colt and shook his head. "Frankly…I ain't expected to *really* meet a fella like you."

"Most don't want to."

"I kin sure enough reckon why."

Looking the Man up and down in crisp deliberation, Sheriff Blaize fell back on his heel and holstered his gun all the way.

"It is not my custom to work with mercenaries of any sort, as I prefer to work with those I know and count among my friends. However…I am not at all opposed to the notion of makin *new* friends."

Adding this with a glimpse at Miss Felder, Blaize slid

one hand into the pocket of his waistcoat and used the other to tend to the cigarette in his lips.

"How'd you feel like doin a job fer me?"

"Same job you jes promised to set that Chrysler punk on?"

"Ah, give'im a hiding in fronta the fellas and he'll forget all about whatever spooked his cattle, if you'll pardon the expression."

The Man made no comment. Only holstered his gun and stood with his thumb hooked in his belt, listening to the proposal.

"I got three hundred heada horses I'm about to be runnin up toward New Mexico a little whiles over the border." Orlena approached with those intense shrew eyesa hers fixed on the lawman to whom they both listened. "Now, I don't know how both or eithera yeh'd feel bout this idea, but I gotta git these horses there as safe as safe kin be. I need a few fellas who kin really shoot."

"No," said the Man, "what you need is one."

Teeth again. A lightning bolt of laughter. A quick look at Orlena to see if she laughed, then a cessation to see she did not.

"Reckon that's true, Jack. Reckon that's true. Moreover, I need a man who kin shoot *and* stay alive between here and there and back agin, and who kin make sure what I got comin back comes back in one piece."

"What you got comin back, Sheriff?"

"A stagecoach," answered the sheriff without elaborating.

The Man nodded. "Long ways. Runnin three hundred heada horses been known to take awhile."

"Fella I talked to reckoned month, month and a half. Ride back should be faster."

"In my experience, the ride back is usually the more dangerous one."

"Why's that?"

"It's when you got the money."

"Sure enough, brother…but them Comanche that worry me ain't as innerested in gold as they is in horses. And anyway, you ain't bringin back gold or nothin else likely t'attract attention. However…I do not want to take chances."

Felder's sister fidgeted, her arms wrapping around herself as the wind picked up across the desert. Gonna try to run in the next month? Ain't nowhere to go except home to bury some bodies…or to see Jimmy.

"Seems to me Jimmy Felder could git awful far in the month and a half to two months it sounds like this trip'll take…assumin he knows to be on the run."

The sheriff's features sharpened as they had briefly in the stagecoach. Looking over his shoulder at the dozing driver and then back between Orlena and the Man, he said, "Listen…since neither onea yeh know this town and are parta the current gossip pool, I'll level with yeh's both."

Orlena leaned in; the Man listened impassively.

Lorenzo murmured, "We had a problem in the area around Sandspur this past week. I thought at first glance it was Comanche, but now talkin t'you folks I think Jimmy Felder's lost his damn mind and gone on some kinda spree… that, or he's jes killin folk Comanche-style to throw me off. Almost worked. Sure am glad I met you two."

Her lower lip disappeared into her mouth. "I'm afraid fer my brother, Sheriff."

"I am, too, and fer my town. So…how about we make a little arrangement, Jack?"

The Sheriff and the Man leveled their stares.

"You deal with my business fer me," suggested the Sheriff, "and I'll handle yers in the meantime."

"I want to kill him myself," said the Man. "I ain't fixinta run all over creation on yer behalf only to come back here and find him already swingin from the rope."

"I think I kin keep him available fer you, but if I must shoot him, Jack, I will—particularly havin heard Miss Orlena's harrowing tale, or the general outline of it."

"So long as I may speak with him first," she said, distant dreams of escape surely still swirling through her mind. "And if you kin keep him alive fer me to speak with, you kin keep him alive fer Jack here to kill."

Nodding, Sheriff Blaize extended his hand to the Man. "So, Jack—deal? You run these horses and bring back my stagecoach, and I'll keep Miss Orlena safe while we look fer Jimmy Felder. Hell! I'll even throw in some bullion fer yer trouble—that's two times the pay, from Orlena *and* myself."

"Money don't mean nothin to me," said the Man. "Not as much as Jimmy's head. Where yeh gonna stay in town, Orlena Felder?"

Before she could answer, the Sheriff hastened to respond through those omnipresent flashing teeth.

"Jes so happens that the very parlor house where you folks had yer shootin match is the same I and many others choose fer our habitation. Fine food and drinks, comfortable rooms."

"Plentya women to choose from," said Orlena stiffly.

The Sheriff laughed a little, adjusting his hat and saying, "That all depends on what a gentleman comes lookin fer, Miss Orlena…I reckon there are a whole heapa places where a man could find a woman if he's lookin fer one. Sometimes"—his smile changed—"even when he's not. What do yeh say, Jack? Let me put Orlena up in a room somewhere, mebbe at the hotel since she seems to find the Pearl objectionable, and we kin help each other out."

The Man regarded Orlena. She did not look at him because she did not care to, but he anticipated she was not likely to cause him a problem—and that any problem she tried to cause would make little difference for the Man. Whatever the sheriff was transporting back obviously required careful discretion, and it would not be wise for him to turncoat on a man with a faster gun than his.

And then, well…based on her decision to lie on Jimmy, she saw what was at stake.

Orlena's choices were cut-and-dry. She could sell out her brother, or could lose anything from her freedom to her land to her life.

It was Jimmy's life, or Orlena's.

And Orlena had already proven herself too selfish—too tenacious—to make the wrong choice.

The Man took the Sheriff's hand.

"When do we leave?"

10

ID ORLENA REALLY want her brother dead? The thought was the first to fly into her head when she stirred in her new bed; her second thought was how rich and deep her sleep had been for the first time in well over five years.

But especially in five years.

Her eyes opened to a new room that gave her stomach the inertia-lurch of an expected step found absent. Rather than her accustomed home of wood boards with furs hanging on some walls and trophies on others and embroidered samplers on others, this one—this very European, plastered room prettily wallpapered in gentle gold, with a single blue wall bearing windas to overlook the town—washed over her like a kiss on the eyelids of a sleeping child.

She had nothing to do.

Her cramps did not bother her at all, if they were still present that morning. She had been in the hotel three days, and in that time her bleeding had faded to negligible levels.

Using the money from the house on top of what she had gotten for the horses but had no need to use while staying on the sheriff's dime, she purchased clothes that the seamstress had managed to turn around in forty-eight hours. The black dress, anyway. The one that made her look like a widow.

She was a widow, of course. But she did not feel like one in her heart.

Some great, awful mistake had at last been rectified. Orlena played the part of the widow because she had to, but in the morning cool of her room, with her mind uncoiling from its customary anticipation of work, she was not a widow. She was not a mother in mourning.

She was someone who had been freed from a great ailment. Someone who was never supposed to be wife or mother, but who had been thrust into such conditions by evil hands. Those conditions were now gone; the evil hands, gone longer.

The only person who knew anythin objectionable about her now was runnin around somewhere in the wilderness with the Stone Hill Gang, plannin who the hell knew what kind of job.

With that in mind, Orlena had to wonder if there was more to her decision to go along with the Needless Man than simply maintaining the length of her own life. The last man who knew. Maybe it was best, yes, to get rid of him.

With her black dress on and her hair coiffed high, Orlena joined the other guests of the hotel for breakfast on the first floor. She did not engage in conversation, which was respected, and the other guests—a couple of cowhands who migrated in and out of town with work, a salesman of some kind, a few others with whom she had not made acquaintance—were just as happy to avert their eyes from the reminder of death she presented.

After eating in silence, Orlena daubed the corners of her mouth. The Mrs. of the place came swishing in.

"Ms. Felder," said the lady with a somewhat mischievous look in her crinkling eyes, "somebody's here to see yeh."

Dread tucked itself in a knot against her diaphragm; Orlena thanked her hostess and rose, knowing if she did not meet the Needless Man when he came to call then he would fetch her.

Her palms beaded with sweat. Would he be good as his word? If she did seize the chance during this next forty-five days to flee as far as she could get, would he really find her?

Yes. She did not have to ponder on it. But, after wiping her palms against the front of her dress and letting herself into the porch of the hotel, she stopped dead.

Sheriff Blaize turned to face her, his wide-brimmed black hat pressed to his chest and giving her a glimpse of his neatly parted blond hair.

"Miss Felder! Good mornin. I do hope I ain't callin too early."

"No." While they shook, his palm warm and broad but not nearly as rough as her husband's (dead husband's), Orlena used her free hand to dip in a slight curtsey. "I'm used to gettin up early, Sheriff—much earlier than I got up today."

"A much-earned rest after yer harrowin experience, I am sure. I wanted to let you know that yer friend, Mr. Allen—"

"He ain't my friend," she informed him quickly, keeping her tone as even and factual as possible.

This still earned her a strange look, but it was a look less of suspicion and more of a kind of calculating relief. "Well, that may be so, but I was wonderin if perhaps you cared to say bon voyage while he and the resta the fellas set off with the horses."

"I believe he and I have said all we need say t'one another until we know where Jimmy is," she answered.

His smile—his laugh—made her heart flutter in a way that was almost like fear. Certainly the feeling of desire in her hands was very much like fear; yet the impulse to flight, when defied, produced such crackling electricity between herself and the Sheriff that she ached to feel it forever.

"You certainly is a razorblade of a woman, isn't yeh, Miss Felder…well, perhaps if you ain't interested in seein Mr. Allen off, you'll oblige me fer a walk?"

His brows knit above sharp green eyes. She lowered her head, arms folding around herself. Her eyes focused instead on his rattleskin boots.

"I reckon it kain't hurt," she told him with only the briefest glance into his face, so as not to lead him on by prolonged assessment of his features.

Was it so wrong to lead him on now, though? Now that she wasn't married anymore? Bit of a harlot move to flirt with a sheriff right after her widowing, but was it not the living and liberty of men she craved? Had the men at that bordello the other night shown the least abashment about consulting her figure for their abject fancies?

Even the sheriff seemed to be doing the same thing once she'd fetched her shawl and hat and joined him for a stroll through slow-waking Sandspur.

"Yer gaze is very direct, Sheriff," she told him stiffly, pressing her shawl closer around herself and turning her stare forward again. "I find it disconcerting."

"I do apologize, Miss Felder…I was jes seein if you look peaked after spendin three days inside like that."

"Counted them, did you?"

"Each one," he told her, smiling while she repressed one of her own. "Particularly if I am t'assist you in the matter of justice, would you not agree it behooves me to know where y'er at and what y'er up t'on a given day? Jimmy's still out there."

Her bosom heaved with the electric conflict of it. His earnest, boyish look as she found him by the water pump. Her brother.

"I reckon that's true enough, but people'll talk if they see us together often."

"Hell, the gossipin old biddies round this place'd talk about they own mothers if they could find somebody to listen."

"Then it may be they are already discussing my arrival to the town."

"I would not doubt it."

"Do you attend church services, Sheriff?"

"Mind you don't keep up with all this 'Sheriff' business. Call me Lorenzo…and I confess I do not attend services with any particular regularity or relish."

"Nor I, but I am beginning to consider it if I will be staying here in town."

"Well, you might wanna wait."

Orlena took his tone and found him grim.

"Remember I told yehs about that—business?"

Over her shoulder lay a porch where an older man, reclining to read a paper in the morning light, pretended as though he were not observing the activities of the sheriff and this strange widow.

"The business around Sandspur, you mean."

"Uh-huh. That business. Well…it would seem Preacher Taft's got the bad enda that business."

Orlena's mouth contorted in shock. "Oh, he was the one who married Bert and me! What happened? Why?"

"By no means am I certain. Was hopin you might know somethin about that, if it is indeed related t'yer…former associate."

Difficult to tiptoe around the subject with the town havin so many ears.

"It would be nice to go someplace *private*," she said in frustration. "I am quite sure yeh have a reputation to protect, but—"

"I'm only savin yers. Truth is, Miss Felder, Sheriff's office is more of a cheap bed fer a drunk man to sober up in every day. There ain't a crime in this town that I do not see and deal with swiftly, and becausea that I am somewhat relaxed in how I do my work."

"If you mean you do most of yer business outta the Pearl to get away from pryin eyes, I done heard that already."

Laughing with the shake of his head, Lorenzo adjusted his hat's brim and squinted down the street ahead of them. "What did I only jes say about gossip in this town? Three days you been here, and already I reckon yer opiniona me to be as down low as a snake's belly."

"A snake might be the right choice. What's in that coach Jack Allen's bringin back, anyway?"

A funny look cross Lorenzo's face. Had she offended him? Some men did not respond well to—but, no.

He smiled, his teeth lovely and straight and white except for a slightly crooked cuspid.

"Well, Miss Felder, you stick around here and help me arrange Jimmy's capture, mebbe I'll tell yeh."

Shivering beneath that smile, Orlena changed the subject as best she could. "I know a little about where he is," she began, but his warm hand fit to the curve of her back and made her jump.

"Let's wait until we're at my office, Miss Felder, if you please...right this way."

Although she had not enjoyed her first visit to the Pearl and had in fact been somewhat startled by the brazenness of it all, Orlena found it was rather preferable to be around a group of gainfully employed women than a bunch of reekin drunks let outta their cells with the comin of morning. At any rate, the parlor house was much less objectionable when it was not bursting to the seams with those very drunk men who later wound up at the sheriff's office.

Meyer, who seemed to inhabit one of the Pearl's rooms, swept the floor on their entrance. With a look of recognition, he nodded graciously at Orlena, took in her black garb, then lowered his eyes back to his sweeping.

Orlena followed the sheriff and found the ballroom-sized first floor belied a veritable second-floor maze of corridors to rooms of various sizes—some clearly better than others. At the far end of the hall, Sheriff Blaize took a left and smiled in bright, polite surprise.

When she reached him, so did the two girls at whom he had smiled while they came down the other side of the hallway. Birdlike greetings of pleasure to see the sheriff had been on their lips, but as the pair and Orlena lay eyes on one another, the greetings faltered. Their smiles, however, remained in place. They were polite, they nodded; Orlena nodded, too.

Then they went their separate ways. Orlena, eyes full of perfectly smooth brows and tight, high cheeks and giddy smiles and French imported perfumes, and cosmetics, and pearls, and silk, and freedom, and the body as something to be enjoyed and not detested, followed the sheriff quietly to his office around the bend.

"I hope yeh aren't especially offended by the accommodations," he told her while gesturing toward an armchair. "The truth is that the Pearl is the first place I'd put up just about any guesta mine on accounta the quality of service—food and drink and housekeepin, I mean, of course."

"It's pleasant once it's quiet," she allotted, avoiding any hint of her reflection in the polished mirror to her left while she made her way to the chair.

His hat removed and hung on the rack, Blaize covered the length of the room to settle in the corner of the sofa and fold his hands between his knees.

"I am not morally opposed to prostitution," she added defensively. "I jes do not relish the idea of being around a bordello full of busy customers at any time of night…I do appreciate yer suggestion of Mrs. Paulson's hotel, however. It is a very pleasant home."

"Ain't it! You know, Mrs. Paulson got her loan t'open that place from the lady what runs this fine institution."

"That so? How interesting."

Most men could not perceive when a woman did not give a hoot about what they were saying, and Orlena had been fully prepared to shut off her brain and let the Sheriff windbag at her for a few minutes. Lorenzo, however, was more alert than that—a smile still settled mildly upon his face, he nodded and assured her, "That's right, she's an innerestin lady—but I find you much more innerestin, Miss Felder. Especially right now."

Orlena sat up at the slight double entendre of his interest. He leaned forward with his voice pitched low.

"Preacher Taft got found with his belly cut open, stuffed with the coals that helped burn down his mission. Ol Comanche trick…onea the reasons I thought it seemed like them. Yer brother got any particular ire gainst Taft?"

"None I know."

An honest answer to a question that was not relevant at all to the truth. The truth that she knew at once who had killed the preacher, and why.

Another death. Because of her.

Orlena sat back in the armchair, the fingertips of one hand spread against her chest.

"I confess," she murmured, consulting the empty chair set across from the sheriff's desk, "I do not know what to make of this."

"I know it is quite a lot to take in, Miss Felder."

Lorenzo took her free hand in both of his. Orlena flinched before she settled in his clutch.

"That is why it means so much to me—and why you must understand it is so important—that you are here and able t'assist me in my investigation."

Once she got used to the sensation, the feeling of his hands around hers made her heart hammer in her ribs. His hands on her hand made her wonder about his hands on her face, his thumb on her mouth, his palm on her waist. She let him keep hold of her while she spoke.

"I confess I know precious little, but I will tell you what I told Mr. Allen when we agreed to find Jimmy and see him dead."

"Perhaps you could recount the night of Jimmy's invasiona yer home? I know it may be difficult, but—"

"No." Her eyes darted away and her hand slipped out of his. "No, it's—I kin do it."

Her every thought for the past three days had been dominated by one of three things: Jimmy, the Needless Man, and a combination of the two. As though symbolic of this, she had steadily knitted together the narratives of her two nights and made of them one overlapping tapestry. Her favorite thing had always been to guess the way the stories she was readin would develop, and that knack allowed her to fold details into seamless fiction.

"It was—it was night. It was probably eleven at night. Or twelve. And I woke up, and—"

"You know what woke you up?"

She shook her head. "I thought I'ws havin more—troubles, as I had been enduring fer the prior night, but now I'm not sure what it was that awoke me."

"Coulda been Jimmy, you mean."

"Coulda been," she agreed with a nod, her mouth tight and her hands in awful want of something to do. Orlena slipped them into her shawl and bunched them in the fabric, her arms around herself. "Coulda been Jimmy, yes, and—I got up and, if you will excuse me, sought our facilities. And, when I stepped out again to go back in the house, suddenly there—"

Rustle.

Click.

Don't move.

Orlena's lips trembled. Her body surged with the same fear of death that had gripped her when the Needless Man introduced himself by pointing a gun at her. Her voice cracked as she went on.

"—there was a gun pointed at me," she said, her eyes glossing over.

Mouth firm with sympathy, Sheriff Blaize lowered his eyes from hers and patted his person for a handkerchief while she went on.

"And I turned and it was Jimmy. And I said, 'What are you doin here?' And he said—he said, 'Shut up and get in the house.'"

The way the sheriff's eyes fixed upon her when he handed her the handkerchief unnerved her more than she had expected it to. She felt a thinness to her story that she had somehow not perceived before presenting it to the lawman. Was it thin enough to poke holes? She had to be careful to avoid excessive details.

"And I tried to talk to him a little, but—but he told me he'd already killed our rancheros, I don't remember how many anymore. I sent the coffin-maker from here out to meet whoever's left and undertake the rest. He said he'd tell me how many fellas is still there when he's back."

"Three," answered Blaize. At Orlena's surprised look from behind the handkerchief she used to dab her eyes, he explained, "Hell, Orlena, you think I wann't gonna ride out t'yer ranch and take a little look around jes as soon as I woke up the mornin after we met? Good thing I did. Fellas left over there did not have the least idea of what to do…kain't say I blame em too much."

"Yes. I understand. Ah—"

Orlena hiccupped out a genuine sob and pressed the handkerchief to her eyes.

"He brought me inside and—he wanted money. No, wait, I'm sorry—he wanted money first, and I hit him with a lantern and ran back inside screamin fer Bert."

The whole night endlessly unfurled itself again and

again, a hideous tapestry sewn in great red detail behind her eyes. Orlena grit her teeth, the Sheriff's sandalwood scented handkerchief grinding into her forehead along with the rotation of her palm.

"He came out with his gun and—and that was it. Oh, God! Jimmy was jes faster."

"I'm so sorry, Orlena."

"And the *boy!* He hurt the boy because I begged him not to take the money. Oh, God. He don't care. He don't care about anythin—he's evil."

She had found herself talking about the Needless Man without realizing it, but the sheriff applied her lamentations to Jimmy.

"But he spared you, Orlena. His sister."

"Yes." Calming a little, Orlena wiped a few more tears from her eyes before drawing the bunched handkerchief down from her face. "Yes, he did."

"Why'd you reckon that is? Ain't spare his little nephew or his brother-in-law."

"I reckon it's on accounta he still has some use fer me." Once more thinking of the Needless Man. "It ain't outta love or generosity or nothin like that. Sparin me was crueler than killin me, sheriff, and more convenient…especially since that Allen fella came ridin up."

She did not mean that in her heart. None of it. She was thrilled to be alive and she was, in a closed room, relieved to be freed from her old life and its rancid secrets—but, in some ways, it was true. It certainly was true for her depiction of herself as a mournful widow, who wetly regarded Sheriff Blaize and added with a small, brave smile, "I'm sorry, listen to me. I mean—Lorenzo."

Stirred from his brooding contemplation of her wept testimony, Lorenzo regarded Orlena and smiled just a hair. "Sounds a lot prettier comin from you than 'Sheriff,' Miss Felder…that is a harrowing, horrible night you have jes described. Y'er very lucky Mr. Allen arrived when he did."

"Yes," was all Orlena said as the door to the office opened.

McLintock, stepping into the room, stopped halfway over the threshold.

"Orlena Felder? Sam Hill! That you?"

"Mr. McLintock!"

Her heart fluttered at the familiar face, met all of one time a while afore Jimmy got sent to the hoosegow but remembered now when she needed him. Moustache a touch grayer, eyes a bit more lined—but, by God, it was the very same McLintock what was runnin round with Jimmy and the Stone Hill robbers all them years ago.

Though Orlena rose from her seat to offer the deputy her hand, the mood changed along with the focus of her mind. Sooner or later she would have to speak with McLintock about the Stone Hill Gang and where they might be found, if he still had even the least idea. She suspected probably not, him bein a deputya Lorenzo Blaize since around the time of Jimmy's capture. He'd made the smart move. The reality was he likely didn't know anymore.

And if he didn't know, she'd be dead in a little over month.

"Thought I heard somethins bout you comin into town. Sorry now I been out the past two days. How are yeh?"

"Fer Chrissakes, Wilt," began the sheriff under his breath. Ignoring him, Orlena maintained her forced smile and looked between the men.

"Well goodness knows, I have been better—but I am glad to be makin the acquaintancea the sheriff, and gladder still to see you again, Wilt."

Her smile was a little more real for a few seconds. At least, until she set her hat upon her head.

"We shall have to catch up sometime…but I do fear I have worn out my conversational capacity fer the mornin. If you fellas would excuse me."

11

LORENZO DID NOT try to walk Miss Felder out of the Pearl. He knew better.

And, anyway, he was too damn mad.

Quiet as he could, Lorenzo shut the door of his office and studied his hand on the knob.

"I think you know damn well better than to let yer own damn self into my office without knockin when I am conductin business, Wilt."

"Sorry, sir. Never know what kinda business y'er conductin in this place. Mebbe if'n yeh'd do sheriff's business outta the sheriff's office I'd keep it straight."

"Jes tell me what the good goddamn it is yeh want, Deputy."

"Meant to hear how it went seein off those Natives this mornin. It was today, wann't?"

"Sure 'nough were. You hadn't been outta town this last two days, I'da had half a mind to send yeh with em."

"Lucky fer me, I'ws up north lookin around fer more signsa who done in Taft."

"Then y'er wastin time. I know yeh liked the fella well enough with all the damn time yeh spent prayin too far from town fer me to give yeh work, but to be frank I ain't cryin many tears. What with that place burned down I expect to see yeh round Sandspur and doin yer job more."

McLintock snorted slightly. "Guess I really did come in at a bad time."

"You ain't know the halfa it. You wanna bea use to me and git outta town awhiles, how's about you run by onea my ranches and pull off a couplea cowhands. Orlena's ranch is gonna need all the help they kin get fer the next few weeks, least till she kin hire new mena her own. Then we oughta start workin on the Stone Hill Gang again; I let em go too long. You know where they're at these days?"

"If I knew, Sheriff, I'da arrested em and had yer job by now."

Sucking a tooth, Lorenzo reclaimed his hat and said, "Well, you git any word about yer old friends, you let me know."

"Yessir, I surely will. Say, uh—"

Lorenzo paused by the door to shoot his deputy an irritated look.

"Give them scorpions a try yet? Must be a damn good time fer a fella to let a mean little bastard like that sting 'im."

"There's a whole hell of a lot more t'it than a good time," Lorenzo said tersely. "Didn't you hear 'em the other night? The Natives think the scorpions kin teach yeh things."

"You believe em?"

"I ain't tried it yet."

The office door shut behind him.

After pausing in the hall to stuff his irritation away,

Lorenzo made his slow way to his room. It was the last in this hall, isolated. Alone behind its shut door, he leaned against the winda and looked out over the town.

Fer some reason what stuck with him was not Wilt's interruption, but his comment about Lorenzo's choice of office.

Was life changing, or was Lorenzo? He had begun seeing things differently at some point, though he was not sure when or why that shift began. His elbow against the winda frame to allow him to prop his forehead on his fist and watch Orlena make her way down the road, he realized at the very least his enterprise had changed. Seemed that, as a man who was called a 'criminal' by lawmen became more and more successful, his crimes tended to become indiscernible from the normally functioning components of society. That thin line between usury and makin a livin on loans; the negligible difference between robbin a man of his land by burnin down his house or claimin he owed back taxes or stickin him on a reservation.

Miss Felder paused to contemplate a side street with those calculating eyesa hers.

He took in every step, the dignified fluidity of her movements dispassionate yet commanding. All men who passed her took care to tip their hats and bid her good-morning, though whether she responded or not, Lorenzo could not discern.

His business was changing along with his goals. Oh, the Pearl and its management was plenty concerned about the development of the town, with its beautification and water supply and the expansion of the library, all of which were recipients of her generous donations and all of which had helped keep Sandspur's perception of the Pearl more positive than negative. No doubt.

However…Lorenzo could see the handwriting on that there wall.

Just like the railroad was an inevitable, reality-shaking development that connected more of these fine United States every day and threatened to leave Sandspur outta the picture if it did not develop quickly enough, certain other changes were similarly inevitable. Public perception toward bordellos was already tense and only bound to get tenser. There was certainly a small but strong-minded contingent in Sandspur that cared little for the Pearl—and, for that matter, Lorenzo. His career was reaching a point where, if he was to maintain his title, he was going to have to make more consistent and subtle use of lieutenants to manage his various business interests…and he was going to have to invest in goods less visible than female bodies.

McLintock had a point, though. Still had to try the damn product.

Lorenzo shut the curtains and slid open the dresser drawer where the scorpions shivered in the light, their tails bobbing. After one had died in the cigar box he improved the size of their quarters and shut them up with a little dirt and a handfula cockroaches that seemed to need replacing.

After assessing them, he grimaced. Another had died and the remaining eight meandered about, not yet having noticed its deceased state but soon to consume it. Well… let em have that, then put McLintock on cockroach duty. Lorenzo sure was curious to see how the eventual scorpion 'farm' would be formatted when the Brave returned with a coach of the creatures.

But who *would*, among the common people, choose to take a scorpion into their hand and allow it to sting them once or twice, let alone the three times required for what was considered by the Natives to be the truly intoxicating purpose of the scorpions? Clearly, somebody smarter than Lorenzo was gonna have to figure out how to get the venom out of the scorpion and into the human body through a method as convenient as the imbibing of alcohol or tincture.

You didn't walk straight up to the damn cow and stick its teat in your mouth.

But the fact that the Natives *did* choose to experience the venom through the sting was part of why it was all so intriguing to Lorenzo. It told him that, whatever the experience of the triple-sting was like, it was more than worth it. That medicine man's whole arm had been covered stem to stern in scars, and if Lorenzo had to guess, the old man's whole body was similarly marked.

The method of ingestion was certainly not appealing… but boy, that venom must have been.

After testing the lock on his door, Lorenzo returned to the drawer of wandering scorpions and used a gloved hand to pick the arachnid of his choice.

What an ugly thing! Its exoskeleton glittered with the indigo-black iridescence of certain Western birds—but the color was, on the scorpion, merely an insidious method by which the world-maker could camouflage itself from predators and hapless human feet alike. Its pinchers grasped the air before it and its little legs rapidly wiggled without purchase while it hung by the tail Lorenzo pinched.

Mouth firm-set, Lorenzo lowered into his bed and rested the scorpion in his gloved hand.

Though agitated, it did not sting him immediately. Instead, as though surprised to find itself released, it sat in his hand and seemed to settle. Its claws lay casually upon the heel of his palm. Its tail receded slightly, that stinger at ease. It was about the length of his palm and the first joint of his fingers, not including the tail or pincher-arms; these nasty little weapons rested dangerously near to the exposed wrist skin between glove and sleeve.

Exhaling, his motions slow, Lorenzo drew his sleeve down another centimeter to expose more skin.

Animating at its sudden perception of movement, the scorpion tensed. It raised its tail.

"Go on, you little bastard," he said with a twitch of his fingers to urge it forward.

The scorpion obliged him—albeit with more enthusiasm than he had prepared for.

One-two; one-two. The scorpion's firebrand stinger struck him in pairs, each time pumping its venom straight into the exposed blue vein in his flesh. Lorenzo yelped on the first pair, his body reacting so viscerally he had to grip the bed to keep himself from flinging the thing away; only when it managed its second set of stings did he yield to the urge, flinging it across the room with a gasp and a hard clutch of the stings' locations.

Was he in trouble? Those Natives had said that enough stings would be deadly to a man. Was four that many more than three? Was he going to regret this? Should he be callin on the doctor before—

Before?

Before the hot flame of pain around his wrist stung up through him in those icy pulses?

Before his limbs grew heavy and feverish, and his joints ached with inflammation?

Before an alien gravity forced him to lay his heavy body down into the mattress, and he did, yielding to the intense push, the great weight, of something that was not the simple force of his home physics?

His mouth fell open, eyes fixed on a ceiling that narrowed to a pinpoint amid a crucible of shifting, glittering shapes closing in around him. These strange objects danced like diamonds of every color, pressing together, twirling around, and gradually closing over the ceiling as though they were a curtain

His body had been similarly dissolved, as dissolved as the ceiling that was really nothing at all and never was, but he did not feel concern because it became at once apparent to him that a body did not matter. Anyway, his focus was consumed by the voice that calmly addressed him.

Was it a voice? Yes-no. Some entity communicated with him some way. He felt the presence and basked in its teacherly warmth, comforted by it as he was unnerved by the shapes.

"Safety," he felt-heard. "You are safe."

He did not feel safe. The rapid gyrations of the shapes, which changed their forms and colors more quickly than the eye could stand, seemed somehow urgent. The urgency of a parent waking their child late for church.

Was the urgency related to the shapes, or to Lorenzo? He remembered his identity very abruptly; only as a consequence of wondering what was watching the shapes. In the self-awareness of watching came profuse and frightening questions. How long had he been watching? How long had he been here? Was he going to be here forever? Where *was* he? When could he go back? Was there a back to go to?

Was he always here, and the other place where he thought he was just some kind of thin dream?

Lorenzo cried out for help, desperate for an exit. The shapes swirled and thrashed around him, hastening to expand around and then fly past him. As though he rode through them upon the back of a rapid horse.

"Patience," said teacher-entity. "Patience."

"Let me out," he tried to stutter through the heavy gravity. "Please, let me go back—I want to go back, I don't want to be here."

"Yes, you did; or you would not have come."

The voice boomed all around him as the shapes folded together, swallowed by the same gravity that turned his perception around.

Those very shapes, he realized, were the teacher-entity speaking to him.

Now, in response to the panic, teacher-entity took on a different form. Lorenzo—at the very least, his disembodied perception—stood before a tall, thin man whose skin was black-blue as the scorpion. The eight eyes upon his bald head all placidly regarded Lorenzo without need for a point of focus. This being stood unclothed in a space that was bright and vibrant and, Lorenzo found, only permitted him to proceed backwards or forwards. Left and right had never existed.

Lorenzo shook, his entire body vibrating at some great intensity of speed or pressure or both.

"You may come and go as you please," said the creature. "It is a choice."

The creature did not mean visiting this place in his mind or even through the scorpion, Lorenzo realized, but rather through death.

"Is this death? Am I dead? Oh, God! Did that thing kill me? I want to go back—please, help me go back!"

"You chose to be here now, and so you are. We have waited for this visit for many centuries."

"Please, oh—"

It was difficult to talk but the words dragged out of him as screams; much as he, still crushed by that gravity, managed to drag himself forward through the two-dimensional space. Toward the entity who stood still before him, eight or nine feet tall and regarding him impassively even as he made an interdimensional ass of himself.

"You gotta help me—I ain't mean to be here—"

"You had to come here so that we might know where you were," said the creature. "We are coming for you now."

"T'help me?"

"Yes."

"Oh, yes! Please—please, God, help me."

"We will help you. You will remember what you have forgotten. You will be safe until we find you. Have patience."

"I will—I will, please. I jes—I want to live!"

Though unable to push himself up very far, he managed to at last grab hold of the scorpion-man's calf and crane his head. His eye got hung up around the creature's enormous phallus, ribbed like the hateful body and curved like the tail of the arachnid with whom this being appeared conjoined. Lorenzo realized his own dick was hard, or at least pulsing with ice-cold waves of ecstasy. Maybe that was all he'd have felt if he'd stopped at one sting.

How strange that the base and animal body could create all this! There seemed to be some secret in the demon's penis and Lorenzo wondered if it could be extricated from his own sexuality; if he could grasp the secret meaning behind the fact that sex, whether loving or commodified or assault or celebratory, could create life. Created him. Created *all* the beings from this side of the planet to the other.

Beneath the weight of this deep meditation, Lorenzo collapsed at the entity's feet and hyperventilated into a plane that soon once more danced and shivered with pulsations of color. Gradually, along with the receding of his panic attack, those shapes reconstructed the world around him: the floor along which he'd dragged himself while hallucinating he was in another dimension; the door slammed off its hinges, its lock broken on its frame; Meyer the bartender, shaking him by the shoulders while a couplea girls held each other and watched in horror.

"Sheriff," Meyer was saying, his tone sliding into a sigh of relief as they locked eyes. Releasing Lorenzo, Meyer sat back on his heels and asked, "Jesus, Sheriff, you all right? You git some bad whiskey somewheres? Let me gitcha to a doctor."

The freshness and beauty of it, suddenly! The vibrancy of being alive. Of smiling weakly at cute women who giggled and whispered t'each other. The grandfatherly concern of a good man. Memories and future and being Lorenzo Blaize.

He sighed in contentment, too tired to get up.

"I think I already seen one," he said, waving his hand. "Don't you worry none about me, Meyer, y'all kin shut the door on yer way out…oh, and, uh, mind the scorpion somewheres round here…trust me, you don't want to find him by surprise."

12

HORSES CASCADED THROUGH the desert. A storm of dust encircled them amid the beating of their hooves. All around, men shouted to their own beasts or two one another. Their voices had to be pitched an extra decibel or two to compensate for the bandanas worn against the grit and wild smell of the mustangs. Their own horses showed signs of weariness after a long morning ride. The Needless Man patted his upon the side of its neck when it tossed its head in agitation to be urged into a faster gait.

He had made his way through the Texas desert before, but its vastness never lost its staggering quality. So much of it was relentlessly flat, which made the trip easy for a leg; but, as they drew farther northwest, the terrain became more visibly mountainous. Beyond that would be the Guadalupe Mountains to navigate around, and as a result it would be a long, arduous trip with some zig-zagging north and south to get the horses where they needed to be with minimal casualties.

The Needless Man did not like the path, but running them horses up mountains and back down was, suffice it to say, impractical. His presence at the drive was heavily necessitated by this long path, he could see; at the very least, they required the presence of someone who was used to killing.

Not to say the other fellas were estranged from violence. That Roaring Bear fella, for instance.

When they stopped for rest, the cohort of horses milling about to graze, the Man unsaddled his horse and watched from the corner of his eye. The stagecoach, naturally at the back of the drive, came to a stop at the camp's edge. Roaring Bear stopped beside it to dismount and help down his elder. The medicine man rejected him with the wave of a hand and a few words in their language, laughing a little, then catching the eye of a nearby ranchero.

"These coaches are a peculiar way to travel," he said. "Don't they make you feel like you are at sea somehow? In a great ship. It's how I've always imagined sailing to be, anyway."

The ranchero snorted. He shook his head, apparently unable to relate to the imagination of the medicine man and too entitled by his lifelong relationship with the technology to be particularly impressed. With a similar chuckle and shake of his head, the old man made a gesture of dismissal toward the young man's back. He turned away to his Tribesmen to find a place to rest.

In the week that they had traveled, the rancheros had developed quite a rapport. Many of em already knew each other. Bout two thirds Black or Mexican; one third, the sort what made the first two thirds go hide in woods and barns when census came round so folk like Orlena didn't pay as much in taxes on their workers.

On this particular trail ride, however, seemed like things was a bit more equitable. Fellas for the most part laughed and chatted without discrimination while the expedition's cook went to his work, a fire crackling in minutes and lunch soon on the way. The Needless Man had watched them all from the outside, minding his business and keeping his thoughts to himself as was his custom. He had not spoken more than three or four words at a time in seven days, and it was a feeling of freedom that he enjoyed.

Of course, much as this quality had made Jimmy deeply uncomfortable, the other men in the drive had a natural limit of acceptance. As quiet as a minority of the other rancheros could be, (older ones, especially; the war vets), the Man couldn't help but think it was something else that made the dullard nicknamed Spud try to make him a target.

A few groups talked and ate here or there, the Natives conversing in their tongue just on the edge of the camp. The Man was the only one aside from the cook who sat by himself, and even the cook went and joined a few other rejects.

Only the Needless Man ate in silence. Accordingly, it was only the Needless Man who recognized the sudden silence of a small group near to him while he scanned the terrain for possible problems.

The present problem stared at him with six eyes and three dirty faces you couldn't tell was white if somebody paid you to guess.

"You ever talk, boy?"

The Man looked over at them.

Chrysler, in the middle, took swig from a tin cup while the grinning yokel beside him waited for a response.

"Too stupid, I guess."

"Nah," said Chrysler, his gaze flicking between the Man and the idiot. "He ain't. I'm tellin you to watch yer mouth, Spud. He'll shoot a new part straight down the middlea yer hair."

Refreshing to know Chrysler could learn a lesson. Friend couldn't. Laughed stupidly again and swallowed the spoonful of beans he had just crammed in his mouth.

"Shit, you ain't needa be smart to shoot good!"

Setting his empty bowl aside, the Needless Man stood in silence. The yokel kept speaking with his head turned toward his friends.

"I known plentya Grade-A mor-ons what'll git a target from six hundred yards away yeh put a gun in they hands."

His hand stilling the buckle, the Man slid his gun belt from his trousers and doubled it over so that the bullets, while heavy, were at least on the inside.

The third guy, his eyes huge, said, "Hey, Spud—"

"In fact, I usedta know a feller down in North Carolina 'fore the war. Had this little monkey he done imported from Af-rica, and you know what he—"

Spud gagged as the Needless Man dragged him by the collar from the rock where he was sitting and threw him face-down in the dirt. Chrysler and the third fella cried out, but they weren't half fools enough to intervene by doin much more than flyin up outta their seats and standing there with looksa horror.

Nobody in the camp much inclined to stop him, either, though everybody watched as the Needless Man threw his whole back and shoulder into mercilessly beating the screaming Confederate whose flailing hands were bruised before he could draw his gun. Spud was quickly reduced to raising his arms over his face and turning himself onto his stomach to let his back and ass take most of the blows. Entire camp had grown silent aside from his cries and the repeated snap of the brutally heavy leather into his hide.

The only other noise worth the least attention was the laughter of the Brave, whose mirth signaled the sufficiency of the beating.

While Spud wept, the Needless Man unfolded his belt and fit it back around his waist. He took the time to buckle it and then, as the camp around gradually returned to their lunch with an uncomfortable (or occasionally amused) series of murmurs, the Needless Man used the toe of his boot to roll the idiot over.

Spud cried out in pain as his welts pressed to the ground through the rough fabric of his shirt.

"You fight in the war?"

"Wh—what?"

"You fight in the war? Fer the South?"

"N—no! No, sir, no, I—I'ws ten, I'ws too young."

"Lotta boys lied bout bein that young so they could join up and ain't nobody in the South fixinta stop em."

"N—no! No, no, sir, not me, I didn't. I swear. My—my mama wouldn't let me."

"Ain't think so. Didn't seem to me like you'wsa man who ever did a damn thing in his life, good or bad."

Shoving Spud back into the ground, the Needless Man collected his bowl. Chrysler and their third pal helped Spud up, eyeing the Nameless Man warily as he navigated around them.

"Here's yer bowl," said Needless to the cook, showing him that he set it beside the fire before making his way back to his horse.

Ain't no more bothern swattin a fly. These things were to be expected. Ignorance knew no creed or color, but it did persistently manifest in a certain type of white boy who had been part of any even slightly well-to-do Southern family prior to the war. The Needless Man reckoned if he'd built an unsustainable business on the backs of slaves and budgeted a lifestyle that assumed free labor would always be plentiful, he'da been pretty upset, himself.

They did not realize how lucky they were that the war had not been won by an American answer to General L'Ouverture down there in Haiti.

Not that it would have made a difference to the Needless Man. Even in that society, he would not have fit in. In a Black world, he would have been perceived as non-Black; in a White world, he was certainly non-White. The Mexicans did not generally feel comfortable around him, and he had to confess he had not yet made the acquaintance of a great many Asians during his time roving the United States because his paths did not intersect with their business sectors very often.

But the Natives understood him. He did not adorn himself with the pretensions of the average, materially hungry man whose blood ran from the stock of a different continent. With no home, no name, no property, the Needless was as in sync with nature as a man could be while still engaging with society as required. As a result, he and the First Peoples of the Americas had something in common.

It was that common nature that caused Roaring Bear to approach the Needless Man one day after his public beating of Spud.

"I'm surprised they have not yet attempted retaliation against you."

Hands at ease on the saddle horn while his gaze raked the distance, the Needless Man said, "Ain't nothin they respect like violence."

"Still, you should be careful. The sort of man to make an ill comment is petty. A petty man is dangerous."

"I did not realize yeh spoke English."

"I prefer to keep it to myself."

"Makes two of us."

The Brave chuckled. He scanned the prairie while the Man did. "Seen anything lately?"

"Not a damn thing but Wells Fargo…and I kinnot help but find myself suspicious of that."

"It is suspicious," agreed the Brave. "This region belongs to the Shis-Inday, but I have myself seen few traces of them."

"You seen traces, though."

"Only an area here or there where an encampment may have been…like us, they must carefully disguise evidence of their habitation if they are to avoid attracting the undue attention of Comanches."

"Or Colonels."

The Brave shook his head. "We are so desperate for assistance that I do not think we would shy away from embracing the help of the cavalry. We were forced to retreat from many Comanche attacks and have been in hiding on our sacred grounds since. These horses, I hope"—he looked upon them with palpable love as they surged along under the guidance of the men—"will not just gain back our lands, but preserve our lives."

"Well—and I don't mean to disappoint—I wouldn't be so sure the land'sll be anybody's but the Federal Government's a whole hell of a lot much longer."

"Then we will have something to sell to them, at the very least."

"Assumin they pay yeh fair…wouldn't hold my breath."

Night fell. Only time the sky didn't look blue was when it was black. The Needless Man sat up cleaning his guns in the semi-dark at the far perimeter of the campfire. On the other side of the camp, the Natives had congregated near the stagecoach. The Braves stayed up softly conversing in a combination of murmurs and sign language.

Every once in a while the tattooed fella, Roaring Bull, would make a glance toward the Man. By these looks, the Man knew that he was going to have to speak again that night.

Sure enough. Once about half the camp had settled down for sleep, the talkative Brave crossed on silent feet among the men.

The Needless Man kept quietly workin the dust outta his Schofield.

"What did I tell you." The Native squatted down on his heels beside Needless, murmuring, "Your friend has been eyeing you tonight."

"Ain't jes you?"

"I have been trying to decide whether or not to speak

on the matter…whether or not I believe my own instincts. I do. He is looking for an opportunity."

"Well," the Man turned the broken open gun in the light of the low fire, "I reckon I oughta give im one."

The Brave returned to his family. The Man studied the gun before snapping its cylinder back down into place, its extractor clicking ready. He turned the barrel in the soft light. Scratched up by years with the lawman. Reliable.

Loaded gun back in holster. Hat low down on face. Pantomime of sleep.

Two hours.

Snoring, farting, thrashing cattlemen all around.

And silence over Spud.

The Man removed his hat from his face and quietly rose to his feet. He affixed his gun belt around his waist and silently crossed out of the camp as though to answer the call of nature in the dark.

Went quite a ways away.

Decided to take a piss after all, just to pass the time and to set the bait.

In thick darkness that was no small walk—perhaps five minutes of footsteps loud enough to telegraph his position to any damn snake—the Man whipped his dick out.

He listened.

Beneath the rhythm of draining on the earth.

Beneath his heart and the wind.

Yes.

There it was.

The grind of dirt under a boot.

The Needless Man tucked himself away, then turned to smash his fist into Spud's face. All one smooth motion.

Shocked, Spud managed something between a gasp and the beginning of a shriek before the Needless Man closed his hands around the little coward's scrawny neck and squeezed his arteries down to nothing.

Spud's eyes bulged, each orb as bright red as the face that was, even in the complete darkness of night, growing by the second less red and more purple-gray.

Spud's tongue lolled fatly out, twitching in his mouth while his limbs flew in all directions.

The Needless Man did not abide Spud's kickin, nor his weak punchin. He forced him down to his knees.

Capable of only noises of strain, Spud clawed at the hands around his throat. Then he lowered his arms and for all the world seemed dead.

The Needless Man counted in his head.

One Mississippi.

Two Mississippi.

Three—

A hand from the darkness, followed by a body, leapt into the Needless Man's vision.

He lunged back as far as he could while keeping his hands around Spud's throat.

Relaxed.

The Brave crouched behind the dying man, having stopped him from reclaiming the gun dropped on his failed surprise attack.

Spud's bulging eyes rolled lifelessly toward his empty brain.

His hand went limp in the Brave's grasp.

Together, the men lay the body down into the dirt and looked at one another.

Next mornin it was the hum.

Anybody seen Spud.

What about you, you seen Spud last night.

Nah, I ain't seen him.

Found five minutes away with his scalp yanked off and hanging, a messa hair and congealed blood, from a nearby cactus.

Poor son of a bitch.

The Needless Man spat in the dirt near the body. He looked over at the resta the search party.

"Guess them Comanches is around after all…we better partner up at night from here on out."

Ain't nobody argued.

13

I T WAS NOT that Orlena did not feel badly about the boy. She did.

She always had.

But she felt worse that the boy had been conceived and born—that God had allowed a life to come into the world in such a horrific way. That a child had been forced to serve as a conscious, feeling reminder of Orlena's shame.

During her early weeks in Sandspur, she therefore ignored as best she could the nag of guilt, the wondering and loss, the fear that there would never be another: all the usual emotional experiences endured by a parent who had lost a child. But she was not alone. Many women Orlena had known had lost a child, and in fact most childbearing women had lost a child through that point in human existence. She held those notions in her heart, along with the memory of the Needless Man firing his revolver and the boy falling down.

Wann't her revolver, was it?

Her thoughts plagued her day in and day out. She lived two lives concurrently: the real life, the physical life in Sandspur; and the life her memories and body expected her to be living with her family. She dreamed of them often. Woke up crying once or twice.

Almost never cried in real life.

But, every day, it was easier. Every day that Orlena became more calibrated to her new existence, her center of gravity shifted away from the cattle ranch and the past. Instead, her center began to settle comfortably into Sandspur. To the future.

And, of course, to Lorenzo Blaize.

Orlena was not sure if she could rightly say she was in love with Lorenzo yet. It was too soon and her heart, torn open by the immediate loss of her family and the probable future loss of her brother, was too exposed. Too prone to emotion. She could therefore not yet safely say whether the way her heart sped in Lorenzo's presence was love, or mere loneliness for the embrace of a handsome man with charisma and jes a little sorta somethin that gave him more dimension than Bert had ever had.

But, oh, hell…her heart *did* flutter to see him walk into a room, or to walk into a room and find him already there.

These events occurred with increasing frequency. Morning walks with the sheriff became a ritual. Each day, after breakfast, Orlena would step onto the porch. There he'd be, hat in his hand and his eyes drifting across the town, a low whistle occasionally on his lips. To hear the door, he'd turn and smile. The whistling would stop.

"Good mornin, Miss Felder! Certainly is a fine day, is it not?"

"Yes, Lorenzo. It certainly is."

She had been nervous that he only buttered her up to extricate information from her, but that fear proved unfounded after a few weeks of their acquaintance. He inquired only once more about Jimmy, this time asking if she might have the least idea where her brother was stayed. She repeated the same vague details that Jimmy had shared with her and, as she had demonstrated for the Needless Man, whistled the bird call.

When its final note had fallen from her lips, Sheriff Blaize had that small, somehow mysterious smile on his face.

"Now that sure sounds like one beautiful bird, Miss Felder. Reckon I see why that Allen fella was plannin on haulin you with'im to see Jimmy. Seems pretty damn risky, but ain't no lawman or bounty hunter with lips soft and small enough to make a birdsong like that."

Her face burned red hot whenever she thoughta him sayin that! Oh, sometimes she sincerely fanned herself in the presence of the aptly-named sheriff.

By far and away, Lorenzo was the most interesting man in town. More interesting still when Orlena heard tell he had, for the first time in three years, started doing business out of his actual sheriff's office.

"Well, Miss Felder"—he squinted into the cloudless ocean of blue unending above them—"sometimes somethin happens and a man gets to thinkin on his image…worryin on it. Reputation's all you got, and I been thinkin lately that the need to protect a reputation might jes be what makes a man grow up. I don't know yet…between you and me, I ain't sure I'm there all the way."

"I don't know nobody who is," she said with a gay laugh. "Mr. Winston what runs the pharmacy across from your station, his jokes are worse than any little kid's. I purchased some sorta medicinal mint tea from him the other day, fer headaches and all, and he says, 'Looks like you'll be makin a lotta money soon, Miss Felder.' And I say, 'Why is that?' And that old fool, he says, 'On accounta it's a mint!' Get it—like a treasury, you know—"

"Oh, I see—" Throwing back his head to laugh, neck

extended, Adam's apple prominent and bobbing, teeth flashing with his tongue, with his smile touching his eyes. "'Old fool' is right! Man don't have nothin to do all day except think up bad jokes, and ain't nobody there to stop him till he hires somebody to help him someday. Shucks, Orlena"—he caught her attention through her laughter with that warm utterance of her first name, her mirth softening slightly—"I sure do love yer laugh. It's a beautiful sound—I ain't git t'hear it enough."

Flushed from her cheeks to her high neckline and beneath, Orlena uttered a more nervous laugh. She lowered her head. "What a thing to say so suddenly, Lorenzo."

"I'm sorry, Orlena. I kain't help it."

"I'm sure you could, but I don't know if I'd want you to."

Their smiles remained upon one another for a few long seconds. Realizing they had come to a stop in the walkway and that there were people coming, Lorenzo offered her his arm. She hesitated only a second, then took it and pressed her hand against his bicep with a soft inhalation at the tension of his muscle.

"Say, Orlena"—once the others had passed, he spoke in a new, low tone—"there's a little thing tonight at another saloon in town. *Not* the Pearl. I'ws jes wonderin, since it's pretty tame there by comparison, and there'll be a lotta ladies dancin and havin a good time, mebbe yeh might like to come with me? I could introduce yeh to some more people. Know yeh haven't exactly been circulatin these past few weeks."

"I had probably ought to," she confessed.

"It's all right if yeh don't *want* to circulate—or come with me, fer that matter. I jes thought—"

"No, no. I'd like that very much, Lorenzo. In fact, I think I have jes the dress."

She had been wearing the black one since her first days in Sandspur, but the green and gold one she had special ordered had arrived at last not many days before—a little faster than she had expected, considering the level of detail. It fit her like a glove and made her feel modern and sexy like a dress never had. A little generous on the amount of shoulder left bare, if you asked her…but she had to wonder how much of that reflexive instinct was just her being stuffy after years of belonging to this man or the other and therefore being forced to conceal herself from the rest of the world.

She wrapped her shoulders in her shawl to make herself feel more comfortable, but then she and Lorenzo walked into the mixer. Plenty of women wearing dresses in styles that were comparable. Not a one of them seemed to think nothing of it, and she wondered at the frightening haste with which styles could change. In the five years she was away from the world, the shift in that world was visible.

Bolstered, she relaxed the shawl from her shoulders. The sweep of Lorenzo's eyes over her made her smile.

Maybe it weren't so indecent, after all…or maybe indecency didn't feel so bad.

"Would you help me with this, Sheriff?"

He smiled somewhat wryly, taking the shawl from her hands with a roguish cock of his brow.

"It's funny, Orlena…I used to think it sounded too damn formal when yeh called me that, but suddenly I think I like the sound."

She swooned a little while he disappeared toward the coat check, her hand on her heart and her forehead all aflame.

Most men were decent sorts, Orlena had generally found. Oh sure, there were quite a few like the bad folk Jimmy ran with. Men like her father, too. Then there was that evil shadowa hers off runnin them horses.

The counter-examples aside, by and large, most men were decent. Many were complicated. Their relationships with women were complicated, too, and stiff. Weren't their fault or even a bad thing necessarily. Jes obvious.

But Lorenzo Blaize was not the least bit foreign to

the company of women. That much was clear. A few ladies cornered him while he was on his way back to her from the coat check, and he greeted them with an ingratiating smile that was no less charming for coming with an excuse to leave.

Then he was before her, offering her his arm. "Well, Orlena, shall we have a dance?"

The band was in full swing and the dancers gay. An entire saloon full of people laughed and sang and clapped along. Lorenzo had an elegant ability to promenade about the floor at the right pace and perfect beat, and when he pulled her into a twirl she felt she could succumb completely. She trusted him.

And the way he looked at her during their ten-step!

Orlena had never had so much fun before. She could relax with Lorenzo. She had never been able to relax with Bert; there was always some formality there. Some stiff understanding, probably on accounta the boy who was quite obviously not as premature as she claimed him to be, that the relationship was largely transactional.

There wasn't anything she wanted from Sheriff Blaize, however. She had weeks ago decided that the only way to rid herself of the Needless Man was to accept that her brother's time had come. This was a matter between men that had expanded beyond the boundaries of the male sphere and impacted her personally. Jimmy was dead as soon as he took that crazy bastard's tooth. Her secrets were dead. Already she felt fresh, and normal, and like she had never a day in her life carried ugly sins of any kind.

Back through the swinging doors three hours later, Orlena's feet danced out and her voice hoarse from meeting everybody in town she didn't already know, Blaize stood on the walkway to roll himself a cigarette. Once it was lit, he dusted the tobacco from his fingers and once again offered his arm to the happy woman reminiscing on the night not yet over.

"While I do not mean to scandalize yeh, Orlena, I do confess the walk back t'yer hotel seems a mite too short fer my likin tonight. May I innerest you in an evenin constitutional? Assumin, of course, yer feet are not too tired."

Glad the darkness did not reveal her blush, illuminated as they were by only the occasional streetlamp and the lights still pouring out of the saloon behind them, Orlena kept her smile polite.

"I do believe nothing would please me more at this very moment, Sheriff."

Her heart pounded as they walked together through the dark streets of Sandspur, infinitely and eerily more quiet than it ever was during the day. A different place. Orlena found herself pressing closer to the sheriff, her shawl thin protection from any wild animals that might be prowling while they drew near the edge of town. One of the things that had made the location attractive to settlers—a manageable, fordable stretch of land along the Pecos River—was also a draw for animals.

"You cold, Miss Felder? Y'er shiverin!"

"No, it's jes—awful dark as you leave town."

"Ah, now, ain't nothin to fret over. Look at all them stars you kin already see!"

Well, he was right about that. Orlena craned her chin and whistled at the vision, the tapestry already well-assembled after only about seven minutes of walking and letting her eyes adjust away from the occasional lamplight lining the dark streets. She was no encyclopedia of constellations, but the moon hung full and bright and she did indeed believe she saw Orion presenting himself for admiration.

At the bridge built over the river leading north of town, Lorenzo stopped. Behind his head, a star shot across the sky.

"Oh!"

Quick as that, the streak was gone: throbbing into life and evaporating all in the same breath, seconds before even Lorenzo's quick turn of his head.

"Shoot," said Orlena, "you missed it! A shootin star—I never did see one before, Sheriff."

"Beautiful as I am sure it was, I ain't sorry I missed it…I'ws lookin at you, Miss Felder. Orlena—"

Her heart leapt with anticipation. Those eyes of his weighed heavily upon her. The sheriff drew near enough for her to smell the whiskey on his breath. Her skin grew hot as he pressed her to the rail of the bridge.

"Would it be very indiscreet of me to kiss you right now?"

As quick and short as she could to get the message across, Orlena shook her head.

Blaize caught her face in his hands and dropped his mouth over hers, the feral swiftness of the movement enough to induce a gasp.

Oh, Lord! Never had Orlena been kissed with such passion. Indeed, she had never known a man *could* feel passionately toward her. As she had in their dance, she succumbed to him utterly. Her gasping mouth permitted the slow coax of a conquering tongue. The closer he pressed to her, the more acutely she felt his body.

His name flowed from her lips in a gasp between kisses. When his mouth left hers, it was only to trail down her neck and push away her shawl. Her bosom heaving, she gasped and let her mind fly to wild notions. It would not be proper to take him back to the hotel…but did he not still sleep nights at the Pearl? Surely nobody there would bat an—

"Sheriff! Sheriff!"

Absolute rage blossomed out of the excitement that had coursed through Orlena's veins from the moment their lips made contact.

Goddamn typical. Whole time she'd been in Sandspur she'd not had one damn opportunity to talk to McLintock alone. In fact, so far as she could tell, he was hardly ever in town.

And when'd he come ridin up, that sonnabitch?

Looking pretty unhappy, himself, Lorenzo drew back from her amid the thunder of hooves.

Deputy McLintock's horse clattered to a halt upon the bridge, finding its balance and coming to a stop with a rapid shake of its head.

"Sheriff, git yer horse and make damn sure yer gun's loaded. Them Stone Hill boys done held up a coach and I need help lookin fer them…and the wounded."

"Hell—whereabouts was this?"

"Folk coming south along the Pecos, waylaid near the starta the hills. They's plannin t'use the Horsehead crossin here but got caught up. Only one fella made it to town to find me, and I done looked, but—seems like it's outta my paygrade."

"All right—Orlena, I do apologize, but as pleasant as this evening has been it seems I'm cuttin it short after all. Let me walk you home right quick—"

"No! It's all right, Sheriff—I'm comfortable going back by myself."

And she was, of course…but as soon as they parted ways, anxiety filled Orlena's heart top-full.

Say something happened to Lorenzo? Right after they'd finally shared a moment of such desire—oh, she could still taste him on her lips!

If she were a sheriff's wife, though, she would have to get used to harrowing evenings like these. Moments of tenderness, shattered by a call to action from urgent circumstances. Long nights spent pacing and fretting.

As she was not his wife, she did not engage herself in pacing; but fret, she did. In her hotel room, she lay in the cold bed alone and stared at the ceiling.

Why did it seem so impossible to live without suffering? Why did she always have to trade something, or at the very least endure some counterbalancing force to any pleasure or freedom of which she might avail herself?

Maybe she was just feeling sorry for herself; but it did seem pretty damn coincidental that, upon her first chance to get close to the sheriff, she had the insecurity of loving a sheriff driven home to her.

Her ears strained through the night.

She turned in bed, her mind aflame with horrific fantasies of the sheriff's murder at the hands of her own brother.

Outside, the sky grew blue with warnings of light.

Seconds before Orlena finally succumbed to sleep, something tapped at her winda.

14

TRUTH BE TOLD, Sheriff Blaize was less happy about being called away than Orlena was to see him go. The opportunity was welcome, but ill-timed.

Yet…it was all the more inconvenient when he woke up in that very same Miss Orlena Felder's bed, as naked beside her as he was on the day God forced him out the womb and into the big, bad world.

Normally this ain't no problem. Orlena Felder was not the first woman of whose embrace he had no memory; even before the scorpion, Blaize hadn't never been no teetotaler.

The trouble was, in addition to having no memory of what had obviously transpired between him and the sleeping widow to his right, he also struggled to recollect anything that had occurred from the time Deputy McLintock and he made off into the night.

Round Sandspur and the brief point in space for miles around where the Pecos grew to bein a fordable river, Texas was still more desert than green; but give it some patience, some miles, some well-pushed horses. Suddenly here come all them grasses, and the hills, and the Pecos growing grander and deeper until, in their pursuit of the Stonehill gang, they were dissevered from the path heavily trod. Instead, they rode into those towering hills and the timber that thickened with elevation.

"Where's that wagon, McLintock?"

The memory of his own question rang in his ears with certainty. He remembered raising his voice loud to ask it while the horses were still at a gallop.

"Think they musta hid it somewheres t'unload whatever it was haulin."

"Think anybody's still alive?"

"Aside from the fella what came hollerin into town fer help, I ain't too optimistic."

The guilty flash of gladness at the thought of some civilian deaths that could, this time round, justify the hangina the whole bunch (that Allen fella, a distant memory now with him weeks off runnin those horses, did not concern the sheriff) was a real emotion, a real impulse to solution that was unmistakable. Real.

Not a dream.

So what the hell else had happened? How in the devil had Lorenzo gotten from out in the middle of the wild country with McLintock to here beside Orlena Felder?

Her stirring body—her stretch, her sigh, the curvature of her twisting neck beneath her fragrant hair—drew him out of his thoughts. Outside the town was already a-movin and the hotel beneath them buzzed with activity.

"Mornin," she murmured, twisting her head to look at him through smiling, sleep-heavy eyes. They shut again. Her head sank into the pillow, one arm curling experimentally against his side between their bodies.

"Mornin, Orlena."

He shifted upon his flank and slid the untamed red curls back from her cheek, his mouth kissing the exposed apple before lowering to her lips. She returned with immediate passion, her slender fingers curling against his scalp.

"I'm glad you had a good night," he told her, smiling a little when at last she tilted her mouth away to catch her breath.

"I had an *awful* night," she told him, unfeigned terse notes tucked into her sensual voice. "You left me all by myself, worryin and wringin my hands till damn near five in the mornin."

That time oughta have helped him pin things down, but it did not. Especially not when she asked, worry in her soft voice, "You git'im?"

He did not know, and that was the scariest gap of all.

Lorenzo refrained from telegraphing any information in any way, maintaining his smile and usual relaxed demeanor even as his brain whirled rapidly around the big, black hole that seemed to encompass the hours between midnight and five in the morning—really, midnight and his waking now.

"I absolutely hate to do this t'yeh, Orlena, but—"

Her sad smile said it all.

"I understand."

"I'll make it up when I kin. I swear."

Their lips met. Blaize sprang out of bed and dressed with Orlena's unabashed eyes all over him.

Yes, ma'am. Had to make it up sooner than later.

"Perhaps, Miss Orlena, since we missed out on our morning walk today yeh might indulge me in another evening walk this night? Round sunset, mebbe."

"All right." Behind her coy smile, an almost girlish hint of soft blushing speckled her cheeks and throat.

"Promise it'll be a better time."

Maybe he ought not to have said that. There were things a man could not control, and Blaize was particularly frightened to learn he could not control his own body—so it would seem.

Somehow, totally unconscious, he had gotten from the hills to Sandspur. Then, into Orlena's room in the hotel.

How? How had he managed the feat of scaling to the second story without even being aware of it? How had he ridden back home?

How had he fought the Stone Hill Gang?

Had he fought?

Lorenzo's mind reeled as he made his unsteady way back to the sheriff's office. The world around him was somehow new and suspicious. People who approved of him smiled and tipped their hats, and somehow he managed to smile back, but that smile never seemed able to last. His body felt weak somehow; this throat ached something awful strange, and he would have written it off as thirst were it not for the notion that the inside of his nose—the inside of his very skull—also seemed to hurt.

Something had happened to him.

He just could not say what.

The sheriff's office and its present state made things only more confusing. Namely, two horses were hitched before it. Deputy McLintock's, of course. But, also, his own.

Lorenzo stopped beside the mounts and marveled up at his. The horse bobbed its head familiarly as its owner stroked its neck.

"Ain't suppose yeh kin tell me the hell happened, could yeh, boy…"

The horse nickered softly, its lip flaring out from its teeth.

The door to the sheriff's office swung open so hard it slammed on its hinge.

McLintock stood there when Lorenzo turned, shock wide in his eyes and mouth.

"Lor—I mean, Sheriff! The hell're yeh doin here?"

"I might could ask the same thing, McLintock…prisoners bein damn quiet in there."

"Prisoners?"

Lorenzo lowered his hand from the horse. McLintock looked at him blankly until, saying nothing, Lorenzo moved him aside with a hand on his shoulder and went into the station beyond him.

He had expected the cells to be overcrowded by the Stone Hill Gang members. At least one or two.

Instead, not even a drunk.

He had been too busy at the dance with Orlena; Deputy McLintock, too busy doing his actual job. Without the two of them, the other deputies might as well not have existed.

The last night sure as hell seemed like it didn't.

Removing his hat to work the brim between his thumbs and forefingers for a few seconds, Lorenzo inhaled slowly. He lowered himself into the seat behind his true desk.

McLintock stood in the doorway, eyes plastered to his every smallest moment.

"Deputy," said Lorenzo carefully, setting his hat on the desk before turning to look at McLintock, "what the hell happened last night?"

"You ain't remember? Hell, I thought fer sure yeh'ws dead…only by what, I ain't exactly sure."

"What does that mean?"

"Well—well, like I said. I jes ain't sure." Hand scratching over the back of his head, the Deputy gestured with his thumb. "One minute, we's ridin into the timber to find the Stone Hill Gang. Then—there was a flash."

In his memory. Yes, there it was. Flickering, gone. Orlena-smell.

He did not understand.

"A flash."

"Yessir, a flash. Thought the trees got caught on fire it got so bright! Then it was gone, and you rode off toward it."

White. White flash. White ceiling. Lorenzo squeezed his eyes shut.

"And you?"

"And I followed, Sheriff, but—"

McLintock's moustache wiggled in consternation. He searched the sheriff's lifting face as though trying to detect some sort of failed test before he went on.

"—but I lost tracka yeh fer jes a minute, and when I came upon yer horse a minute later there was no signa yeh."

"Did you look?"

"Sure did! Course I did—and fer those Stone Hill Boys, too. Ain't find nothin. No trace. Jes yer horse, like I said."

Lorenzo was by now scrutinizing the deputy with the same intensity the deputy had shown for him.

It was not so much that there was anything amiss with the deputy's story. It was that nothing about it—or about the night—seemed to make any sense.

Lorenzo only barely remembered the vague impression of a light when reminded. He did not remember riding off.

And he really did not understand how he got back into town by dawn on his own two feet when he was startin way up yonder in them hills you couldn't even really quite see from Sandspur.

"And you brought my horse back?"

"I'm sorry, Sheriff, I jes didn't know what else to do—I thought fer sure the Stone Hill Gang had got yeh, or even some In—some Natives, but…ain't nobody tried nothin on me. Ain't nobody up there so far as I could see."

"And the cohort?"

McLintock looked at him blankly.

"The missin folk with the wagon."

"Oh! Oh, uh—nossir, no, I ain't seen no signa them or the coach."

Exhaling slowly, Lorenzo did his best to absorb all this.

What the hell was happening?

"How yeh feelin today? Sheriff?"

Lorenzo glanced at his deputy through the fog of a kind of stupor.

"Feelin tired, but I also ain't feelin like I walked back to town all night if that's whatche mean."

"And—you ain't hurt or nothin?"

"Not so far as I kin find," he said, disregarding the odd sensation in his throat. "Don't understand what happened… not at all."

"You don't remember anything?"

Something in McLintock's tone—Lorenzo didn't like it. Couldn't say why.

Sparing the deputy one more brisk glance, the sheriff rose from his seat and set his hat on his head.

"Sheriff," said Deputy McLintock as Lorenzo slipped past him again, "where yeh goin?"

"Out to do my job…you stay here and keep an eye on the town, McLintock. But, mind, if'n I don't come back, you round up a posse to look fer me."

"Surely will, Sheriff," said the deputy to himself, watching in silence as Lorenzo saddled his horse and unhitched it from the post.

Horse ran in good spirits, like it had been given plenty of time to sleep. McLintock had probably turned around fairly quickly when discovering he was the only man accounted for; Lorenzo could not fault him for that. He only found himself annoyed that the deputy had not taken it upon himself to round up a search party right away with the coming of dawn.

That was McLintock, though…never had been a self-motivated individual.

At any rate, having been back in town by two and resting since, the horse raced into the wilderness without the least hint of reticence. Had it endured a frightening experience in the hills the night before, Lorenzo would have expected the beast to be a bit more wary when it recognized their direction. Particularly when they rode into the hills. The timber, and the remainder of Lorenzo's memories from the night prior.

The horse, however, was untroubled. If it had any unpleasant memories, it did not find them deterring. They rode through the trees at a brisk trot, or he did the ridin and the horse did the runnin; and all the while, his hand remained tangled round the reins and ready to steer it out of harm's way at the first sign of danger.

But there just weren't none.

He listened real careful as they made their way through. There was no sound of laughter or men practicing shooting or nonea that; and if it were Comanche runnin round out there, there wouldn't be no hearin to be had.

Ain't be no livin for Sheriff Blaize, neither, if he had in fact been captured by such natives.

He was not sure what he had expected to find in the hills, but he had somehow not expected to find nothing. That was all there seemed to be: hills and trees, dirt and weeds.

While his horse rested, he looked out from a ridge too steep to grow trees. For miles around there was no visible sign of anyone, let alone someone of the criminal variety.

Nobody dead, neither. After spending the afternoon picking around the woods, he rode down around the perimeter. Eyed all the natural places where, thick with foliage, an empty wagon or some dead bodies could be stowed away from prying eyes.

Ain't nothin, once again.

In fact, it struck him only as he rode away that he hardly took notice of a damn bird.

Something was wrong here. Yes indeed, there was something rotten in the state of Texas, but Jesus alone knew what it was.

For some reason, he thought of the creature he had met in the fever dream of the scorpion's venom.

Whatever it was, it had been very smart. It had not said or done anything in particular to promote this impression. Lorenzo jes knew that it was, and that it could help him learn something a normal man could not when left to his own devices.

Why did he think it any more intelligent than somebody in a dream? Well…truth was Sheriff *had* met some awful smart folks in dreams. So smart that he figured dreams had to count as some sorta proof that the human mind was connected to *somethin* other than itself…after all, Lorenzo Blaize was pretty damn smart, but at his sharpest he was not half as smart as somea the folks he'd met while in bed.

So, whatever folks who ain't real were to a fella who was, Lorenzo had as reasonable a measurea respect for the scorpion-man as he did for any visionary dream actor. He was not sold on the Native line that this being was any ancestor of any human's, now…but he could understand for some reason why they interpreted it that way.

It had not made any attempt to explain itself to *him*, after all. He could only imagine it did not make any attempt to explain itself to the Natives. In the absence of its explanation, they made their own.

Lorenzo appreciated the impulse. It might have made his brain a whole lot more settled in his skull if he knew what to call that big iridescent sonnabitch in that infinitely expanding, infinitely narrow space. If he knew what to call that space, period.

But would any explanation he found or received be true? Would it be any truer than the explanation the Natives had settled on after lifetimes upon lifetimes of sharing in some secret knowledge?

Not truer, no…but maybe the same from a different perspective. Something that could offer him information about himself and his own absence.

And if this fella was even half a dream, and a dream was

even half the man who dreamed it, then maybe with that quartera insight into Sheriff Blaize the entity might tell him jes a littlea what the hell was goin on these days.

15

DUST.

Eyes shirt mouth hair nostrils. Dust. Ears and socks and trousers and eyebrows. Dust.

Brain. Balls. Gun barrel.

Soul. Shit. Water.

Dust.

The men were ready to be done. So were the horses. Over their weeks of transit, the herd had been reduced by twenty-three. Too many, in the Needless Man's opinion.

"It is disappointing," agreed the Brave, whose conversations with him had become a regular occurrence. "However, it was inevitable we would lose a few."

Inevitable, too, that they should encounter occasional problems. They crossed paths with an edgy squadrona cavalrymen what had to be satisfied they weren't rustlers and had in fact been willfully endowed with the responsibility of takin the horses to New Mexico. They encountered a group of Mescalero Apache after all, (was that same group, the Man sussed out, that Roaring Bear had called "Shis-Inday"), but the meetin went peaceful and in the end the medicine man okayed the tradea bout twentya the horses fer some food and blankets that went greatly appreciated.

Over all, nobody got sick and nobody save fer Spud wound up dead. Fella did end up with a broken arm, but they got it splinted and sent him on ahead to the nearest town with a frienda his to get it seen to.

Not too bad, all told. The Needless Man felt like he had wasted his time and that Felder had been given ample opportunity to get ahead of him on the chase, assuming he'd been smart enough to run.

Then they reached what shoulda been the last day.

The Man reckoned he was superstitious if that was what you wanted to call it. Signs and symbols, he called it. He read signs in the world the way folk in that old Shakespeare's plays was always seein futures in the stars. Sometimes them signs was so well-written one did not even realize one was readin at all. Not till it was too late.

And sometimes you didn't know what signs you was seein…you jes got the message.

He got a message.

A message in his stomach and his mind as the men on horseback fore and aft talked joyously, their anticipation to have the long job over with obvious. The Natives seemed in a good mood of their own.

Only the Needless Man looked into himself and knew that this would not be the last daya his journey to deliver those horses to their destination.

Fatal moment. A ridge in the distance. Roaring Bear's joyful whoop, his horse rearing beneath his excited gesticulations. The beast galloping forward when it had all its hooves beneath it again.

The sharp stop.

The silence.

A solitary figure, looking over the abyss.

The Needless Man urged his horse ahead, far ahead, and caught up with the Brave where his mount stood stock still.

What looked like a fine place for an encampment contained no sign of inhabitants.

"They should be here," said Roaring Bear. "Unless something happened."

"You know it did."

"Yes."

"Least there ain't no bodies nowheres I kin see."

The Brave stared grimly into the valley, saying nothing.

The Man looked with him.

"We gonna go find em?"

"We must."

"Well…reckon we oughta tell the boys to retrace our steps fer the day, put a little space between 'emselves and here. And to get their guns ready fer work when they make camp."

A whole hell of a lotta bitchin rose up amid the rancheros at the news of the delay. Since it were their horses, the Needless Man let the Natives handle it. He only put in to assure them all, "We ain't find no sign in the next three days, we'll make our way back round."

"You got us here waitin a week then,'" said somebody in an especially bitter tone.

"Only if we don't find em," said the Needless Man without bothering to look for the complainer. "And I most assuredly aim to."

In the end it was decided that all three Natives and the Needless Man would make up the search party. While the rest of the men retreated to set up camp, the chosen four rode off to investigate the prior location of the Tribe. One way or another the scorpions would need loading up, so it was decided that Roaring Bear's brother would drive the coach with his father riding beside him. They made the steady way into the verdant valley and, late in the afternoon, stood at its empty edge.

Flattened grass was the only sign indicating people had spent any time in the area at all.

"This is not good," understated the medicine man, shaking his head.

"Any chance yeh might know where they gone to?"

"There are a few likely places," Roaring Bear agreed, scanning the cliff and hills enclosing the valley before identifying what he sought. With a brisk word in their language, he turned his horse toward his goal.

"Come with me, friend."

The Needless Man obliged him, their horses making an easy way through this pleasant little pocket of paradise. Must have been some underground water, or just a good place to catch the flow of a lotta rain. The gramas grass formed a lush carpet that grew richer near the edge of one particular hill and trees were reasonably plentiful. He could see the appeal right until they reached their goal and the Needless Man understood what it was that had attracted Roaring Bear's People to the valley.

"That a cave?"

"This is where the world-maker nests." A black mouth had opened as they overcame a small rise and got a better angle through a splaying copse of honey locusts. Roaring Bear went on, listing unconsciously toward it, "I am frightened for them. The scorpions."

"These the ones we bringin back? Yeah, I reckon it'd be a shame if somethin happened to em."

"Not just that." The Brave looked at him in a manner that was both respectful and stern, and now the Man knew fer sure he was dealin with somethin religious. "The scorpion contains knowledge—not just the knowledge of my people, but the knowledge of the spirits that made the world. Their medicine, and the medicine of my ancestors are contained in the world-maker. If something were to happen to the species—"

He did not finish his thought.

"That why you folks are lookin to trade some? So somebody else will be breedin em, too?"

"I am afraid that you are right when you speak of how short-lived the liberty of my people is. Our People and the others, we are many Nations; the United States is one big Nation, bigger all the time. A different kind of Nation than our Nations. And it does not think our Nations' ways of living are compatible with its way of living.

"There is hope in my heart that things are not becoming what they seem, but that hope is less all the time. All we may hope for is that our ways will have been remembered by our children and their children, and that they will manage to show those not of our Nations the worthiness of our ways of life. The world-maker volunteered its kind to be traded to the White men for the horses that will save our people, but—yes, friend. I do hope that there will be medicine men among all Peoples someday. Perhaps there already are, and I am not experienced enough to identify them in Peoples other than my own."

The Man listened to all of this in careful consideration before asking, "What's it exactly them Comanche got aginst yer people?"

"Because we will not join them in their war. There is a man, a mighty warrior. The sheriff of Sandspur explained to us his name is, in English, "Wolf Cunt.""

The Man snorted as the Brave continued, "A very serious warrior. He has no love for his White brothers in his heart. In some senses, a futile and petty sense, I understand. Everywhere, buffalo grow scarce. The Peoples have nothing to do *but* attack the White men taking land and food and everything else from us…especially the Comanche. War means something different to us than it does to your People. But to wage war in fulfillment of empty time?"

The Brave shook his head and drew his horse to a stop still some hundred yards before the obscured mouth of the cave.

"An emissary of the Tonkawa approached us seeking advice, knowing that the speech of the scorpion is true and for the betterment of all life; there are times among other Tribes when they are split, or their own medicine men require conference. They find us. We in turn consult the world-maker for them; and to the Tonkawa people, the world-maker said through us that they must shun Wolf Cunt."

"And I bet Wolf Cunt didn't like that," observed the Needless Man, dismounting his horse.

"No. He now believes our tribe is directly opposed to the best interests of the People, and that we are traitors to be destroyed; worse, he knows dangerous medicine, and the bad spirits with which he confers would like nothing more than the destruction of the world-maker's being-ness here with us."

"Them scorpions, you mean."

The Brave nodded, leading the way down a slight slope that the Needless Man observed stopped in a sharp ridge. "They must be defended. If we are to be destroyed, whether by the Comanche or by the pressure of the White men, we must find ways for the world-maker to live on."

The Needless Man reckoned he could see the reasoning for the impulse, but he also had to wonder to himself if it wasn't a waste of time.

After all…if the world-maker had a message to send, and if it were a spirit that really had made the world, seemed the message could be folded into jes about anythin. Seemed like it *was* folded into jes about anythin, in fact.

Ain't no use trynta reason a fella outta his religion, though, so he kept his thoughts to himself.

There was an art to scalin down the ridge and into the hard stone floor of the cave some twelve yards down. Man could easily slip and smash open his own skull tryin, and it seemed to him that the conjunction of boulders down which the Brave led him was still pretty treacherous. Roaring Bear's expertise naturally helped.

Not that it was really worth it, in the Man's opinion. Ain't tryinta be rude. Gold looks different in every fella's eye.

The Needless Man jes couldn't see that gold in the hide of the one or two bluish black scorpions scuttling out of the dark curve of the cave's shadow upon the stone foyer.

"I am glad to see the cave still overflows," said the Brave with a proud look, gesturing in. "There are many layers and, within, more messengers of the world-maker than one could ever hope to count. Here they are endless, but they are also found *only* here; at the very least, if they thrive elsewhere, it is not the will of the world-maker that we should discover them."

An arachnid scuttled near the Man's boot but came to a stop before it got too close. He did not move and neither did it.

It turned away and resumed its hunting.

"Mighty glad to know we won't be headin back empty-handed, Roarin Bear, but what about them damn horses?"

"I can only suppose my People did not remain because they felt they were being observed by Comanche. Staying near the world-maker's home would only simplify Wolf Cunt's mission on behalf of his trickster spirits."

As he spoke, Roaring Bear—who had stooped to stroke with a fingertip the back of a scorpion that seemed amenable to it, or at least that did not sting him—straightened and looked around.

He paused, his eye falling upon a pile of brush cut down and tossed into the pit as though to remove the potential for fire from the field above. Trash. Some kinda nest fer the scorpions.

The tattooed Brave moved it aside and studied the pictograph behind.

A square. Not too big, but bigger than the Needless Man mighta pictured. Sizea his hand or thereabouts. A kind of rectangle with two tall, thin rectangles on either side.

He stood tryinta suss it out while the Brave found a suitably sharp stone and gouged away the symbol until it was nothing but a series of scratches.

"The mission," said the Brave.

"Natural placeta go when y'er in trouble and kain't trust the cavalry," reckoned the Man, thinking without the least trace of irony or shame of the burning church licking flames on his back as he mounted his horse to ride off.

"Yes. Let's you and I go together; White Serpent and my brother will stay here to monitor the world-maker's brood and watch for Comanche. It's quite some ways from here, but if we push the horses we may make it there tomorrow afternoon."

Push, they did. Fine by them, the Needless Man reckoned; them horses had been enjoying a downright leisurely pace throughout the brunt of the trip, and it seemed like they was ready to run.

Two sets of hooves pounded across the plains. Roaring Bear and the Needless Man fell into a kind of breakneck race at times, hunting together when the first night fell and coming back with a few fine hares for dinner.

It felt too comfortable.

The interference was too little.

The nag was still there in his chest as he awoke on the second day of their scouting to the mission.

His eye scanned the horizon as they rode on. There was no visible or olfactory sign of smoke, which would have been an unmistakable warning sign of Comanche presence or warfare. Vultures circled in the distance over a dead thing that, as they passed, turned out to be a javelina.

There was no evidence of other tribes, or of cavalry troops, or any damn thing.

That was what bothered the Man.

Even when the mission stood in the distance about half a day later than they'd have liked, the blots of people moving in and out and all around the building resolving to tribe members the Brave recognized with a whoop and a slap of his hurrying horse's ass, the victory seemed hollow.

His senses turned away from the cheers and the joyful hurrying of men and women and children out along with one of the mission's Jesuits. The Man remained on the horse, nodding to the padre while the Natives spoke among themselves in their language.

"Come down from your horse, friend," urged the Brave. "There is to be a great feast tonight."

"Boys'll be unhappy if we start the feastin without them, and yer pa…and I do not like the thought of sittin round even a night. Best I go fetch 'em back whiles you lead yer folks back down to World-Maker Valley. We'll meet in the middle."

The Brave considered him. "Do you believe we should set out again tonight?"

"Believe *I* should, anyhow…and I sure ain't bringin the horses here, to this mission fulla food. Even more attractive to them Comanche, if they is in fact as imminent a threat as I believe them to be."

Roaring Bear's face, having truly relaxed into a smile for the first time that the Man had seen, solidified once more into a mask of seriousness.

"I have had a sense of that myself, and what I posited before was correct. I have not yet heard much, but it seems Wolf Cunt's scouts were seen in the area. The natural response was to flee."

"Mighty finea the mission to take you folks in. Well…I do not wish to be rude, but I reckon I'll git a chance to unwind a little down the line."

The Brave nodded. The Needless Man turned his horse away and rode off without waiting for his traveling companion's explanation to the Natives, some of whom called after him as though to protest his flight.

The immediate area around the mission was violently flat and barren, but that did not mean there were not places to hide. Boulders and dense cacti and distant mesas made a mess of an otherwise straightforward task. Taska navigatin by himself was fraught with peril, but he had a compass from the dead lawman and a good sensea direction, and a memory like a steel trap.

And he remembered that dead javelina.

That dead javelina had once been a live javelina, and a live javelina needed water jes like a man and a horse.

He rode back a ways, a long handfula hours that represented his first slivera peace in a hot minute. His thoughts cooled off even as the day's heat mounted more and more.

He did not see anything worth noting in those hours. Not until, exploring the area around the dead javelina upon retracing the route to it, he discovered an increase in vegetation and the signs of water to the southeast.

The horse was no doubt tired. He had hardly given it opportunity to rest, let alone given it enough water.

The Needless Man dismounted his animal and, whistling through his parched lip, led it by the reins into the denser foliage. A patch of saguaros were kindly disposed to the beast's safety; the Man hitched it under a few large rocks and patted its neck.

"Jes you wait there, boy, I'll come back fer yeh…"

The Man removed his gun from his holster.

The mesa not far from which he'd parked the horse stood on a slope overlooking a quarry. Water supply was pretty grim all told. Every place in the southwest wanted for rain that year, monsoons later every day. New Mexican desert was no exception, and the Comanche scouts—six—took full advantage of what was still there to water their horses. A ways away, they squatted along the bank in apparent conversation.

Gun ready, he pressed himself down into the rocks as one of the scouts turned his head.

The man gritted his teeth. Conversation stopped while a few pebbles, ground by his boot as he shifted down into place, rolled along the slope. The powder-soft *clack* was all they needed.

All he needed, too.

One of the Comanche murmured something to the others.

No sound reached his ears.

The Man waited, hyper-aware of every one of the six bullets in his revolver.

There was no sound.

There was no sound.

There was no sound.

The Man sprang up and buried a bullet in the brain of the Comanche tryinta take him by surprise, a bone dagger in his hand all the justification anybody needed.

Before the scout had dropped, the Man's left hand had slammed the hammer down three times in rapid succession. Each time, his finger's subsequent twitch had heralded the killing of a man.

Scout collapsed in a heap. Two survivors were already mounting their startled horses and tugging them back under control while they steered the beasts wildly away.

The Man spent his last round knocking one of the escapees off his horse and dead down into the cacti below.

Without a rider, the horse kept on runnin.

Its mounted fellow ran, too.

The other horses, terror in their body language and their whinnies, paced and thrashed and splashed around the quarry's water.

For about thirty seconds, he reloaded his gun and waited for somebody to get up.

Nobody did.

Satisfied, he fetched his horse.

16

LOVING LORENZO BLAIZE was not what Orlena had expected it to be.

Oh, there was no doubt he was just about the handsomest man she'd ever set eyes on, and a fine lover to boot. He was gallant and funny, and his hygiene was measurably better than that of most men.

But…well.

Over the past three weeks since their friendship had taken a, ahem, somewhat more mature turn, Orlena had perceived what she worried to be distancing from the sheriff. Distancing, or a general decrease in interest. Had he gotten what he wanted from her? Found her to be too loose to continue pursuing? Near every night now, she considered the facts.

The drifting began simply. She didn't notice it at first because many men did not really listen when women spoke. Therefore, when she took it upon herself to discuss some amusing anecdote from her life, or the plot of some dime story she was reading, or any other little thing that might have crossed her mind, and the sheriff looked a bit distracted or glazed over, she assumed it was the normal masculine disinterest in perceived feminine concerns.

That was fine. She got bored, too, and so without complaint would change the subject to things like the letters she received from the ranch. Such matters tended to lure the businessman in him back to attention. Would not be very long when they were in each other's company before sneaking off to amuse one another less formally, anyway. Then they'd both be out for an hour or three, stone cold. Exchanging no words until the nightmares visited Blaize.

She hadn't managed to figure out what it was, at first. Thought he was snoring in a stifled way. These hiccupped, high sorts of little gasps coming from his pillow. Round about the third time she tried waking him and he jolted in her hand with a half a shout that felt short as he realized he was awake.

"Jesus," he'd say, or sometimes just, "Thank you, angel," before lowering his head back down to sleep.

Only asked him the once.

"You remember what it is y'er always dreamin about, Sheriff?"

"Hell, Orlena! Best off askin that when I jes woke up. Hardly remember now. Somethin bout—I don't know."

He looked troubled. She waited, curious and keen to unburden him from the worries with which he had not once, on any occasion of their visiting, enlightened or enshrouded her.

"Ain't really sure what to makea it," he said after a few seconds of pondering. "Thinkin, well, there's—me bein in the woods up north, and…gettin stung by a scorpion there."

"A scorpion?"

"And this light. This light comes, and it's like—I knew it would."

His eyes narrowed, slightly unfocused as he stared into the space between them and the muddled contents of dream-memory.

"Like an angel?"

"Nah. Ain't no angel-light. When I think about that light, I—"

He laughed a little at himself, head lowering and shaking. When it lifted, there was the cheeky old Lorenzo she loved. His glittering green eyes crinkled with mirth.

"Unmanly as it sounds, I git scared as shit."

She laughed at his vulgarity and leaned in to kiss him on the mouth.

Soon, they were at it again.

There was so much about Lorenzo that she loved. She loved his charm, she loved his tenderness. She loved the way he loved her. The bad did not outweigh the good, even if she got the sense that he withheld information on his side businesses because they were not necessarily in keeping with the traditional character of a lawman.

But the real problem was that those bad qualities did not stop at boredom, or even nightmares.

He began to arrive late for their evening dates. Twenty minutes at first, then thirty; then, before you knew it, whole hours she'd be there in the parlor of the hotel before Lorenzo collected her for an evening walk that had become inappropriately late at night. On such occasions she would find him rather more disheveled than usual, his hair hastily combed and his forehead clammy with sweat. His apologizes were disjointed or hardly offered and he would not even think to look her in the eye.

On such nights when he was especially late, he had might as well not come at all. His mind would be elsewhere entirely and his eyes unfocused. On an occasion near the end of their relationship she stopped dead in her tracks.

"Have I become so dull to you?"

"What?" The Sheriff snapped out of it enough to somewhat tersely ask, "What's the matter now, Orlena?"

"What's the matter is that this all began as some genuine pleasure. If you no longer take pleasure in my company, Lorenzo, I hardly see why you should be obligated t'entertain me every evening."

"Orlena! Come on now, honey."

His gallant smile was somewhat cowed, but no less genuine for it. Adjusting his hat, Lorenzo told her earnestly, "I'm sorry, now, you know I got work to think about."

"And I wouldn't mind that if you weren't thinkin about work the whole damn time I'm here with you! A time that gets shorter every minute you're late to bein parta it. What's goin on with you, Lorenzo? You changed overnight jes as soon as—as soon as you came knockin at my winda."

She had lowered her voice for this last addition and now raised it again to reasonable levels, saying with a careful study of his bloodshot eyes in the lamplight, "If you are feelin pressured, then please rest assured. I am still only a month and a half out of a marriage with a bloody end. I ain't innerested in rushin into anythin so serious you couldn't stand it."

"I know that, Orlena, I know—look—"

Blaize caught her hands in his gloved ones and raised them, his eyes searching deep into hers.

"I know, damn it. I know I ain't been actin right lately. I knew sooner or later you'ws gonna say somethin about it. And I deserve that. But—you jes gotta trust me, Orlena, when I say it ain't you. There's somethin important I am tryinta figure out…and when I am able to share it, I certainly will."

"What is it y'er waitin to share? Is this somethin to do with Jimmy?"

"Mebbe," said the sheriff, his tone cryptic, his hands tightening around hers. "You jes gotta trust me."

She wanted to. But, as her eyes fell to their hands, the third repeated issue with Blaize drew her attention.

The sores.

She could not figure out for the life of her what in God's name was happening to him. to be perfectly frank, it frightened her; but no such rashes had appeared on her person, so she did not reckon it was anything liable to rub off.

However…that did not make it any easier to look upon the angry red welts that, with increasing frequency, ringed the sheriff's wrists and covered up the heel of his palm. His right palm, in fact, had borne so many of the mean little red marks that it had become textured with a patch of scars she believed were doomed to be there forever. And in only a few weeks!

Whatever was wrong with him, it frightened her.

"Maybe yeh oughta see a doctor, Lorenzo. You're so— scattered lately."

He drew his hands from hers when he saw her lookin at the flesh between his glove and sleeve.

"Now, Orlena—"

"I jes mean to say—"

"I keep *tellin* yeh," he said, firmer now, "yeh don't need to worry over me. It's under control. I promise, you'll understand everything soon."

She sure hoped she would.

She especially hoped she would when she opened an almanac and thought about how many days it had been since she left the ranch. When she had last woken up with blood smeared between her thighs.

Orlena reckoned she oughta have been more afraid of the possibility, but it seemed in other ways like another gift with which she could escape the shadow of her past. Another chance to be a mother, now to a child who was not so— cursed.

Yes. The boy had felt cursed. Through no fault of his own,

through only the circumstances of his making, he had been an ill omen to be rejected by his mother. And that curse had been fulfilled by the Needless Man's coming, when he burst into her life like some baleful force of Fate. He destroyed it. And the boy.

Still thought about him. Always would. Had to get used to that. A whole life of that.

Now, though…maybe things could be different now.

With or without the sheriff.

And she was beginning to think it would be the latter.

The next night, he was an hour late again.

Two.

Three.

Dozed off over her embroidery. Snapped up, looked at the clock and found it chiming eleven at night.

Her blood just about boiled up and steamed out her ears, she was so mad.

After throwing down her embroidery and putting out the lights that had been left on as a courtesy to her, Orlena yanked on her shawl and stormed through Sandspur.

The Pearl glowed with life and laughter. She made her way through to the bar and realized it was the first time she had done such a thing at night since her arrival in the town, with the Needless Man. 'Jack Allen.' Now everybody knew her and ain't nobody so much as tried to look at her, let alone touch her. The men ain't wanted no trouble with the sheriff.

Orlena didn't even question the thought of making trouble with him. In fact, she hoped he was dead so she wouldn't have to be as mad as she was. He sure as hell *would* be dead if the Needless Man got back into town before he'd got his shit together well enough to track Jimmy.

Hell…in jes a couple more weeks, the Man would be back with the sheriff's cargo. Ready to take Jimmy's life. Then, she'd be really free.

It was all feelin more real by the day.

"Miss Felder!" Meyer sounded pleased to be visited. "How are yeh, Ma'am?"

"Not too fine, Meyer. You seen Lorenzo around?"

"Sheriff? Sure, he's up in his office or his bedroom. Glad to see yeh here. I wondered if you'd had a fight, him not comin down tonight and all."

"Not that I'm aware of, but that's what I'm here to say. I don't reckon you could let slip his room key, could you?"

"Door's been broke three weeks…give it a good jiggle, you'll git in."

What the *hell* was going on around these parts?

Upstairs, Orlena turned her eyes away from the customers disappearing with their chosen women into a rented room. The sheriff's bedroom, at the far end of the hall, stood shut. Light faintly indicated he was awake on the other side.

Her breath held, Orlena knocked on the door. Her ears strained for the startled gasp of another woman.

Nothing.

"Lorenzo?"

Orlena tried the knob. It did not yield.

She did as Meyer advised, giving it a violent wrench up and down that made the door give way at once.

Grimacing as it threatened to fall off its hinges altogether, Orlena stepped into Lorenzo's room.

For one reason or another, he had apparently stopped the Pearl from tidying his room for him. The dust burned her sinuses, and the bedsheets were in as much disarray as the man upon them. Half-leaning against the wall, his neck bent at an angle that caused her sympathy pain, Lorenzo lay in a stupor with his mouth open and his eyes so lidded they were nearly shut.

"Lorenzo? Lorenzo!"

Rushing to him, Orlena shook him by the shoulders until she got the slightest twitch of an eyelid. She gritted her teeth. How to wake him?

At the very least, he still shaved: a bowl of water rested atop his open dresser.

Every slightest movement imbued with urgency, Orlena collected some droplets in her fingers only to withdraw her hand with a sharp cry of fright.

Scorpions in the open drawer beneath her arm thrashed to be as startled as she was.

Swearing, shrieking, then swearing again, Orlena flailed her hands and slammed the drawer shut. She stumbled back, her mind racing until movement on the floor once more drew her attention.

Gasping sharply, Orlena yanked her dress up and slammed her boot down on the scorpion that had been experimenting with scaling her.

In the heat of the moment, she did not make the perhaps obvious connection of the scorpions to the marks around her lover's wrist. She could only see the drawer, and the loose arachnid, and the state he was in, and grab him and shake him in a terrible fright while saying, "Lorenzo! Lorenzo, wake up! They've poisoned you—somebody's poisoned you, Lorenzo, with scorpions!"

Lorenzo stirred insofar as his eyelids flickered. His lips moved. Then his head rolled back.

Pale with fright, she stepped away.

"Sheriff—oh, Lorenzo—"

Her face nearly numb, Orlena darted from his room. Propriety forgotten, she hiked up her hem and ran to the staircase overlooking the Pearl's dance hall. There wasn't no sign of Deputy McLintock, who came and went from the town with exceeding frequency and spent most of his days actually in Sandspur playing cards or getting drunk. In all her time living there, her schedule had never aligned to give her the privilege of his company and let her have a chance to do more than say hello to him. If she did not know better, she would have thought him to be avoiding her.

Now, though, it was critical they speak. She raced down the stairs and once again caught Meyers' attention, crying, "Where's McLintock?"

""Oh, uh, I don't think he's been in tonight—"

Without pausing for another word, Orlena forced her way back through the card players and whores. Her head throbbed. Lorenzo needed a doctor—a doctor, and a real lawman. One who could sort all this out.

To her surprise and relief, the sheriff's office was bright with activity. Orlena rushed in, hanging in the doorway and overwhelmed with joy to find not just one but two deputies there. McLintock, and some other she had not met.

"Deputy McLintock—"

"Who's—Miss Orlena?"

"I need yer assistance." Breathless, Orlena clutched the swinging door and said, "It's the sheriff."

McLintock sat up at the desk where he had been reclining in conversation with his fellow. His eyes focused intensely on her beneath his untamed brows. "What's the matter with the sheriff?"

"He's in an awful state, oh—I think he's been poisoned by a scorpion. Yes, envenomated, that's the word."

"I'll go git the doctor," said the other deputy hurriedly.

"But be careful," Orlena called after him, "there's more, more scorpions up in his dresser drawer—who knows if they'll get out, oh—"

Urgency she appreciated to his every movement, the deputy rushed into the night without delay.

When the door had swung shut behind him, Orlena burst into tears.

McLintock tutted and came to her side, one great hand falling upon her shoulder.

"Ain't no call fer cryin like that."

"Oh, but Wilt! It was horrible. There were so many of them. I'm sure someone meant to do him wrong—that's the only way they coulda wound up there."

"Ain't the only way. What'd these scorpions look like?"

She plumbed the depths of memory and shook her head. "I don't know. Blackish."

"Mmhm. Sounds like the scorpions them Natives gave him…promised more fer trade."

Her weeping paused.

"Scorpions for trade?"

"Yes ma'am. From what they were sayin, them scorpions have a venom more powerful than opium, and more beneficial when it comes ta…certain effects. Sheriff Blaize thought it were a reasonable trade to send em horses that might help against the Comanche…seems to me though like he mighta lost tracka that purpose and got a little too innerested in his own supply."

"What do yeh mean?"

"I mean I jes the other day walked in on the sheriff lettin onea those little bastards sting him…and with all those marks round his wrists and on his hands, I'd wager a guess that he imbibes, oh, at least once a day."

A weakness came over Orlena, who unsteadily lowered into the vacated chair of the station's desk. "You mean—you mean he's jes…sittin in his room, leavin me alone so he kin get *drunk*?"

"Somethin like that," agreed McLintock, his fingers sweeping smooth the hairs of his moustache. "Kain't account fer what these scorpions is like, never havin tried em myself, but…"

A new wave of tears burned Orlena's eyes. She fought them back, her elbow propping against the edge of the desk to permit her to shield her eyes with her hand.

"Oh, Wilt—what am I going to do?"

"Now, Miss Orlena…"

"You don't understand. Has he even told you why I've been waiting in town all this time?"

"No, he ain't."

"It's—it's Jimmy."

Removing a handkerchief from her person, Orlena pressed the silk to her eyelids. With an unsteady breath of air, she said miserably, "There's a man. An evil man. I'm only tellin you this on accounta yeh know what it's like on the other side, and you know what you kin and kain't tell t'a man like the sheriff."

"Might be surprised what you kin and kain't tell the sheriff, but go on."

"Well—well, I will spare yeh the details. But this man, if he don't find Jimmy and kill him, he's fixinta kill *me*. He was Jimmy's cell mate, and the Sheriff promised me that in the time this Man was gone, he'd help me find Jimmy."

"To warn him?"

"I don't know," said Orlena, shaking her head, rocking in the chair to a more comfortable position. "I reckon so, or maybe to see him put back in jail. I ain't keen on the thoughta betrayin my blood, but—it's my *life* Wilt. He threatened my *life*."

"I understand."

The handkerchief balled in her fist. She shifted her knuckles to the temple of her forehead. "I've kept all this in me so long—not said a word t'anyone. Even the sheriff don't know the whole story. Now I regret it. And all this time I've been waitin fer the sheriff's investigation t'yield some fruit! Some sign of where Jimmy is. Now I wonder if he's investigated anything except those goddamn scorpions the whole time I been here."

"Reckon he ain't," McLintock admitted. "Not based on what I seen."

Sobbing, Orlena lowered the handkerchief and said through clenched teeth, "Then he's *killin* me. There is no protectin me from this man. If I kain't deliver Jimmy, I am goin to die…and so will the Sheriff's baby, if I am in fact correct about my current condition."

"That so?"

"Yes. I do believe it is so."

Watchin her in some long, careful thought, Deputy McLintock folded his arms. "How exactly were you folks plannin to git holda Jimmy once yeh knew where he was stayin?"

"There's a way," she said. "A whistle we used as children. A birdsong. The idea was, Sheriff and I would go together. I would…draw Jimmy out."

For the third time, to the third man, Orlena demonstrated the whistle. McLintock's moustache wiggled at the sound. Almost a smile. Then, nodding, he said, "Well, that's a mighty fine plan…and you might be the last piecea my own investigation."

Her heart throbbed with hope.

"While Sheriff's been sittin with his thumbs you-know-where, I been lookin into the Stone Hill Gang. I think I know jes where they're at these days, and I been interested in goin up there but I ain't been able to figure how I might git em in the open."

Studying her intently, McLintock said, "I know I ain't no Sheriff Blaize, but maybe yeh'd be inclined to come with me."

"Oh—oh, yes!"

Orlena sprang from her seat, catching one of McLintock's grimy hands and beaming at him in sincere appreciation.

"Thank you! Yes, jes a chance t'at least speak with my brother. Maybe if you kain't capture him without a gunfight I could convince him to come back to town. He's so quick—if that Man really wants to kill him, let him try to do it in a duel."

Of course, as she said this she remembered her brother's wounded finger.

Her stomach tensed as McLintock went on.

"Jimmy does have a fast hand, I'll give him that…come on, Miss Orlena—"

"*Now*? It's practically midnight."

"More so the better. The elementa surprise—we don't wanna ride up on em in broad daylight, when they kin see us comin."

She reckoned that did make sense, but the idea of riding into the darkness to betray her brother on short-notice made her feel ill.

Wasn't it better this way, though? Better to have it over and done with, without a lot of worrying beforehand? Without any definite timeline, after all, she had been able to put the inevitability of the betrayal out of her mind. Now that the moment had arrived without her thinking of it, it was like a slap of cold water in the middle of a deep sleep.

Still mighty awful, in other words…but it was quick, without dread. A simple exchange. Like hacking off a limb so you could live.

Like that.

"Okay," said Orlena, nodding. "All right, yes—let's go."

With the delirium of one of Lorenzo's dreams, Orlena was soon on the back of a horse borrowed from the station to follow McLintock and his light through the darkness north of Sandspur.

The horses had plenty of confidence. So, it seemed, did McLintock, but Orlena was not sure exactly what was about to happen. Assumin McLintock was right and he *did* know where the Stone Hill Gang was keepin itself? They'd just as likely end up shot as gettin a chance to capture Jimmy.

And as for Jimmy…as for Jimmy.

Would he come at her call?

Would he hate her for her willingness to bargain his life?

A little voice in the back of her head told her it wann't right, what she was set to do. She ignored it. Orlena Felder had not survived, had not clawed and bit and fought her way to this point in time, by always doin what folk thought was 'right.'

The night sky sparkling over Texas made her pine for Lorenzo. For a few seconds of relief, her mind turned away from Jimmy and to her new lover. To finding him in his room.

What a sorry state! He had seemed so sick when she saw him—that was getting drunk? And having to let a scorpion sting him to do it! It was clear that, if this continued, Lorenzo would not be the sheriff very long…but it was a damn shame. In spite of his more insidious qualities, and the fact that he, like so many sheriffs, made money by impounding property and collaborating with lower-level organized criminals, there had been something so vibrant and so promising about him.

But maybe it only seemed that way on accounta his was the first face she truly saw when she'd been let out her prison by the Needless Man.

Yes. Maybe that was why she now found herself so willing to sell Jimmy's life away. it was not so much to preserve her own existence as it was to *earn* it. She had been born in a little black room in the bottom of a black pit and now the sunshine was so close she could smell it on her own clothes…but it was still so easy to slip back and fall, fall, fall, die at the bottom in the darkness.

And there, at the lip of the pit, stood not Lorenzo or Jimmy but the Needless Man. A man who just as easily could push her away or pull her up out.

And after all that timea climbin and riskin and feelin death just centimeters away in the darknessa that evil pit, Orlena was willin to take any hand offered her.

They had to have been riding for two hours. The horses were stumbling and showing their wariness at the late hour, and Orlena was deep in fretful thoughts around the time the presidio came into sight through the trees into which McLintock had led them.

"Reckon we better dismount here," he said softly.

"Is that them up in there?"

"Yes ma'am. Old presidio what ain't been used in years. Built by the Spanish to deal with the French, I reckon, long time ago."

That was to be certain. The wooden palisades around the structure had largely collapsed, yielding back to the timber in which the fort had been discretely situated. The fort itself was fairly sizable from what she could see through the gnarled main gate, a cobbled-together replacement for the original means of entry. Within the fortification, it seemed at least a few of the buildings had collapsed. Their desecrated remains of stone and timber told the story of a failed defense.

She looked anxiously at McLintock. "Don't you think I oughta have a gun?"

"You don't reckon yer brother's liable to hurtcha, do yeh, Orlena?"

Her lips pressed thin. She studied the rifle McLintock removed from the saddle of his horse and, nodding in slight determination, she picked what seemed like the path least covered in noisy fallen leaves and tangling, tripping vines.

"Please," she begged McLintock, "Don't let me get shot."

"I'll be right here," he said, sliding behind a tree.

Lips suddenly dry, Orlena wet them with her tongue. She might not be able to produce the bird call after all. Would her brother hear her if she was too quiet? Would someone else? Nobody had found them out by the whistle before, but—

She found herself before the gate and slipped back against the edge of the palisade, her heart fluttering in her bosom like a doomed bird.

Air whizzed past her lips and back over her tongue, her lungs swelling with fullness.

The gate swung open before she could make a chirp.

"That you, McLintock?"

"Ah, hell—"

McLintock's profanity was audible even over Orlena's fright at the opening of the gate. At that voice—Jimmy's voice, asking for McLintock.

"Jimmy?"

"Orlena!"

"Who's that?" Another voice from within the palisades came hollerin out, and Orlena's blood ran cold. She stumbled back from the gate well enough to catch sight of her brother's face through the tree-filtered moonlight.

The horse was so close. The horse was so close! If she could just get on it, she could—

"Don't git too excited, now, Orlena."

McLintock had revealed himself. She discovered this when she turned to race back to the horses: found him there with his rifle pointed at her, as though he meant to shoot her if she moved too far too fast.

It didn't make sense. Then, it did.

"We ain't gonna hurtcha if'n you come nice and quiet. Ain't that right, Jim?"

"Course not, Orlena!"

At the drop of Jimmy's hand on her shoulder, Orlena let out a little scream that made more than a few other men laugh in the darkness around them. She whirled wildly, catching ghostly hints of faces in the trees and beyond the palisades.

With a devious grin at his sister's panic, Jimmy told her, "Why, hell—I'm so happy to see yeh, I may jes make yeh stay a little while."

All the voices laughed again. Especially, as he arrived behind her, Deputy McLintock.

Her grip on the edge of that dark pit seemed about to slip after all.

17

DOCTOR ROBINSON STOOPED over Lorenzo's bed, which was one hell of a bad way to slam back into your body once you'd passed out in the middle of conversing with a scorpion-man. The sheriff screamed in surprise, which made the doctor scream in surprise, which made the deputy come rushing in with his gun already pulled.

"Back up there, brother," the sheriff cried, reflexively wiping his palm across his own chest and attempting to slide up in the bed. His neck stung with a terrible ache and, grimacing, he rubbed.

The doctor leaned back and recovered his sense of gravitas.

"Well, at first glance there certainly doesn't seem to be any lasting mental damage."

"Lasting damage? The hell're yeh talkin about?"

"The scorpion, of course, Sheriff—you were stung by a scorpion."

Lorenzo's disorientation snapped to a far more thorough understanding. He bolted all the straighter, forgetting doctor and deputy alike. Instead, he focused on the dresser.

The drawer had been shut.

While the doctor said something unintelligible, Lorenzo scrambled up to yank open the drawer.

Empty.

"Where are they."

"Sir?"

His gun already put away, the deputy looked anxiously at the boss that whirled on him with the drawer still hanging open from the dresser.

"The scorpions, you dipshit! The scorpions! Where are they?"

"Well—they—I—"

The deputy's eyes flickered away from the sheriff's. Toward something on the floor.

Slowly, the Sheriff followed his look to the dead scorpion curled in the middle of the room.

"You didn't."

"Well—well not *that* one, Sheriff, but—"

"Jes all the resta'em."

The Deputy said nothing. Lorenzo trembled with fury, his brain quivering with the energy of a vicious flame.

If he had a gun on him, he'd have shot both men dead. Lucky for everybody it was across the room there at the rolltop. He didn't think he could get to it before the urge passed or he himself was shot down.

Instead, he slammed the drawer shut with his fist. When it did not close all the way, he jerked it open and slammed it back and forth in the dresser so viciously that the structure whined. Incensed by its protest, he shoved the whole piece of shit over and put his foot through the back.

The doctor retreated quietly out of the room.

Less intelligent, the deputy watched his boss's temper

tantrum for about fifteen seconds before asking with a vapid look, "Should I not of?"

"*Get out.*"

Lorenzo's command had the tone of an urgent, slightly insane whisper. Glancing over his shoulder at the doctor who had already done the same, the deputy cleared his throat.

"I'll…go let Deputy McLintock know y'er up."

The deputy shut the door quietly behind him.

Alone in his room, Lorenzo sank down beside the ruins of his dresser. His eyes watered. He felt like a child and hated himself for it.

That stagecoach was arriving at Sandspur in a bit over a week if everything had gone in accordance with the plans. That was not so very long to wait, except that it was. He had so many questions. The thought of losing momentum—of having no escape from all this—was devastating.

Over his month of prodigious experimentation, Lorenzo had learned damn well why the Natives felt the way they did about the scorpions and the creature on the other side of their venom. This thing—it was a teacher, a mentor. A counselor to all men, like Prometheus in the ancient Greek myths.

More than that, though: it was a warm consolation to Lorenzo.

The space it inhabited, through its infinite containment of all-things and no-thing at once, also encompassed Lorenzo's being. When he was there, he knew beyond any doubt what it meant when Jesus said he offered not death but eternal life: only, the scorpion-man could *show* it to Lorenzo. Whether it had the capacity to *give* remained to be seen, but Lorenzo knew there was some way to express this unity he felt. Some way to achieve the state of visionary consultation with the spirit while sober on Earth, thereby gaining concrete proof of the soul's eternal security.

In some ways, the blissful unity *did* stick with him. For

a day or two after a triple-sting his whole body vibrated with a secret truth fully beyond the comprehension of his fellow townsfolk. Why was that?

He lay back on the floor and decided it had something to do with livin in these houses. In the rigid structure of boxes in boxes. Box buildins in structured towns in structured countries all livin structured ways of life structured by the damn Church. All that structure, that separation—it kept a body from feelin that unity-force that, by definition, surely must have inhabited everybody around Lorenzo as much as Lorenzo himself.

Slowly but surely, it had become all he had thought about: that unity and how to manifest it for himself while also expressing it to others. He had kept his thoughts as contained as possible but had taken to filling the pages of a notebook with diagrams. An attempt to organize his discoveries in a comprehensive way. What he had learned would always make sense to him, but the question was how he could make another understand it…or whether he even should.

After all. For as beautiful and euphoric as were these notions of immortality, it somehow made the mortality of his current form all the more acutely painful. A few triple-stings ago, the world-maker had really fucked him up. The two-dimensional space had folded overhead of him, curving into him, and he had been overwhelmed by a sense of profound, horrific emptiness. He was absolutely alone, and lying to himself.

The further one went back toward that unity, the more one realized the inherent alone-ness of existence was more than inescapable: it was *the* condition. The only condition. The one true constant, the stifling emptiness. It was an emptiness that turned down everything not the scorpion to a painful murmur soon ended.

Hell…that considered, maybe it wouldn't kill him to take a break from the world-maker for a couple of weeks.

McLintock knocked before he walked in, though he did not wait for the sheriff's answer first. If he had an opinion about the state of the sheriff or his room, he did not express it. Instead he folded his arms over his chest while regarding the man at his feet.

"Feelin better?"

"Hell no." Lorenzo rubbed his hands over his face and groaned through his palms, "Fire that feckless dipshit fer destroyin evidence when we're done here."

"I don't know if today's the day yeh oughta be firin anybody, Sheriff."

Dropping his hand from his face to his chest, Lorenzo sighed and studied the ceiling.

"Lay it on me."

"It's Orlena Felder, sir. She's missing."

So evaporated all his angst over the deaths of the scorpions.

Lorenzo sat upright.

"What?"

"Disappeared last night, I reckon." McLintock's normally stoic expression was grimly lined. "Mrs. Paulson heard her go out late last night but didn't hear her come back. Checked the room this mornin, nothin. Let me know on account Orlena is usually back a few hours after she sees you, Mrs. said."

"And you? Where were yeh? What'd you hear last night?"

"Nothin unusual. Thinkin mebbe round about midnight I heard a horse leavin town, but we was too busy dealin with you. Was Orlena who found yeh and told us."

Lorenzo stood up in the solid room that was real and not real all at once.

What was the point of all this?

Because it had to be. It was the only thing that could be. If one cog of the mechanism was absent, nothing else could function.

With consideration for the whiskey beside his gun on the rolltop, Lorenzo crossed the room and unscrewed the cap.

"You believe in God, McLintock?"

"Strange thing to ask a man out the blue."

"Sunday, ain't it?"

"Reckon that's true."

"So?" Taking a swig of the whiskey, Lorenzo offered his deputy some and was refused with a polite hand. He lifted the bottle back to his lips, saying, "Do yeh?"

"Reckon it ain't really a mattera belief."

"How yeh figure?"

"The hell difference is my belief gonna make to Him?"

"Ain't about what belief does fer Him...it's what it does fer you."

With another hefty swig of the burning liquor to chase away morning breath and wake himself up, Lorenzo swished it around his mouth, swallowed, then slammed the bottle down a little hard.

"How bout, insteada firin that deputy, yeh send him down to Miss Orlena's ranch quick as he kin to see if she's gone home."

"And meanwhile?"

"And meanwhile..."

He leaned back against the desk.

"Meanwhile, I clean up my act."

Lorenzo Blaize did not particularly feel like dressing to the nines anymore. That slick black get-up he used to love felt tight and oppressive now. A little like his job, to be honest, and all the things he had done in the past that were not on the level. Much as he was not particularly wild about the structures that made it difficult for him to see over the fence and into the infinite beyond, he still understood that those structures existed because they were in accordance with the operations of eternity. They were structures that permitted or suppressed the greater understanding of individuals depending upon their class, and they represented principles that were expressions of that infinite all-mind's will.

Homes were a structure of security; marriage, of domesticity of course, and that was domesticity in the pure sense of domesticatin. Oneself and one's woman and chilins.

Then, you had the law. An expression of Justice. The hand of balance emerging in the world, palm open to receive the weights and measures of men.

Now Lorenzo saw how unjust he had been in his life. Now he felt like he'd been a real sonnabitch, and when he considered his own attitude toward the position of sheriff back at the time of his election, he grew deeply ashamed. Humiliated, even.

More than making sure Orlena hadn't run away in response to finding him indisposed, Lorenzo found himself overwhelmed with the urge to sincerely repent for his unjust heart.

After emptying the dresser, Lorenzo went down and got some boards and nails and brought em back up and fixed up the dresser. He apologized to it, figuring that if all things were part of the all-mind then he'd done the dresser awful wrong in the heat of the moment. He shifted the nails around between his lips and thought he was losing his goddamn mind, but then wondered if all this feeling weren't why the Natives seemed to think every last damn thing on the earth was some kinda spirit.

Damn…Lorenzo was finding out more and more often that he'd just been flat wrong his whole life.

The deputy returned from Orlena's ranch around half past noon, his hat in his hand and a nervous look in his eyes to speak to the sheriff tidying the rest of the room as he never had in his God-given life.

"Fellas down at the ranch say Orlena ain't been back since she left last month," the mousy deputy said.

"They say she ain't been back…she ain't been back."

Lorenzo finished tucking in the corner of the blanket and lowered himself upon the edge of his newly-made bed.

Something in him deflated.

He had been trying not to think too much about her today, and now he had nothing else to think about.

"You ain't seen no other signa her? Not since she found you and McLintock and told yehs about me and the scorpions and all?"

"No, sir, I ain't seen her nowhere. Reckon she's moved house?"

"Then Mrs. Paulson would have seen fit to mention all her belongings had been disappeared overnight, I do believe."

"Oh. Reckon that's true, sheriff."

With an anxious look at the spot where the scorpion once lay dead, the deputy began, "Sheriff—"

"You will have t'excuse my unpleasant demeanor earlier, Deputy," said Lorenzo, springing up and grabbing the broom he'd borrowed from Meyer. With this tucked under his arm, he bent to take the bed by the footboard. The deputy belatedly sprang to the headboard to help move it as Lorenzo continued, "I had something of a rude awakening. Was not anticipatin none of that…and those scorpions were somewhat important to me, yeh see."

"I kin certainly see that now, Sheriff…ah!"

The deputy dropped the headboard so Lorenzo jerked to a halt and turned a somewhat aggravated eye upon him. Said deputy pointed to the corner beneath the moved bed, his face excited.

"But it looks like you still got one! Look—"

Sure enough.

Here he thought the ones that had disappeared over time had all been cannibalized. At the time of the deputy killin 'em they numbered six; now that he thought about it, Lorenzo reckoned he'd only ever seen three of em dead with his own two eyes. First one dead had just out and out disappeared.

And here he was, stinger high and claws at the ready.

"Poor fella! You ain't gotta be scared, little brother. Hold on now…deputy, run on down and git me a jar."

Five minutes later, the little world-maker had a new home, some dirt and sticks a poor compensation for the size of the tiny terrarium.

"I know it ain't the Taj Mahal," he told the little fella, who had calmed down significantly but still seemed ready to fight for life at a moment's notice, "but once I git yeh a couplea roaches I think you'll manage a little whiles longer. Deputy?"

"Yessir!"

"Find my friend some roaches," he commanded, carefully placing the jar into the deputy's hands. "I got work to do."

His hair combed back, his hat on, his crisp white shirt unbuttoned at the collar and unadorned save for his sheriff's badge, Lorenzo stepped out upon the walkway of Sandspur and looked at all the people. *His* people. Good people, and tolerant. Always lookin to see the best in their boyish, slightly metropolitan sheriff.

The people pained him because, without knowledge of their immortality, he reckoned that someday they'd die. Did folk understand in this world where death was written in every bullet, oozing from every disease, burning in every fire, that the promises of Christ were literal even if the stories of the Bible were not? The thoughts plagued him. On his way to the sheriff's office, it occurred to Lorenzo that, as the hand of Justice in the world, his responsibility was to keep life comfortable and stable enough so's these folks *could* have a shot at thinking deeply enough to meet with God's true messages. Ain't matter what they prayed or what they imbibed. Only that life was secure enough to allow the truth.

That was his duty here, his position in the array of cogs. Protecting these people; protecting Orlena, the thought of whom stung him with love and love-pain for something he knew would never work out. He wasn't sure why.

Sheriff's office was empty. He got on his horse, fully aware for the first time ever of how good it was to pet a loving animal and completely observe its existence as a being on Earth. He did away with the spurs on his boots and loosened the bridle for the horse's greater comfort. Together, they made their way around town.

Nobody had seen Orlena Felder.

Nobody. Not since the evening prior.

With each indefinite response, Lorenzo's heart sank more.

Come supper he'd asked about half the damn town; as much of it as spoke English or could at least cobble it together. Nobody had seen Orlena or had any idea where she'd got off to.

Frankly, he had expected this. The sheriff had not expected anybody reputable (that was, not drunk at the time) would have seen Orlena up and about at eleven thirty. That was about when McLintock and the other deputy had reported her barging into the sheriff's office to beg for their help. The other deputy had gone and got the doctor, who'd apparently stayed an hour and then come back around for that rude early morning awakening.

What had happened after that hour?

"Gosh, let's see." The deputy, having delivered the scorpion's cockroach-enriched terrarium, sat across from the sheriff at his office desk. "Nothin really very excitin happened…folks goin to they rooms, y'know."

"You stayed with me all night?"

"Yessir, sheriff. Had to be sure you was gonna make it."

And he'd almost fired this fella on an angry impulse… one of his most vital lessons was still learning to not let his emotion get the better of him.

"Y'er a good man, Deputy. McLintock didn't check in with yeh, though?"

"No, Sheriff, not that I remember, although—"

"Although?"

"I may have—dozed off an hour'r so's."

His lips pursing in a combination of humor and disappointment to have no new information, Lorenzo leaned forward in his seat.

"Guess I have to hope he's forgettin somethin…if that ain't the case, and the last time he saw Orlena was—"

"Sheriff!"

The door slammed open and, as if summoned, Deputy McLintock barged in with a wild look in his eye. Both men sprang up from the sheriff's desk while, panting, McLintock said, "I got some real bad news."

He passed over the bundled shawl, which Lorenzo rightaway saw was both bloodstained and Orlena's. His heart clenched in anxious anticipation of what he was about to see; McLintock lay the bundle upon the desk and stepped back as though anticipating a snake.

"I was jes runnin my horse up north a ways lookin fer some sign of Miss Orlena, and on the way back I noticed this lyin on the bridge back to town."

Dread in his heart, Lorenzo reflexively patted his person for his gloves only to realize he had left them in the jacket abandoned in the hotel room. With one long, steady exhalation through his teeth, he used a kerchief to peel back the gummy, slightly stiff layers of fabric enclosing the small chunk of woman's scalp.

Outside, somebody laughed at a joke on their way out of the pharmacy.

Lorenzo lowered slowly into his chair.

He almost struggled to see through all the dried blood to the natural color of the strands.

The deputies looked on with haunted expressions before McLintock began, "Lorenzo—"

"She ain't dead," said Lorenzo softly.

"What?"

Swallowing against his dry throat, he leaned forward and inspected the clotted mass of hair. Rich hair; beautiful, wild, thick, vibrant, red hair.

And, oh, Christ—when he looked at it close, real close, it weren't no slicea scalp at all. A stripa animal meat: blood from the same, no doubt.

Lorenzo leaned back and exhaled real slow, his brain's tension slacking at the assurance that it was only a message and not proof of action.

"Sheriff."

At McLintock's intonation of his title, Lorenzo stood straight up from the desk. He looked around the office with new, clear eyes.

"She ain't dead yet; this ain't more than a sample. Somebody git me a rifle and enough ammunition to take on an army."

"What does this mean, sir?" McLintock made no move to arm himself while the other deputy scurried off. "Who yeh reckon has her?"

"Somebody who wants me dead," said Lorenzo, checking his pistol before holstering it and giving his gun belt a slight adjustment. "Or worse than dead. Whoever they are, it's somebody that wants me to come to them. Deputy, go git Meyer and a fewa them young fellas what fight fires fer us. Tell em they's deputies till I say they ain't anymore. I want em meetin me by the bridge, ready to go in a half hour."

"Where we goin, sheriff?"

"We are about t'embark on a systematic sweepa the goddamn countryside until we find whoever has been causin all this chaos. I got a naggin itch that says that church burnin, the Felder escape, and Orlena's kindappin are all related, and as I am mighty tired of such events occurrin in my town, I aim to put a stop t'it if it takes us a montha campin in them goddamn hills."

"How about that time yeh jes…disappeared?"

McLintock's question succeeded in drawing Lorenzo's attention. The sheriff looked at his deputy grimly while McLintock arched a brow.

"You think that's related to all this, too? That some Comanches knocked yeh over the head or some such?"

"I think I better tell you that once I have solved the mystery for myself, Deputy McLintock…till then, it's all speculative. You stay here and watch over the town whiles I and the posse look around. We may be gone a few days, so be prepared…but, if none of us have returned in two weeks, I reckon you oughta take it upon yerself to do somethin."

An hour later, the posse was arranged at the bridge. Supplies had been packed and every man had at least two guns.

Lorenzo had the scorpion with him. It was content with its remaining cockroach in its terrarium, which was itself safe in the horse's saddlebag. He knew no other way to see to its care than to bring it along, but the trade-off came in the enormous pressure he felt to care for the scorpion's well-being.

Little like bein pregnant, he reckoned.

Why did he feel so disheartened before this search even began? Why did, as his horse stood upon the Pecos bank opposite Sandspur, did this sense of great woe come over him?

He weren't gonna git nowhere thinking like that, but he couldn't help it. As the posse ran off into the evening and spent their first hours searching into the coming of dark, Lorenzo had the acute sense that Orlena was near. Near, and in danger.

And he could not allow her to endure the same fate as her family.

On the second day of their journey, nothing of interest captured the imagination of the search party. That general malaise that had settled over Lorenzo right away infected the men. The countryside laughed around them, hateful oceanic desert yawning out into one oblivion while the rising hills and their timber teeth invited a great many deaths.

And mysteries.

The third day, Lorenzo and the six men with whom he had split off came across the presidio.

He had not known it to be there, truth be told. The limestone with which its remaining structures had been built indicated that the overgrown path—littered with trees at least as old as Lorenzo's dead daddy—had once been worth traveling, and had indeed been used by many in that period. Yes: though it was like the rest of the area clustered with new-old tree growth, the presidio was substantial enough within its fortifications that if it had survived it might have blossomed into a cozy little town out here in the hills. Coulda run Sandspur outta business.

It also provided a convenient location that Lorenzo reckoned he'd be usin if the shoe were on the other foot and it had been him that got run outta town durin that fateful election.

The presidio's back gate had not been repaired, but the front looked damn near new. As telltale a sign of habitation as a glass bottle on the ground right near the entrance, or the obviously used beds discovered in the barracks Lorenzo and Meyer cleared with their guns ready to shoot at the least sign of movement.

But there weren't no movement.

"Maybe whoever's been stayin here has moved on."

Meyer's suggestion did not ring true at all, but Lorenzo kept that to himself. "Mebbe," he decided, looking around. "Or mebbe we jes walked into the Stone Hill Gang's house while nobody was home."

"You really think it's them that kidnapped her? Then where's she at?"

Meyer's touch of grandfatherly emotion spurred a bit too many of Lorenzo's feelings. The sheriff cleared his throat and slid his gun into his holster. He stepped back out of the barracks and into the open air of the presidio, where other members were already collecting in an empty-handed group.

"Well, Meyer…I reckon if it had been Comanche what got her, then her *real* scalp'd still be hangin from some war chief's belt somewheres insteada the fake bein delivered to the doorstepa my town."

Some discussion was had in the center of the ruined presidio. The hours were wearing on and the men were tired. If they were going to be caught sitting around when the Stone Hill Gang came back, they'd be at a disadvantage.

But, the place empty as it was—now that sure seemed like a good goddamn opportunity.

By dark, the posse had regrouped. Arrangements had been made. Working in shifts, the rescue party organized themselves to keep tireless watch over the old fort. For as long, anyway, as it took to satisfy Lorenzo that the place was uninhabited, which many of the men protested it must have been.

"They got what they wanted, ain't they," said one of the protestors with a spit into the dirt. "Got a woman—yer woman."

"And why yeh reckon that is? To git me out here and take a shot at me. So, why ain't they?"

The men looked around at one another. Meyer, hands spreading, suggested, "On accounta they wasn't anticipatin so many men to be with yeh, Sheriff?"

"No," said Lorenzo, his eyes narrowing through the darkness in which they operated without so much as a lantern. "No. They know this land. If they could kill us here, they would and do it quick. But they kain't—soemthin's keepin em. I jes ain't sure what."

The men murmured among themselves and warily took up their arms, splitting off into the first shift of sleepers and watchers.

Lorenzo, sleep as far from his mind as it had ever been, stayed up among those watchers perched up in trees and hidden in the dark. Together, they all waited for the least sign of life that did not announce itself.

One would have expected at least a bear.

It occurred to Lorenzo the next day of their watch, on reflecting upon this oddity, that he had once before been in the woods and expected at least one animal to be seen amid the timber. Certainly at least a squirrel or a rat in the old presidio.

This was just like that time. That strange time when McLintock took him up in the woods and that great flash came. When Lorenzo woke up in bed next to Orlena for the first time.

Orlena! Oh, Orlena, where was she? What had them sonsabitches done with her while they was off raidin and robbin and killin? Whatever she suffered, Lorenzo could not help but hope she knew he'd be lookin for her.

It therefore felt almost disloyal when he took his horse out to pick their slow, careful way through the night in hopes of confirming his suspicion about that absence of sound.

This did not take long.

As the horse emerged upon a ridge overlooking miles, stopping short with an irritated whinny for the rider that nearly got them both killed by making it wander around at night, Lorenzo patted the horse's neck.

"Sorry, brother…needed to make sure."

This was just the place McLintock had taken him.

Lorenzo had not noticed it at first, partly because he was so focused on the presidio but also because they'd come around it a back way. His half of the search party had arced around the bases of several hills and explored a great deal of timber that had a way of blending on a man after awhiles.

But this view, such vastness illuminated by an entire universe of twinkling stars—he remembered it from being there during the day. He just hadn't ridden far enough into the trees, or in the right direction long enough, to find the presidio by his own self.

That, or something had kept him from it.

With a glance down at the horse's saddlebag, Lorenzo turned his mount back toward the trees. Five minutes later, he whistled to announce his arrival to camp. Meyer sat up and looked at him through the dark, about to lay back down until the sheriff rode up.

"Something wrong, sheriff?"

"I'm fixinta go take a look at somethin not far from here and jes wanted y'all to know I oughta be back by morn."

The barman looked queerly at the sheriff. "This somethin onea us oughta see to along with yeh?"

"Git yer rest; I jes don't want you wakin up at the next shift change and gettin all in a tizz lookin fer me when I'm well and fine on the other sidea the hill."

Nodding once, Meyer settled back against the tree where he reclined. "Don't do anything I wouldn't."

Lorenzo laughed a little, looking fondly upon the man as he did, and urged his horse on toward the trees with the scorpion still in his saddlebag.

"Meyer, my friend…I could say the very same."

18

AS AGREED, THE Needless Man went on back to the horses by his own self. Being alone was such a relief that, were it not for Jim's imminent demise, the Needless Man surely would have been tempted to ride off and leave everybody in the lurch.

But cooperating with the sheriff was too clean and easy a way to get his hands on Jimmy; particularly if Orlena held up her end of the bargain, which he believed she would.

So, his attention tuned for signs of more Comanche scouts, the Man made his way back to camp. Ain't greeted with cheers so much as impatience, but a few fellas seemed pleased progress had been made. Made camp with them one night before they all returned in one great drive to the grounds where, sure enough, the Tribe had remade the essential sites of their home. A handful of able-bodied young men used tools not unlike butterfly nets: pouches with leather backings, with which they pushed the scorpions en masse into the provided crates.

Each time they did, more of the hand-sized arachnids scuttled out of the writhing darkness to take the empty space.

Roaring Bear, hard at work at the bottom of the pit, broke from the rest when the Needless Man called down to him.

"Back already, my friend—we've barely arrived, ourselves. The packing's only half-done."

"Encounter any trouble on yer way back here?"

"No. The way was clear."

With a call to his fellows, the Brave mounted the stones stepping up toward the ridge and hauled himself into the grass. Easiness in his features and posture. Back with the family.

"That is a beautiful sight," he commended of the horses that grazed throughout the paradisal little valley in the middle of a harsh hike. "For all the trouble we had finding a man both willing and able to help us, it has been an easier journey than I feared."

"That's what I want to talk to yehs about."

The Man recounted killing the Comanche scouts by the quarry. And the one that got away.

Roaring Bear's pleasurable smile faded by the word.

"And as glad as I am to find you all alive and well," the Man summarized, looking out among the People, "I cannot help but find it an ominous sign that with five of six scouts dead the Comanche have still not made a move."

"Because we did not have what they have been waiting for."

"Why kill one group or the other when you kin kill em both in a bottle like this'un, and take the horses all at once?"

"Exactly."

"Yeah," said the Needless Man, adjusting his hat and studying the happy People mingling with the rancheros, "I been thinkin that, too."

"Perhaps we ought to have remained in the mission."

"Cornered there, cornered here…what's the difference."

The Brave's glance—toward the scorpion cave— expressed the difference damn well, but the Needless Man paid it no mind. The old medicine man came over to greet Needless and explain that the small group of men riding off around the ridge would be back with good hunting game within a few hours, if the world-maker were willing.

That, it were. Each Brave returned with a sizable sampling of venison, and the ranch hands whooped and hollered long before the Natives.

The hunters looked honored, all the people were gay. Real sight for sore eyes.

Fellowship. Relief. Men helpin one another.

Revelries lasted long into the evening hours and too well beyond nightfall for the Man's comfort. The Brave was primed at a high level of alertness for everything beyond the fire where, with a dance of thanks for the horses that would save their lives, the People invoked their sacred spirits and blessed the rancheros and even thanked the venison.

And it was all real nice.

Eventually the victory celebration settled down, and the tepis erected in a flash that morning by the well-practiced Natives became filled not just by their owners but also by a few rancheros availing themselves of friendly Native women who had been very grateful, and who were probably also excited by the prospect of having a child that did not obligate them to any one particular man of their tribe.

The Needless Man did not accept the advances of the woman—women, probably—who showed him attention. He did not perceive it as other men did, and he meant what he said t'Orlena, at any rate. Women brought trouble. They kept a man's mind anywhere but where it oughta have been.

And the Needless Man had a whole hell of a lot on his mind.

Polite as he could, he rejected the offer of a tipi to sleep in. "Always sleep better with the open sky overhead," he said, truth after his time in prison. "And, anyway, I git restless in early mornin. Don't want nobody bothered by the sounda me rustlin about with the tipi."

The medicine man had attempted to fawn on him a little more, but Roaring Bear understood exactly why the Needless Man intended to sleep outside the tents—assuming he slept at all. The glance they exchanged while parting ways for the night said so. While the Brave helped his father to bed, the Needless Man settled himself down not far from the remains of the firepit that had been killed for the night.

Then, the waiting.

In the dark, with a silent hand, he cleaned the shiny new Winchester rifle he had inherited from Mr. Mayfield.

The wind haunted the valley with its moan.

Next, he unloaded the revolver. Cleaned it. Loaded it again. His gun belt had been replenished on his arrival to the other men. He ran his hand along the bullets and felt for open slots, finding none.

A ways away, far on the edge of the encampment, the horses took their well-deserved rest.

The Needless Man slid his revolver back into the holster along his thigh, then lay back with the rifle slung in his arms like a baby.

His eyes shut but his mind remained steel-hard awake, running hot in the cold of desert night.

Again, the howling wind.

A man turning over in a tipi.

Slight tug at back of eyes. Cool darkness so good. Calm. Breathing slow. Chest unbinding.

Something scratched around in the dirt beside the Man's head.

Eyes flew open. Head turning, then jerking back.

Black and blue scorpion—black, blacker than black in the night—contemplating his face, caught in the act, waving its claws at him in half-hearted threat.

Or expression of some kind, at any rate.

The Man sat fully up, the sleep falling from his mind.

His eye trailed around the ridge demarking the shore of sky's ocean.

Along this path, there were no stars.

The silhouettes of horsemen blotted them out.

Silent, the rifle still in his arms, the Man rose in the dark and moved at a crouch behind the nearest tipi. No activity along the ridge: not seen. How many? Hard to tell—enough to line the ridge.

Too many.

The Man whispered into the flap of the tipi into which the Brave had retired about four hours prior. "Hey, Roaring Bear."

Easily as wound up as the Man, Roaring Bear darted out of the tent with a knife in his hand and an intense, knowing look in his dark eyes.

The Needless Man said nothing. He only touched the Brave's shoulder and gestured toward the ridge.

Roaring Bear's nostrils flared.

"Quick as you kin, git everybody awake and git em to them horses. The rancheros…well, tell em to fight, but I won't hold my breath."

The Brave looked shocked as he took the Needless Man's meaning. "You can't stand off against the Comanche."

"I done it before," grunted the Man, making his way back over to his grazing horse. "Reckon it won't be so different this time round."

"Wait."

The Man paused. Roaring Bear hurried over and placed the knife into his hand.

Nodding, the Man slid it into his boot. "I'll do my best to keep a clear path out the valley…but these scorpions sure as hell coulda picked a better place to breed."

His horse greeted him familiarity, ears twitching with

the sounds of distant animals unknown to it. The Man mounted and urged the beast around its fellows, his eyes always on the warriors looked down across the Tribe's camp.

By moving at a slow trot, they had almost made it to a spread of desert willows—and one or two people had quietly emerged from their tipis—when the pounding of hooves and an ominous rising hum announced the coming storm.

As the hum rose to a crescendo of high, wild war whoops, the Man leveled the rifle and aimed through the darkness.

Like a wild, roaring avalanche, a flood of Comanche rolled around the ridge and into the valley.

Find the target. Slam the lever. Pull the trigger. Find the next target. Slam the lever. Pull the trigger. Find the next target. Slam the lever. Pull the trigger. Find the next target. Slam the lever. Pull the trigger. Find the next target. Slam the lever. Pull the trigger.

Take a second in the smell of gun smoke to slide one two three four five rounds in and recalibrate.

Five riderless horses for at least a hundred others still steered by whooping braves, some of whom had torches. The Needless Man fired for the lights. Aim. Slam. Pull. Aim. Slam. Pull. Aim. Slam. Pull. Aim.

Arrows whistled through the air and one struck hard into the ground by his horse's hooves. The beast reared and he held on, balancing his weight forward while the startled animal hammered back down upon the ground and charged forward in a fright.

Best it did. More arrows shot into the turf where it had stood. The Needless Man leaned up in the saddle and slid a few more bullets in, the nearing cries of the Comanche already drowning the panic of the Tribe.

"Hey, Allen!"

Chrysler, maybe. Couldn't tell one voice from another now. Aim slam pull aim. The horse galloped wildly. He lifted the rifle against his shoulder to pull at the reins, slowing the beast enough to redirect its path before he hammered his heels in and got it goin again. It now charged with more deliberate stride straight for the Comanche mounts, the fastest of which were all of eight hundred yards from the camp.

Slam pull aim. Slam pull slam. He ejected the cartridge, loaded two more rounds, then let the rifle rest while he drew his revolver from its holster.

The front line of Comanche horsemen met him, surpassed him, and drove their horses into the camp behind him. Three warriors, their faces and bodies painted red and black to resemble demons, assumed they had it easy facing down this one man. A tomahawk swung through the air for the Man's neck.

The Needless Man ducked and, while rising, twisted to aim the Schofield at his assailant. Then, his assailant's companions.

While three horses went riderless into the chaos, screams of mortal anguish rose from the encampment along with general noises of panic and chaos. A tipi collapsed as a horse was driven through it. Someone inside released a terrible bellow at the trampling. A handful of the Tribe's horses had been successfully mounted by their legal owners, but more were scattering away from the encampment as the shouting Comanche riders swung torches and short arrows at their hooves.

The Needless Man's eye swept from one torch to another. A rider thundered past and, sliding to the side of his steed and hanging on as naturally as walking, he swept the torch in his hand along the foliage that made the valley so hospitable to the Tribe.

Shot the bastard in the head a few seconds before the lawman's horse took an arrow straight through the neck. It collapsed forward beneath the Needless Man with a wet noise of agony.

Cursing, the Man rolled away and got his gong rung by a hard slam into the ground. Two seconds later he stumbled up, sparing little more than a glance at the horse he was quick to shoot in the head.

A few warriors charging the newly dismounted Man soon joined him on the earth, a hell of a lot more immobile than he was.

The Man broke open his Schofield to sweep away the cartridges and thumb six more bullets into the cylinder.

More fires took hold on the other side of the camp. A small group of Tribespeople, their horses terrified, took their chance to flee. The Man focused on clearing the way for them, taking out a few more riders and, when he couldn't take out a rider, a horse or two to keep their route at least navigable. One of em still ended up shot by some Comanche's gun.

This was far from the worst thing that was happening within the Tribe. The encampment had dissolved into absolute insanity. When the Needless Man swung around to keep his sights trained on a certain target he counted no fewer than three tipi already smoking, five or six tribesman dead in the grass, and at least one mother visibly struggling to bear her child, panicking in the blanket with which she'd covered its face, to any riderless horse she could reach.

Her flight stopped abruptly and her face contorted in a scream as, swinging a club, a Comanche took direct aim at the blanket in her arms.

The Needless Man turned his aim to shoot the horse. Losing his club, the rider was pitched straight into the embrace of a fire from which he emitted a dying wail.

The mother wasted no time hurrying on.

The Man wasted none, himself.

Another horse, its rider dead, went dashing by.

He got hold of it at just the right moment, flinging himself upon its back and gripping its mane even as it galloped on to escape the gunfire and flames.

He didn't let it. The Needless Man forced it back into the fray, into the swarming Comanche riders that flooded the camp without end. Every once in a while he would catch a glimpse of one of the rancheros in the midst of a skirmish, or Roaring Bear helping an evacuee onto a horse, but for the most part the Man was focused solely on his own business.

The business of stayin alive.

He did not make it out unscathed. An arrow caught him in the thigh and he raged, shooting the sender of the unwanted gift before tearing its sharp head from his flesh with a roar. Another Comanche warrior rode near, taking aim with his spear.

The Man dove from his horse's back to miss the spear and fired his last few rounds. The Schofield broke open and he touched his gun belt.

Nothing.

His nostrils flared. He glanced down the half-second it took to confirm he'd worn through every last scrap of ammunition, then turned his attention back to the small band coming at him through the smoke. One of these riders raised a bow, another arrow notched in its embrace.

The Man rolled away from it, the abandoned spear in his hand when he sprang back up. Ten yards between him and the riders: he ran toward them, leaping, the spear's vicious tip stabbing in and through the neck of the archer's horse.

Down went the horse: the archer managed to roll upon his back in time to see the Man jam the spear through his heart and take the bow from his hands.

Ducking the axe of the next Brave to make it to him, the Man extricated the quiver from the dead assailant's body and took aim.

Notch pull aim release. Notch pull aim release. Notch notch pull aim release.

Best part of bow and arrow was killin two men at once.

Sweat and the blood of other men soaked his shirt.

He paused to tear it off. When it was gone, a number of Comanche were coming at him on foot. He spent his last few arrows on them before abandoning the bow in favor of the nearby lost tomahawk axe.

He swung it into the nearest warrior's neck with a snarl. With it still stuck just beneath his opponent's chin, he ducked a strike from someone else and took his bleeding, gagging, half-beheaded opponent down with him, then jerked the blade out and nailed it into the guts of the opportunist. His free hand raised to catch an arm bringing a club down over his head from the other direction, and with one fluid motion he jerked the axe out of the second hostile's stomach and into the ribs of the third.

The falling trio gave way to a camp wreathed totally in flame. Cries of horses and women and children and dying men rose together beneath the relentless crackling of flames. Around the Needless Man lay at least twenty dead Comanche; in the distance, beyond the fire, there were many more killed by his hand. Had to guess the total between sixty and eighty. The rancheros had not slacked, and had each of them killed a minimum of ten raiders if they were still alive. The total number of the dead on the side of the Comanche had to already number close to one hundred. It likely exceeded.

Yet still they surged, driving their horses to leap through the flames.

The Man accepted it. This was just a fact of nature. They would come and come and he would kill and kill. The killing became fully automatic, a matter of course. The colors black and red signaled his tomahawk's coming down, signaled the inevitable splatter of brain and blood. His torso glistened with these signs of violence; with sweat, and the spittle of screams.

He kept killing until, as constant as they had been, the Comanche whooping stopped all at once.

Only the hot crackling of the fire and the weeping of the People remained.

The Man whirled, his bloody tomahawk still tight in his hand.

Flames licking around the camp revealed horsemen lining the perimeter as they earlier lined the ridge.

A Comanche warrior stood across from the Needless Man, in size if not in brutality a match for the encampment's most successful defender.

The Needless Man regarded him for a few long seconds. Regarded the spear in his hand, most especially. With only the briskest glance to either side of them, he turned the tomahawk around and tossed it upon the ground.

The warrior stuck his spear in the dirt.

Each sprinting fast as a horse, the fighters met head-on and hand-to-hand. The grip of a hand soon turned to the grip of a shoulder. Face-to-face, teeth-to-teeth. Hateful lovers.

The Comanche was heavy. With a throw of great force, he slammed the Needless Man back down into the earth to the excited whooping of those outside the fire.

Bracing his feet, the Needless Man bucked up and over. He rolled the Comanche onto his back and slammed an elbow into his face.

The Comanche warrior released a howl of pain that was somehow muted by his broken, bleeding nose. Sitting up, the Needless Man intended to give him a few hard clocks in the skull, but the tomahawk he had abandoned in good faith now swung for his head. He twisted just enough to catch the warrior's wrist before impact.

Jaw tight, the Man took hold of the tomahawk's handle to wrench it from the Comanche's hand.

The bastard was tough and kept a hard hold of it.

Without even thinking, the Man lunged down to bite into the Comanche's wrist.

Blood spurted into the Needless Man's mouth. The warrior unleashed another howl of pain, releasing the tomahawk to instead slam his arm up against the Man's mouth. The Needless Man stumbled back, tomahawk in his hand, and barely managed to avoid a fistful of ashes and burning pitch flung from the edge of the nearby fire—straight for his eyes. The Comanche shook off his burning hand and pushed himself up, stumbling unsteadily to his feet.

There was nothing unsteady about his charge, however.

The Brave's hard shoulder slammed into the Man's diaphragm and left him breathless as he was hammered back down into the earth. He lost his grip on the weapon. One big fist slammed down into his face.

Blood poured from his nose and flooded back down his throat to his mouth.

The tomahawk had flown a few inches too far.

His arm extended, blindly groping for it while the Comanche landed another punch. Another.

The Man choked on his own blood, lifting his head and spitting a mouthful out to catch his breath. His feet dug into the terrain against the pain.

As he braced his hand against his own leg to give it some support in bucking the Comanche away, his hand made contact with another handle altogether.

Roaring Bear's knife looked awful good while arcing into the Comanche's neck.

Shocked, the warrior reached up to lamely touch the handle sticking out of his jugular.

His breath coming in a haggard gasp, the Comanche slid the dagger from his neck and produced a surprised sort of choking sound. A fan of blood sprayed wildly across the Needless Man's face.

Eyes rolling into his head, dagger falling from his hand, the Comanche collapsed upon the ground beside the Needless Man.

Panting through his mouth while blood continued pouring from his nose, the Needless Man found his balance and got up to his knees. Then his feet. He stooped for the dagger with one hand and gripped the Comanche's head with the other.

Every breath taken through a waterfall of his own suffocating blood, the Needless Man slammed the tip of the dagger into the skull of the Comanche. He sawed.

The entire top of the warrior's skull cap came off, glistening, along with the scalp. It dangled, red and pink and black, from long tendrils of bloody hair that the Needless Man hurled with an animal scream into the Comanche on the other side of the fire.

Quiet settled over the camp, and over the Comanche who had cheered the brawl until the Man had his clear advantage.

A horse jerked into motion beneath the guidance of the rider that forced it to vault through the flames and pace around the battlefield.

Like the others, he was decorated in that demonic red and black paint, and his weapons were either traded for or of elegant construction. Feathers ornamented his hair and belt, but there was no seething wildness in his eyes or carriage. His eyes had a hard, calculating sort of intelligence, and they were set in a face that was almost effeminate.

His horse pacing, Wolf Cunt studied the Needless Man.

With a scornful glance up at the burning camp, then across his own dead Comanche, the disgraced medicine man turned his horse around. He forced it back through the fire.

A victorious whoop echoed through the Comanche, whose horses all turned to follow Wolf Cunt's.

Blood still pouring down his open, panting mouth, the Man remained there with the knife in his hand and fires burning all around him.

Behind him, a set of mournful cries echoed through the valley.

Reluctant to turn his back on the fire until he was damn sure the Comanche were not due to return, the Man stepped a few feet back. He looked over his shoulder toward the sound.

The old medicine man had been shot dead with a few Comanche arrows.

Roaring Bear crouched over him, weeping.

The damage was beyond reckoning. Many were dead and some had been kidnapped, particularly younger members of the tribe. It was impossible, for now, to tell who had been kidnapped and who had made good an escape. Nine rancheros had died. One was mortally wounded.

No raiders returned to finish what they had started.

The next morning, with the fires out and his scorpion-scarred brother left behind to guide the tribe, Roaring Bear helped the Needless Man and the remaining rancheros pack the undamaged stagecoach with hissing crates.

Tears gathering in his eyes, Roaring Bear rode his horse alongside the coach. He had not said a word all morning.

"At least this ain't happen at a time when you would have had to stay," said the Needless Man.

It was more consolation than he had ever offered anyone.

19

THE FIRST WEEK of her captivity was the worst.

In truth, more terrible things happened to Orlena in the eight days after they came up out of the limestone mine hidden on the presidio grounds. Other terrible things would go on to happen occasionally throughout the course of her life.

Still, those three days in the claustrophobic darkness of the abandoned mine were truly the worst in her life.

First three nights with the Stone Hill Gang had been fine. Good, even Nice seeing her brother again. Seeing him free and easy and excited for his future. McLintock ain't relayed the details to nobody on the night he tricked her into coming there with him; only said with a look at Orlena, "Old cellmate's sniffin round fer you, Jim."

"That so? Shit, let'im. I gotta git him back fer this, anyway."

Jimmy flipped two thirds of the bird (healing not so bad after all, thanks to whichever one was the man with medical training) while everybody laughed. McLintock only smirked as he went on.

"He's on that trail ride what we busted you out fer."

"Hell, then it's *two* birds with one stone! Sounds good to me."

Orlena weren't so sure about that, but she was happy her brother was happy and happier still that McLintock did not feel inclined to publicly relate her betrayal. She had the feeling he understood better than even she did what would happen if the truth got out among the Stone Hill Gang.

And she also got the feeling that, if McLintock had stuck around the whole time, none of the ugliness of the second week would have happened.

He was damn lucky he spent so much of his time commuting back and forth between the presidio and Sandspur under pretenses of this investigation or that visit to the church. His pattern of coming and going meant that, on the third day, he had long-since left with his package. Orlena's shawl, and a chunk of hair that had been cut from her head and knotted up into the skin of an elk what had been their supper that night.

In the time since the deputy's departure, she had been treated fairly, but warily.

"I don't reckon you oughta wander too far from me, Orlena," her brother confessed with an apologetic tone the first night. "Fellas is mostly all right, but you never know how a man livin outside the law's gonna be when he's got some whiskey and only one woman fer miles."

The message was clear. She acted accordingly, sticking near the shack that was Jimmy's quarters. Ain't no room for two people in there. He tried to get her to share the bed the first night but gave up real quick and took the floor. Sometimes, they laughed.

But there was no laughter in Orlena's heart. That shawl and her hair had been sent off for a purpose that could backfire on the Stone Hill Gang. Every second of every day and night, she prayed that it would. Prayed that Sheriff Lorenzo Blaize would come bursting in to save her before things became too horrific to bear.

At the very least, she hoped she wouldn't have to see him get shot.

Third day. She and Jimmy were playing Beggar My Neighbor out in front of the shack. A few of the men went about the business of improving the presidio, others were sleeping well into the day so as to be alert at night, and a handful were gearing up to go shoot some game for the rest of the crew. One man whistled a song while strapping his rifle around his shoulder.

His whistle was what kept them from realizing until near a minute had passed that nature had gone mute.

"Sh," hissed somebody.

Jimmy and Orlena stopped their game, freezing with the cards in their hands and exchanging looks that went back to their shared childhood.

Somehow, in the minute of the whistling, the forest had fallen silent.

Every bird had stopped singing.

No wind quivered a branch.

The timber held its breath.

Exchanging a constellation of urgent looks, the men— Jimmy, included—abandoned their current activities to convene in comparable silence at the center of the presidio.

Her ears straining, Orlena left the cards to shamelessly creep after her brother and listen to the conversation.

"—Indians? Must be. Shit, Jesus, must be everywheres fer the birds to be so quiet."

"Now, hold on jes a second…let's see if they start back up…"

Everyone waited.

Every eye scanned the trees, the palisades, the gate.

A great wave of creeping fear washed slowly up over Orlena.

She could see it coming upon everyone there, one man at a time.

Another minute passed.

Still, no sound. No nothing.

"You ain't think it could be the sheriff and his men," posited somebody.

"Then we'd hear 'em. It's gotta be Indians. You ain't never hear a Comanche till he's stickin a spear straight up yer—"

"Okay," said another man, looking annoyed. "The sheriff and some half-wit deputies is one thing. Comanche raid is a whole 'nother."

"Probably why this damn presidio got left in the first place," muttered Jimmy.

"Ain't lyin. Somebody grab some food and somebody else git some blankets."

Folk hurried to obey. The speaker turned his eye on Orlena.

"Do somethin bout yer sister, Jimmy. We're goin in the mines."

Her stomach turned inside out.

Jimmy looked back at her and then at the other man, grim displeasure all across his face. "Suppose it really is the sheriff and his posse? We'll be stuck in there till they leave."

"It's a risk I'm willinta take. Listen to that."

Silence.

Nothing.

A great intensity of absolute nothing through which the human mind flew, each explanation for it worse than the last.

"All right," he said. "Orlena…I'm sorry. Jes gotta make sure y'er gonna cooperate. Ah…sorry."

Sorry ain't feed the dog.

Breathing was next to impossible. In addition to being enclosed in the darkness of a tunnel whose entrance was treacherously sealed by boulders and disguised with the ruins of a shattered old wagon, Orlena was gagged by a dirty contrivance of cloth and rope and restrained around the wrists. Occasionally her brother would let her out of the wrist-bindings, but he would also closely ensure she did not yield to the oppressive urge to remove her gag.

Especially when, at the end of the first tense hour, the watchers peering through a small gap in the seal of the tunnel let out hisses of disappointment.

"It *is* the sheriff," said somebody up there.

Thrill leapt through Orlena's entire body. She leaned forward while somebody else asked softly, "Now what the hell do we do? Move one of these rocks and they'll hear us move the rest. We're done."

"Real sorry Orlena," he murmured to her in the darkness of their hiding place. "Looks like we're waitin awhiles."

"How long we gonna be down here," groused one of the foulest smelling, worst shaven bastards in the Stone Hill Gang. "Ain't took enough food down here to live more'n a couple days. Indians'll stop through a night at most when they find there ain't nobody or nothin here. A posse on a manhunt fer us? They'll have us in here a week if they think we're due back from somewheres else."

"And if we come up outta this mine it will most assuredly be like shootin fish in a barrel," said another gang member, who had earned a small bit of favor in Orlena's mind by way of not leering at her. "If we come up, we die and that is it. But if we wait, well, hell! Better to struggle and live than rush and die. I ain't arrogant enough to come on up outta here."

That may have been a perfectly fine point, and in another situation Orlena might even have agreed; but, with her breathing stifled by both the seal over the mine and the gag in her mouth, it was just a little difficult to get on the level with them.

There was no way to tell time in the mine. The men would, every now and again, look out from the boulders. They would watch through the hole for about three minutes before, agitated, sealing up the tunnel again.

"They're still sittin in the trees and patrolling once an hour but I ain't seen that damn sheriff in a day," said one of the men one time. Orlena made mental note, re-oriented herself in time, and listened on while the watchman continued. "Why the hell are we sittin here like cowards? Without the sheriff, this posse's jes a buncha hicks with guns."

"Wait," urged the patient one. "Jes wait."

A small stash of jarred preserves got broken out two times a day, along with old biscuits and newer jerky, too. The first day, Orlena had not been permitted to eat anything because of her gag; but this second day, with the food broken out in front of her, a wild hunger swept her body and she complained inarticulately through her bindings.

Her brother, sucking a tooth, glanced over at the other men gathered around to split food among themselves.

"Say fellas"—Jimmy worked his eyebrows in a somewhat theatrical manner, nodding toward his sister—"yeh mind? If we're gonna be down here much longer, ain't right to starve Orlena."

"Take her deeper in the mine," grunted one of the sixteen men. "If she screams, y'er both gettin shot."

Much to Orlena's displeasure, her brother led her down the hewn and lightly reinforced tunnel before liberating her. The darkness was no darker, but somehow the mere knowledge that they had descended farther served to heighten her anxiety. By the time Jimmy had removed the gag from her mouth, her palms were slick with sweat.

"I really am sorry about this, Orlena."

"The *hell* you are," she hissed right back, her eyes blazing with fury for her no-good, low-down robber of a brother. "If you was the least sorry, yeh'd let me walk up outta this mine and go back to Sandspur."

"Now, you know I kain't do that—I thought I explained myself pretty well. We needed you so we could git the sheriff here."

Orlena sneered while shoveling marmalade-smeared stale bread into her mouth.

"Seems like it worked too well."

"Yeah, well—*somethin's* wrong out there. Birds still ain't singin. Ain't jes the posse. You kin feel it, kain't you? The fear."

She didn't want to acknowledge the uncanny feeling she got when considering the now multi-day silence over the presidio. Instead, she took the whiskey bottle from his hand and changed the subject.

"You comin to my house flipped my damn life upside-down so hard and so quick that, so far as I see's it, every last onea yeh bastards owes me fer cooperatin."

"Cooperatin, hell. If this is cooperatin I'd hate to see yer fightin."

"You keep givin me this lip, Jimmy Felder, and you'll see it jes fine."

Unexpectedly, Jimmy laughed and lowered his head. "Ah, damn, sis! I sure missed you."

"Rest assured, Jimmy, I ain't missed you. Mattera fact, I been mad as hell at you this last near two months."

His face fell. She felt a little spatea guilt, but not near as much as when he said with the air of a kicked puppy, "Now what you gotta go talkinta me like that fer? You ain't missed me at all? What the hell happened back at the ranch once I passed through?"

The Man behind her, gun pointed. Death so close. Death in her house, her husband's blood and the boy's blood together on the floor.

It was all so long ago.

"I ain't care to discuss it, Jimmy, I told you."

"But why the hell you ain't still around home? You didn't have a fight with Bert on my account, didjyes?"

"No, Jimmy, it's not—" She inhaled shakily. "It ain't that."

"Then what? What is it? I haven't understood fer a month and a half what the hell McLintock's been talkin about. You bein in town, steppin out with the sheriff? Makes no damn sense."

Orlena squeezed her eyes shut and exhaled slowly. "I'm surprised McLintock ain't tell you."

"Nah, he ain't the sorta man inclined to say what he knows."

When Orlena opened her eyes, her brother's were fixed on her. They slid away only after a few seconds; only to tend to the next bite of food.

"Somethin happen, Orlena?"

Her teeth ground together in her skull. With a reluctant glance up the slope to the entrance of the mine, she told her brother, "Why don't you let me tell you once we're out? Able to walk around and speak like reasonable human beings?"

An aggravated little smile darted over her brother's mouth. He tilted his head as he took a bite, thinking to himself before saying, "You know…there ain't nothin I hate more than knowin I gotta wait to hear bad news."

Lowering his morsel, Jimmy leaned toward his sister.

"Did somethin happen to him, Orlena?"

Her eyes slid down to the limestone floor.

"What happened?"

"Yer cellmate," she said. "That big sonnabitch. He— surprised me, and…"

"And?"

"And—after he was finished with em, he said he'd do the same to me if'n I didn't help him find you."

She braced herself for an angry response. Instead, she received the cool question, "Did you agree?"

"Hardly had a *choice*, now did I? Of course, I said—oh, but Jimmy, I didn't mean it—"

"Yeah…sure yeh didn't."

Surprised by his tone, Orlena balked at the sudden, almost hateful stoniness of his features.

"Bet you wept tears fer yer poor brother every good goddamn night you spent with Lorenzo's dick in yer mouth."

The same sparkling rage that must have been sweeping through Jimmy's body coursed also through Orlena's, settling in her bright red face. "Now, hold on a damn minute—"

"I don't think I have to! God damn…when McLintock told me yeh'd been pallin around with that slick sonnabitch, I swore to myself it had to be so's yeh could keep him occupied. Hold his attention away from me. But now—cooperatin with Rhodes, lettin the Sheriff give it to yeh…and you ain't even kept my son alive, besides."

"*Yer* son!"

That was it. Orlena snapped under the comment, her body springing to slap him so quickly that she was shocked he managed to grab her arm. Wrenching her wrist from him, she grabbed a tender point, investigated a sure-to-be bruise, and glowered at him as she said, "He ain't never been *yer* son. You ain't hardly clapped eyes on him but the once—"

"You know I came around to see that boy plentya times when I'ws in hidin the first time."

"Even though I asked you *not* to."

"Why in the hell should I have refrained, Orlena? Only reason I'ws in hidin was so you didn't have to."

"And you ain't *needed* to hide! You coulda done the time fer me and already been out! Ain't nobody woulda thoughta hangin you if you ain't hooked up with these Stone Hill morons. Instead you hid from the law, got a longer sentence with new crimes, and got us in this mess by lettin the boys bust you out fer yet *another* crime. When you went free too soon, yer leftover guilt followed you to my house. *You* killed the boy, Jimmy! You sister-fuckin, backstabbin, tooth-stealin sonnabitch."

His nostrils flared. She could not tell properly in the dark, but she swore his eyes might have been watering.

Without further comment, Jimmy affixed the gag around the back of her head.

She did not get to eat for the remainder of her time in the mine. Jimmy did not speak to her and did not untie her wrists. Weak and exhausted, her limbs tingling with numbness and her shoulder twisted back for so long she couldn't even tell the muscle pain from her headache or the tension of the rope around her wrists, all Orlena could do was rub her hands in her bindings and keep her fingers wiggling as much as possible.

The second day passed into the third day and the restless, pacing men were beginning to fight over their games of cards. Tensions mounted by the hour. When dinner came around and there was only enough food for a mouthful or two apiece, everybody blamed Jimmy for giving Orlena some scraps.

"You better watch what the hell you say to me," he told them all in dark response, "or I might jes lose my knack fer wranglin coaches."

"We ain't gonna *need* yer knack if we kin jes cap that sheriff in the head and leave him dead in the dirt," one of the more short-tempered members of the group said. "I say we shoot our way outta here come hell or high water and hunt him down like a dog."

A few others agreed; Orlena groaned inwardly at the thought of another man losing his life over her. Lorenzo! Oh, Jesus.

At the mouth of the mine, a few men pushed the peephole boulder aside to peer into the twilight-illuminated presidio. The argument continued, the level-headed man from before softly going on to his companion, "We already waited here such a long time. Kain't be hungry when yer asleep—why not let's jes rest and—"

"And then what? Wake up with no food? Then what'll we do, smartass?"

"Well, then we kin talk about how to git outta here and git an advantage."

"What'll be different between tonight and tomorra mornin, aside from the fact that we will all be that much more famished and that much more ill-prepared to fight?"

"God willin, somebody'll have putcha out yer misery in yer sleep."

While the bad-tempered man drew his gun, practically spitting like a feral tomcat, the patient one laughed and set his hand on his own weapon.

The men by the front of the mine looked over their shoulders.

"Hey! Boys—"

"Kain't you see we're *busy* here, Alfred—"

"Listen," said the fella, once again looking out from the mine.

They did listen.

Somewhere in the forest, a bird sang.

"They're gone," came the whisper from a watchman.

Eyes slightly wide, the short-tempered fellow turned around and hurried up to the front of the mine.

The entire gang held its breath.

For twenty minutes, everyone waited.

For twenty minutes, Orlena prayed.

At last, the short-tempered fella strained to push away one of the boulders. A few men helped him.

Orlena glanced sidelong at Jimmy, who watched only the opening seal of the mine.

Guns ready, the three gang members near the entrance stepped out into the open sky. Cool, rich, fresh air flooded the chamber and Orlena shut her eyes, her breast heaving with each rich inhalation through her nose.

After a five-minute sweep, it was the bad-tempered man

who let out a happy whistle and called from the center of the presidio, "Coast's clear, boys!"

Relief rippled through the Stone Hill Gang, all their profound consternation relaxing into brotherhood at once. "Bet those sonsabitches ate all our damn food," somebody groused merrily, picking up his hat on the way out of the mine.

"Git up," said Jimmy with a jerk of her arm.

Orlena rose. He looked like he debated removing the gag from her mouth before doing it.

After working her jaw, she forced out a bright, shiny smile.

"You look jes like Daddy when y'er treatin me like shit, Jimmy."

"Go on," he told her, shoving her toward the entrance of the mine without unbinding her wrists.

If spending three days in that stifling dark had been the worst time of her life, surely leaving that abysmal prison stood among its single greatest moments. With mouth and nose alike she took great, gasping breaths of fresh air and trembled to look up at the stars. To have nothing overhead but stars!

The relief was not to last.

While she marveled, Jimmy had a word with some of his friends and only then returned to unbind her wrists. "Sounds like they leftcha a little food to cook us after all, and the posse never found the whiskey."

"Look how mad you are. Was that boy really worth so much more than me, Jimmy?"

"Ain't jes him. You ain't even able to see it, is yeh?"

Jimmy looked at her in a way that was—insulting somehow. Like a kind of pity mingled with disgust; as though he, the criminal, were the morally righteous of the two of them.

"After all I done, yeh'd still trade away my life if'n it meant savin yer own skin. Go on. Git cookin."

And so, after all this time, there Orlena was again: crouched before a stove, blowin the fire to life, haulin cast iron pots of water, sweatin and cookin and cuttin herself by accident.

Yes, yet again.

She had a breakdown and cried two different times, but the third time Jimmy came in to tell her she was takin too long. She told herself it was just all them fucked up emotions what came with pregnancy. Ain't nothin was gonna happen that Lorenzo wouldn't save her from eventually.

She kept cookin.

When it was all done, she brought one dish at a time out to the center of the presidio. A fire had been built in what was a risky luxury, but worthwhile to the men. Somebody had gotten out a fiddle and everybody was drunk. The fiddling stopped while Orlena served the food and for about an hour things went all right. Jimmy didn't say nothing to her, the men liked her food, and she was allowed to eat on accounta there being plenty.

But then, after dinner, the men kept drinkin.

Men drinkin too much made Orlena damn nervous. Blame her daddy fer that, and a lot else besides, but there weren't nothin on God's green earth that made a man as dangerous as drinkin. Oughta have stuck by Lorenzo and his damn sedatin scorpions when she thought about it now.

Round this time she tried to suss out how a body could leave this presidio and take they chances in the woods without nobody payin mind. It was hard to look around without having her gaze caught by the men—especially Jimmy, who knew that Orlena cwas a prisoner to be watched.

Unfortunately, the other men largely agreed.

As soon as her eyes raised toward the presidio gate, she realized that foul-tempered sonnabitch from the mine had been takin advantagea the fire to fill his eyes with her. The fiddler had taken up the instrument again and somebody else had dug out a harmonica. A few men clapped or danced while others enjoyed the music and drank themselves to sleep.

"Whatchu say t'a dance, Miss Orlena?"

From the staring man. She'd known it was coming.

Orlena looked helplessly at her brother, who ignored her. Throat dry, she endeavored a smile and said, "I—I don't—"

"Oh, now, you ain't about to tell me yeh don't dance! Every woman kin dance. Ain't matter if she knows how, man good enough'll teach her…or jes drag her around in circles awhiles."

She rubbed her sweaty palms off on her dress. A few other men were looking at her. Jimmy was not.

"I—I reckon it kain't hurt nothin," she said with a reflexive glance to the gun at the robber's hip.

His ugly smile revealed he was missing a cuspid and an incisor, among many other, markedly rotting teeth.

While Orlena forced herself to stand, Jimmy stood, too.

"I got the urge to stretch my legs and enjoy a smoke… see you boys in a whiles."

Orlena felt like she was going to be sick all over herself.

She hoped she would be, because then maybe when the bastard who took her by the hand and led her toward a more open area might have been repulsed enough to stay the hell back. As it stood, he pulled her too close. Now her vomitous inspiration was the rotten bone smell of dead teeth lodged somewhere in the back of the man's hideous mouth, reeking out beneath the whiskey stink.

Her face turned away, Orlena tolerated moving with this foreign body in what was more or less the rhythm of the music. Like a human makin a dog appear to dance by holding it on its hind legs and leadin it around, the robber swung Orlena back and forth and even attempted somethin resemblin a dip. She was so limp and unhelpful, focused on bein anywhere but in her body, that he almost dropped her.

"Careful, now… You don't gotta be so cold, you know, Miss Orlena. We ain't the formal sorts out here."

A couple men laughed. Orlena said nothing.

The bastard with the dirty mouth put a dirty hand on the back of her head and wrenched her around until she was forced to look at his dirty face. The intolerable smell of his rotten breath panted at her with every respiration.

She imagined how good it would feel to beat him almost to death with a gun before shooting him right in the face.

"Ain't nobody gonna judge yeh none fer havin a little fun," he said with a gross chortle. "Least, I ain't."

He went for it.

Orlena smashed her forehead down into his nose before his mouth could quite make it to hers.

"Ah, shit! Little cunt—"

One of the bastards laughed. Somebody sighed and got up, muttering, "Better find Jimmy."

While the tooth-challenged desperado stumbled back a step to rub his nose amid watering eyes, Orlena darted for the presidio gate.

A bullet whizzed past her feet before she'd made it fifteen steps.

"Jes where yeh think y'er goin, cunt," asked the sonnabitch through that rotten mouth.

20

LORENZO MUSTA BEEN there with his eyes wide open and some kinda dastardly annoyin bird chirpin in his ear for damn near five minutes afore he realized he'ws awake.

He looked for his winda to get a sense of the light.

There was no winda, but that fact did not settle into a mind preoccupied by the pain it caused him to lift his head. It seemed almost like something stuck between his nose and the back of his throat was jerking down against the bone.

He gasped, then retched to realize something *was* stuck down his throat.

Lorenzo raised his hand, frantic to remove whatever it was.

Several thin black tendrils, like long horsehair worms unwinding from a grasshopper's corpse, curved out of his arm and up toward the ceiling.

Was it a ceiling? The space seemed all-white, totally formless yet somehow familiar. Each thin little tendril plunged into him by way of a scorpion sting, either new or scarred over; his heart raced and, unsure what to make of it, he pulled his arm free of the contrivances that looked a hellofa lot like wires.

And he screamed.

Brutal little needles had been the means by which those wires were affixed into his flesh. The sensation made his skin crawl; the act of gagging made the tube up his nose and down his throat tug down against his cartilage. In fact, it was yanked hard enough by his esophagus to make him feel like he was going to have a nosebleed.

His wrist already dotted in blood, he used his newly freed hand to pull the wire from his nostril hand over hand, retching all the way until he got the idea to blow while he yanked. That sonnabitch came right out then, though he still felt like somebody had been punching his nose from the inside.

As to the rest—he wanted to get a good look at it all, but before he even could they came rushing in.

Lorenzo screamed.

It was one thing to see the scorpion-man in the fugue state of a vision induced by the scorpion venom, when a man had no body and was liberated from spacetime and his entire being *was* the self-knowingness of the godhead.

And he had recently felt that way, he vaguely remembered.

But he couldn't place the feeling right there and then. Waking up afraid, in three dimensions, in his body, with time flowing as normal and all his senses poised to full awareness, and *still* with the scorpion-man—*men*—there before him.

It was by pissing himself that Lorenzo realized a tube had been stuffed up his dick, too.

Before he could rip it out and do himself real damage, one of the creatures held him down by the shoulder. Another pressed a hard mask over his face.

Lorenzo opened his eyes and looked around the room where he sat, fully dressed except for the hat placed on the white table beside him.

All white again. Nowhere to set the eyes. Eyes. His eyes hurt. Mighta closed em if he weren't afraid for his life.

He touched his thigh and found his gun absent.

A strange hissing noise drew his alarmed attention to the wall opposite a great big painting of the planet Earth, apparently depicted from space. A panel roughly the proportions of a door had opened there. He braced himself for another imposing scorpion-creature to walk in.

Instead, there stood one of the most beautiful women he had ever seen.

No—no reason to tone it down. She *was* the most beautiful woman she had ever seen, and that was not hyperbole. Her every feature was perfectly symmetrical, her eyes large and set slightly too wide apart from one another upon her face; yet, this oddity added an unearthly element to her beauty that only intensified it. As she smiled and glided across the room, long white hair tumbling down her back amid the pinkish gauze gown she wore, the willowy proportions of her limbs peeking out seemed somehow alarming.

Everything about her was alarming. Her beauty was alarming; her presence in this place, this hell, was alarming.

As she took a seat in the sofa across from him, the door through which she had entered again hissed shut. Lorenzo withdrew his kerchief and mopped his brow. The environment was stiflingly humid, more humid than any day before the breaking of monsoon season. He loosened the collar of his shirt a little, asking, "They take you, too?"

"I am among them." Her words were stilted and her mouth produced the sounds with an odd contortion, as though she held space for a marble somewhere in the back of her tongue. "I am like you; and also like them."

Though he took her meaning, he could not help the furrowing of his brow and the long investigation of her features.

"Yeah," he said, taking in the great black eyes that contained no irises and the vaguely triangular shape of a face that seemed like it could have referred to the scorpion-men. "Yeah, I reckon I kin see that."

"You are not like them, Sheriff Blaize."

"How is it you know my name, ma'am? Beggin yer pardon."

"You told me last time we took you away. Do you not remember?"

The room was humid, but Lorenzo's mouth was very dry.

"No ma'am," he told her, feeling as though he were a young child speaking to a kindly adult woman. "No ma'am, I do not remember. You will have to forgive me."

Her lips expanded in a bright white, wide smile that was genuine but also extremely strange. Like she'd seen about six smiles in her whole damn life.

"That is common."

"Oh."

"Yes."

"Common when—"

"When we are interested in someone."

"Ah. I see."

She went on smiling.

Lorenzo had never been so uncomfortable in all his life.

Certainly never so frightened of a woman.

She frowned as the thought crossed his mind.

"I am sorry, Sheriff. You were afraid of me last time, as well."

"Was I? Oh! Oh—no, no, I'm not...afraid. It ain't *you*. It's jes—I'm *afraid* that I am...mighty disoriented. Jes what is goin on?"

"The last time we took you, we told you how to contact us when you needed our help."

"And—how was it that I was to do that?"

"The scorpion. The woods."

"And I did?"

Smiling once again, the woman nodded. "Just as we programmed you to, Sheriff."

Sheriff.

Lorenzo's mouth opened.

At last, he remembered.

Orlena.

Yes! Hell. He had been out lookin fer Orlena with the boys. They found that ruined presidio with the supplies in it, and—and Lorenzo had realized it was that place from last time, with that bright flood of light like what he was always seein in his dreams—

"That's right," said the woman in musical approbation. "Yes, my love, that's right."

"'My love!' Wait jes a minute—"

But the woman laughed as though at a precocious pet, shaking her head. "You will remember soon enough. The promises I made to you. How we made love last time, and how, after we were through, I told you all about where I am from. You told me you wanted to go. Do you remember?"

No. But, somehow, it all rang true. As though he had once dreamed what she described.

"It was not a dream, Sheriff. This is not a dream. This is more real than your old life."

"I kin see that," he said, correcting, "that's to say, I kin see that y'er perfectly real. It's jes—"

Her happy face once more sobered. "What?"

"It's not really a very good *time* fer me to have come back here. I mean…I didn't even know what I was doin. I was in the middlea this whole thing—"

"Looking for Orlena. Yes, Sheriff. You came intending to consult us about her; but, as I promised you when we brought you aboard, she will free herself."

Too quickly, her movements certainly arachnoid in their pacing, the woman jerked into motion. She glided across the room and, before she knelt beside his chair, he marveled to reckon her at least seven feet tall. With her kneeling, their faces were level.

"She does not need you. The world does not need you. You can go, Sheriff. Go with me."

"Go—go t'yer home, yeh mean? But—where?"

"Far from here."

His brow knit.

"Now?"

"Yes."

"And come back when?"

"There will be no need for you to come back when you have followed me home. I will make you so happy! All earthly pleasures are pale shadows of what I can give to you, Sheriff."

Well…didn't sound so bad, really.

"It is far from bad," she said upon his thought. "You will be so proud to have me for a wife, sir."

"Hell, I reckon any fella what gits to call himself yer husband'll have a conniption on the spot fer joy." At her pleased smile, he smiled a little himself and let her fit her hand over one of his.

Damn! Some hand, bigger than his. Beautiful shape to it, though. Skin so soft. What a perfect woman.

"I jes kain't imagine why yeh'd want anythin to do with a human man."

"I was born to humans," said the woman. "But it is more ethical to bring human men to us than it is to use human couples to breed our children."

"I, uh…kain't really argue with that. Even if I don't understand quite what you mean."

"That is all right. You will someday, when you have come with me and seen our ways."

"Yeah. That is, I'd like to. Sounds real nice. But—I mean, what about Orlena?"

"As I said. She will be safe without your intervention."

"But will *she* come to the place where you folks are?"

The woman shook her head.

"She will not be brought to us. Few are selected for the honor, for so few that are brought aboard can win one of our hearts."

"And I am glad you find me charmin, ma'am, but it's jes—I kain't go without Orlena."

The woman's smooth brow furrowed. He felt like he was ruinin a worka art.

"But why? Am I displeasing to you?"

"No! No, of course not. Jes—I have a duty. And it's not enough fer me t'hear she'll be safe. I have to know she's safe. I have to be there if she needs me. And…truth is, you may have taken a shine to me last time we met, but I don't remember none of it. What I do remember is spendin the last month and a half in the company of Orlena Felder—and failin her."

Lorenzo's eyes sagged from the woman's unearthly face to the floor beside her, sorrow weighing his heart.

"I really messed things up. I been so focused on the secrets you people kin tell me about reality that I wann't payin any attention to the realitya my own life. T'a woman I been fallin in love with and neglectin. And I don't see how I kin possibly come live some wonderful life somewheres else when I ain't even lived my own life back on Earth."

"But Sheriff—you don't understand."

He looked up to find her beautiful brow still knit with the same concern.

"There will never be another opportunity for us to evacuate you safely from this place before your body dies. Do you understand that?"

"You mean—"

"If we send you back to Earth," said the beautiful woman grimly, "you are very soon to die. Deputy McLintock will shoot you."

"McLintock! But he's *my* deputy."

"He is a petty, evil man who has only cooperated while waiting for a chance to kill you without evidence. Had we not taken you the first time we did, you would have been murdered. And you will be murdered if we send you back."

Somewhat rocked to hear all this, Lorenzo worked all these facts through his mind while staring into space. The woman took his face in her long fingers and turned him to look at her.

"Perhaps you do not remember, Sheriff, but I do. I remember, and I love you, and I am pained to return you to your death. But—if that is what you wish, I will act in accordance with your will."

"I won't let McLintock kill me," Lorenzo said in firm false confidence. "And, even if somethin does happen—I jes kain't abandon everythin I ever known. Not so suddenly."

Her eyelids shut, tears flowing down her cheeks.

"I understand."

"Hey," said Lorenzo, garnering a look from her, "but… is there some kinda reason we kain't have a good time afore I go back?"

She hesitated for only a few seconds before leaning in to kiss him.

Lorenzo stayed with the strange woman in her humid apartment for somethin in the ordera fivea her days. It seemed as such. He was not sure of the time. He did not worry about time. It upset him, in fact, to think about time.

So he didn't think about time.

He just had a good time.

Then, when that good time felt like it had gone on long enough and he was confident he had given her something to remember him by, he told her it was time for him to go.

She begged him as she had that first—second, he supposed—time they'd met.

He was sorely tempted to comply.

No man wanted to die.

"Father, Father, why have you forsaken me," and all that deeply depressing horseshit.

But…well, hell. Lorenzo reckoned he understood that old carpenter better than he once thought he did. After all… Jesus coulda saved Himself any time He wanted.

And He didn't.

If Lorenzo had really been put on this Earth to serve Justice, there weren't no justice in runnin from cause and effect.

"I wish you would stay," said the woman very sadly, watching him dress.

"Wish I would, too. I jes kain't."

She nodded, turning her face away against the pillow. Sighing, Lorenzo climbed upon the bed beside her one last time. She peeked mournfully at him and he ran his thumb over the ribbon of her lower lip.

"Sounds to me like you ain't need me around anyhow, angel…and who knows? You scorpion folk may be smart, but only the Good Lord knows it all…mebbe we'll meet agin someday."

She smiled against his palm, her eyes closing.

The door hissed open.

Before Lorenzo even stood, the scorpion-man crossed the room and pressed that stinking mask against his face.

Lorenzo bolted from his desk in the sheriff's office of Sandspur, his head whipping wildly around.

A tremendous loss—a loss beyond description, beyond any possible measure or reckoning—settled over his head.

Laughing to somebody else outside the station, McLintock shoved open the door and tromped in with his head turned away.

The old badge on his vest had been replaced by a shiny new star. *SHERIFF.*

Catching sight of an unexpected body in his periphery, McLintock whipped his head toward the threat.

He stopped dead still twelve feet away from Lorenzo.

"Lorenzo?"

"McLintock," said Lorenzo, his hands down at his sides. He did not have to check. He could feel the weight of the gun, back where it belonged.

"Where the hell you been?"

"Dealin with something." He jerked his chin toward the badge. "Looks like you been well in my absence. How long was I away, exactly?"

"Over a damn week! We thought you was dead."

"I ain't."

With a long, cautious look as though to determine whether Lorenzo lived or were some ghost, McLintock stroked his moustache with a slow hand.

"Truth be told, I'm damn relieved to have yeh back. Me, sheriffa this place? That's a whole hellofa lotta responsibility. I am not a particular fan of the highly visible power positions what society offers, if'n yeh understand."

Those noises in the distance.

Was that gunfire?

Lorenzo rushed to the winda behind the desk, pressing his face to the glass and struggling to see down the road.

"But, you know…havin enjoyed it fer a week, I have come to see it is a position with some real fine virtues. Awful lotta respect. And then, well…there's no small amounta money in it, if'n you play yer cards—right!"

Lorenzo whipped his gun from its holster and spun to shoot right as the bullet caught him in the lower back.

Deputy McLintock watched his own gun fly from his bloodied hand and did not hesitate to flee after it, sweeping it up on his way from the station.

With a shout of agony, Lorenzo careened against the wall.

Grimacing against the pain, he followed McLintock out the door with a trio of wasted bullets. Sweat beading his forehead, he touched the wound in his back and raised the hand before his face.

His palm was slick with blood.

Outside, the fracas nearing the town of Sandspur was ever more clearly gunfire; whinnying horses; shouting men.

Oh, yeah.

Here Lorenzo had almost forgotten he was expectin that coach.

Somehow, it sorta ended up the last thing on his mind.

21

THE WHOLE WAY back, the air was thick with the kinda vile heat that foretold monsoons. That sweet, sticky sorta under-layer got caught up in the dusty wind; a fine haze occasionally settled across the sky for an hour after sun-up.

But Texas was too hateful a state to permit such luxuries long. Any kiss of humidity ramped the heat up to a miserable level so that, on the way back home, the Needless Man watched one ranchero drop off his horse from heatstroke. Had to tie the bastard down for damn near twenty miles afore they reached a homestead with a well and a bed.

Another lost day.

Neither the Man nor the Brave—nor, for that matter, anyone else who had survived the Comanche raid—had the least desire for the return trip to be lengthened for any reason.

This meant, of course, it was doomed to be. Without mustangs to police, the trip should have been easier.

The problem was, of course, that damn stagecoach.

Ain't nobody wanted to drive the godforsaken thing, fer starters. Who in the hell would? Damn thing fulla scorpions. Needless Man sure as shit wann't fixinta hassle it too much, however sacred the little sonsabitches were. He'd been stung, though not by these; and he did not need to be stung by these, based on what he'd heard.

He knew what he knew. Whatever else remained to be revealed would be revealed by what came upon him, and not what he pursued.

Round the time they got down to Red Bluff Reservoir and followed the Pecos River back down into Texas, the humidity increased. Cicadas or some such croaked all hours before it cooled enough to shut em up, and every mornin the men awoke itchin the bitesa nasty skeeters and other bugs makin homes along the banksa the river.

This far north, the river ran at the base of a steep gulch: wild beneath them, with vicious rapids that would only reduce to fordable levels quite some ways along the line—one of them places, significantly, the location where Sandspur had gone up. It was on the other side of the Pecos from where they pushed their horses along through the sticky heat, and where Roaring Bear watched the stagecoach's every rock with hawklike attention and paternal concern.

The Man had not known what to make of his friend's grief until the Native went off into the hills one night and came back with his hair chopped off. Smell of a nastily burnin fire still on his clothes. Grief did strange things; strange things, or perhaps expected things.

As the depths of the bluffs overlooking the Pecos and the wildness of the river steadily resolved, no relief came over the men. The shellshocked exhaustion that had left them so quiet for the first few days gradually gave way to a wariness.

No Comanche scouts followed them. The Man and Roaring Bear rode out many times at many hours in pursuit of the matter. They were confident that Wolf Cunt had continued to pursue the remaining tribe; or, more likely, had gone ahead along the Pecos or through the hills in pursuit of some other last act of vengeance before the inevitability of a reservation was thrust upon his people.

There weren't no comfort in the absencea the Comanche. There weren't no comfort in nothin. The man slept fairly well at night even with his thigh throbbing fer the first days to the reservoir, but when they stopped off to deal with the fella what had the heatstroke the mister of the house had offered bandages and some kinda salve that seemed t'have done the trick. Didn't plan on puttin pressure on it notime soon. But it worked.

Other men who survived the raid had not done so without an injury in most cases. One had outright lost an eye and was not lookin very good, if one might pardon the pun; but he held on, and did not take an opportunity to stop. Needed the money too bad, the Man reckoned.

And the rest of em?

Regret in every face. The grim affects of veterans fresh from a new mind-wound of trauma.

Surely their due compensation was not worth what was taken from them. Whether the rancheros or Roaring Bear, the cost of obtaining the unobtainable (that big fat payday for little work; security for a fading Tribe in a world hostile to its values) had proven life-altering.

And the Man had paid only with a little arrow stickin out his thigh.

He paid so little at the raid because he had already paid. Had loaned, in fact. To someone whose day was coming.

The only payment the Man expected was something what was already his.

And, as promised, he *would* get it from the job…only, in a way he had not quite expected.

They were about three days away from Sandspur when the fella lookin sick on accounta his lost eye began lookin all the sicker. Pale and shakin on the backa his horse like it weren't the surfacea the damn sun out in that bitch. Every man had been keenly aware of his condition, but at the day's first break Chrysler took one look at him before addressing the rest of the men.

"We oughta left him back at that farm. If we keep goin at the rate we're goin, Harvey here's gonna be dead before we reach Sandspur."

"If we push the coach too hard—"

Chrysler shook his head, speaking over Roaring Bear and raising a hand. "I ain't sayin that—I'm sayin if somebodies else kin drive a coach I might kin run on ahead with'im and we kin stop off early at McCarney."

The Man nodded. "I ain't been lookin forward to takin a day out the trip to dig this fella's grave."

Harvey, holding himself amid the chattering of his teeth, said nothing.

Chrysler asked, "How bout it, brother? Let's gitcha back. If Lorenzo has a problem with it and don't pay yeh all he should, I'll shoot'im m'self."

The sick man laughed a little, weakly, and nodded.

So it was that they were down two more men. Chrysler and Harvey rode off faster than the stagecoach would let 'em. As another driver climbed up into the seat with a reluctant glance over his shoulder for the coach itself, the Man counted the remaining rancheros.

Seven; plus the driver, eight; plus the Brave, nine.

And the Needless Man made ten.

Ten was not a whole hellofa a lotta guns to have when things got bad.

Two days out from Sandspur. That haze stayed on more than just an hour. Now it stayed on for two or three.

Then that hateful blue sky again. The thickness of that swampy heat. The beaming sun mocking them, always right in a man's eyes. Everybody dirty, sunburnt, parched. Even the horses wanted whiskey.

Another dark night. No fires. Too risky.

Woke up shivering.

Sky still dark.

Back along the trail.

A buzz gripped the air.

Everybody knew it; ain't nobody dared say it.

Needless Man savored it.

Finally.

The last day.

Such a long day. An endlessly long day made all the more endless by the knowledge that, at the end of the long day (and it would be a *long* day) they would find themselves crossing the bridge to Sandspur and, at long last, divesting themselves of their responsibility.

No signa Chrysler or the dead body of Harvey anywheres on the trail. No signa nothin but the expected.

Last day. It was the last day. The magnetic pull of Sandspur dragged them on even though their mustangs flagged after so many long days.

One last long day.

One last day.

The stagecoach rocked steadily behind its horses, the noise not unlike the rushing of the river that had reduced from a roar to a steady lap.

The morning haze did not dissipate after two hours.

"It may finally storm," observed Roaring Bear, watching the sky.

"Mebbe," agreed the Man.

It surely had been months since Texas had enjoyed rain. The storms were behind schedule. With the Pecos substantially reduced and the river's width growing manageable, now would be the time some great big monsoon would crack down to flood out the banks and wash the damn stagecoach away.

"Let's push," said the Man, urging his horse.

"But the coach—"

"Brother, if this damn thing loses a wheel and rolls over now, I'll collect all them damn scorpions myself."

That ain't happen, though. The terrain got rough at moments, especially as they were met mid-morning with the very tip Sandspur's northern hills. Lucky the coach driver was not very inept. He managed to keep the horses going and the stage balanced so the scorpions ain't have too rough a ride.

Not until they were almost into town, anyway.

With a long break to compensate for the push on the horses, the men did not reach that slight widening of expanse between river and mountains that signaled the opening of Sandspur's valley until it was almost nightfall. At the very least, the fingers of dusk had crawled just over the edge of the horizon to darken the thickening haze.

When comin round a sharp bend in the turf revealed their path sloped to the far-distant but visible town of Sandspur, the men let out a cheer.

The Needless Man glanced up at the sky.

Shootin star.

"Sky's cloudy," he said, still staring up at the space where the tail had been. As though to correct Nature itself.

Reminded hima that scorpion what woke him up.

Somethin rustled in the timber on the hills not six hundred yards from em.

The Man's gun was in his hand and a round lighter two heartbeats later, when a man hidden in the trees let out a pained bellow that signaled his own last heartbeat was not far off.

"Robbers," called the Man while the rancheros looked sharply at him. "Protect the stage."

A sharp whistle from the trees signaled the surging forth of riders from the shadows of the timber, their pistols firing wildly enough to spook a few horses and provoke the violent rocking of the stagecoach. The Man put a bullet through one of the riders just as a ranchero got shot from his steed. Another was dismounted when a laughing bandit rode past and lassoed him down to be viciously trampled.

"Eight," said the Man. He shot another two riders from their horses, then had his attention pulled by a pair riding up on either side of the stage driver.

The Man urged his horse forward just as Roaring Bear put a bullet in one of the two. While the remaining robber called out for his friend, he raised his gun to shoot the Brave in revenge.

The Man came up on him and spent the last round in his Schofield in the back of the bastard's head.

Roaring Bear urged his horse to loop around the coach and double back through the robbers closing in around them. Looked as though they intended to drive the coach into the river and pick the rancheros off when it was immobilized.

Pacing the driver, the Man called, "You git this thing any faster?"

"Fast as she goes without bustin an axel at least," shouted the driver over the din. "We still got five minutes to Sandspur!"

"I'll see what I kin do."

At his slap, his horse galloped forward and followed the loop opposite the one taken by Roaring Bear. While he rode, the Man ejected his cartridges and pressed six bullets into their chambers.

Just as he'd snapped it closed, he was met with a robber who got damn lucky he ain't closed his gun a second sooner.

The men locked eyes, just briefly. Robber's intense blue stare pierced from the holes cut into the black strip hidin his identity along with his bandana.

Then their crossed paths separated, and the Man leveled his gun with another robber comin his way. He knocked the bastard back from his horse with a vicious shot in the kidney that made him lose balance and go down amid a very familiar scream.

Chrysler.

"You no good sonnabitch," said the Man before turning attention to Roaring Bear's call.

Followed the Brave's pointed finger over his shoulder to the stagecoach.

The masked robber had ridden his horse up alongside it so as to clamber atop and kill the driver from behind.

Cursing, the Man stopped his horse short. The beast reared up in a slight panic. As it settled upon the earth again, he patted it, whistled, and sent it blazing off along the stagecoach with which the riderless horse still galloped.

The Man, his gun holstered, ducked a bullet from a robber that had overtaken the coach and shot from ahead. When he straightened up, it was only to get his horse alongside the one the masked robber had abandoned.

With one hand on the back of the saddle, the Man carefully stood upon his horse's back.

The earth rushed beneath them, the horse alongside his not always perfectly in stride.

Another bullet whizzed past him.

Used it as his queue.

With a careful jump, he landed upon the back of the robber's horse and hauled himself up to the roof of the coach before he could lose his balance.

By this time, the masked robber had dodged a few shots from the driver and a couple from Roaring Bear. In fact, he was already down in the seat beside the driver to wrestle the gun away.

Hand really oughta have been on the reins anyway.

The revolver let off two rounds before the robber managed to twist it from the driver's hand and shoot him with it.

While the driver's body fell into the road, the Man crawled to the front of the coach.

The robber whirled around and fired the gun.

It clicked empty.

While he cursed and hurled the useless weapon away, the Man leapt down into the seat beside him and kept him from unholstering his revolver with a tight grip of his hand. Hand didn't feel right, and seemed especially sensitive; the bandit cried out. His gun suffered the fate of the driver's body.

Incensed, the bandit turned back to the Needless Man just in time to have his head smashed back against the hard wood of the coach.

The masked robber slumped back in the seat

The Man snatched up the reins without hesitation, regaining control of the speeding horses that had careened off their path at the shepherding riders. Gritting his teeth, the Needless Man drew his gun and turned to shoot a robber comin up on his side. Then he leaned around the coach to make another count.

Two rancheros, the Brave. Still somethin like seven bandits.

The Man snapped the reins to navigate the horses against the flow of the ones leading them toward the Pecos.

"Allen!"

Roaring Bear's call came with a gesture to the hills.

The Man ducked.

A rifle's bullet smashed into the wood of the coach behind his head, splinters flyin every which way.

By the time he had leaned up, Roaring Bear had driven his horse close to the coach. So close that the horse's blood spat across the rear wheel on the impact of the bullet to its neck.

Down went Roaring Bear along with his horse. Left there in the road, crushed or trampled.

Two rancheros.

There'd be time to think about death later.

The Man turned, leaning up in his seat to shoot any man what came too close. Some other wiseass tried to climb onto the coach and fell off by his own damn failing.

The bridge to Sandspur opened into the town.

Holstering his gun, the Man kept a tight grip on the reins and pulled hard as he could against the resistance of the horses. Soon they yielded, breaking through the flow of their shepherds, and the two remaining rancheros cheered and whistled as the coach resumed its path to Sandspur.

The four horses pulling it clattered over the bridge and to the other side.

As wild spates of gunfire cracked out not just behind them but ahead of them, the Man had to wonder how widespread the robbers' assault was.

Dust kicked wildly up on either side of the coach. The horses beat a path through the streets to the sheriff's office and were always nearer to that gunfire.

All the while, the robbers took their shots at him and bored chunks outta the coach.

The Man urged the vehicle around a sharp turn, rocking with it and grimacing as it bounced on its wheels.

One of the crates thumped.

His eye fell on the distant sheriff's office just as the masked robber, conscious again, yanked the gun from the Needless Man's holster.

Dropping the reins, the Man ducked a shot and slammed on the brake.

The coach's wheels were sharply immobilized. Horses dragged it a few feet before stopping so violently that both men in the driver's seat were whipped back and forth.

Gun went flying.

When, dizzy and pale, Jim Felder looked up, his mask and bandana had been left askew.

Their eyes locked.

Jim realized what had happened, and that he had no

weapon, and that the man who sat beside him was going to kill him.

Without a second of hesitation, Jim scrambled down from the coach and booked it. Not to the lost gun. As far from the ensuing gunfire as he could, clearly aware that his friends could not or would not do anything to protect him.

Looking after his gun in annoyance, the Man leapt down and hissed slightly as he landed on his wounded leg. He got the gun up just as Jim, having stolen a horse minding its own business outside the sheriff's station halfway down the street, rode off into the night.

The Man pointed his gun at the vanishing figure but did not take his shot. More shooting continued behind him. Gunfire was being exchanged between sides of the street.

Jim would die when it was Jim's time to die.

For now, ducking behind the coach, the Man reloaded his gun.

22

JIMMY DID NOT come back and see Orlena until many hours after the first few rapes.

He stepped into the stables where, with swollen eyes and a body aching head to foot, Orlena lay in a nest of unformed plans.

"You left," she whispered hoarsely when that slim and blurry view of the ceiling was interrupted by her brother's face.

"Ain't done me no good helpin you yet," he said.

"Do yeh understand…what they did?"

"I reckon I kin figure it by the looksa yeh."

"And you don't care."

"Whenever I git to carin, a little voice in the backa my head reminds me yeh spent this last near two months fixinta see me dead to git Rhodes off yer back and the Sheriff in yer bed."

"You ain't got nothin to do with what's between me and Lorenzo. He's kind to me."

"Then he better watch out. Ain't no good comesa bein kind to yeh."

"You ain't never been kind to me without a reason to be kind to me, Jimmy Felder, and you damn well know it."

"Now—"

"If you had, I wouldn'ta had to kill Daddy myself."

Jimmy ain't say nothin to that.

Nothin except that, "I did the time fer yeh, ain't I?"

"Yeah. Yessir, you did. Yes, my brother, you did that time fer me…once you had to…and only so's to make sure yer boy, our boy—the child we created together when I jes wanted to know a man could touch me without hurtin me—only so's to make sure he had a mother."

"And because I loved you, Orlena."

"No. If that were true, yeh woulda done it years ago. Woulda done it fer me. You did the time only becausea the boy. And I knew you would. I knew it would be the only way. I knew otherwise yeh'd help me, maybe. Treat me the way I treated you while you'ws on the run. But, unless you had a damn good reason, you wouldn't go down fer me."

"The hell you talkin about, Orlena?"

She crooked a finger, her voice too tired to project all the way up to his height. He knelt beside her, his expression hard as he listened.

"I mean, Jimmy Felder, you absolute *son* of a bitch, that my boy ain't never was yer child. Not no more than he'ws Bert's."

Jimmy said nothing.

Orlena found herself smiling, though her face hurt to do so. It was a small price. Paid gladly to hurt him now: when the thing that would hurt him worst and most efficiently, while she herself was incapacitated on the floor of the stables, was the stark truth of it all.

Of his wasted life.

"I—I knew I'ws pregnant already. And I couldn't do it.

I couldn't do it anymore. It was too much to think that all those things he did to me could bring a life into the world. And what if that life belonged to a girl? I couldn't—I couldn't.

"So, I decided to kill him. But first I needed to make sure you'd help me the way I needed…cause in all the years of our lives since he came back fucked up by that damn war, you ain't never said a cross word to him bout the way he treated me. I knew you ain't likely to kill him, or to go down fer me if I killed him…but if you thought the baby in my belly was yers…"

"Y'er an evil bitch," said Jimmy.

"I had to survive."

"And you cost me my life! Two years on the run, three in prison, more if I hadn't been busted out—I only joined the Stone Hill Gang on accounta otherwise I'd be dyin on my own out in the woods while I'ws on the run! You bitch—you bitch!"

"You ain't sinless, Jimmy Felder. Used to be, when a sister wrapped her arms round her brother's neck a little too tight, feara God'd make him tell her 'no.' But you ain't said 'no,' Jimmy. You said 'yes,' 'yes,' 'ye—'"

He punched her in the mouth and left her in the stables to moan in pain alone.

For a long week, bad things happened to Orlena.

She took solace knowing that her body had not miscarried the baby she believed to be growing in it. She reminded herself that many worse things had happened to women all up and down the plains.

She paid special care to move her hands when she was alone. To touch the hay and count to ten and recollect those memories that she could stand to.

To remind herself that she was alive.

She was alive.

Only Death could change that.

Days passed. Activity picked up outside. The men practiced their shooting with religious frequency.

Inside the stables, Orlena practiced sitting up. Gradually managed to limp on her own two feet.

At night, she crept out to wincingly steal provisions of water and jerky. One of the men caught her one time but ain't say nothin. Stood before the gate to make sure she didn't try to leave.

She had not planned on it. She could not navigate the woods at night in her current state. Her vision got a little better every day, but she still could hardly see as normal and her body required very ginger steps. Small steps. She was afraid that any big motion would hurt the baby.

Then again, it was clearly withstanding all this better than she was. Or, maybe she wasn't pregnant…but she had a good sense that she was.

Especially near the end of the week, when she started wakin up nauseous even though she was hardly eatin more than a fistful of food a night.

As well as the baby was holding on, though, Orlena was dealing with a closing winda. Just because she had not lost the child did not mean she would not lose the child if she couldn't have relief from this harrowing state.

She began to ask herself how she could force her way out. How she might manage to kill all the men in the presidio without any of them fending her off. Cook for them again? Poison them.

They probably expected something like that.

And then, one fine night, the fellas had a party. That was what it sounded like, anyway. A lotta hootin and hollerin and clappin round the fire. Smells like cooked meat wafting on the air.

Orlena sat herself up a little when she heard McLintock's laugh among them.

"Reckon it ain't long afore they's back," he said to the rest. "And if Lorenzo ain't back by now, I don't think he's comin back."

"Bet he got himself ate by a mountain lion," somebody yucked.

"More like fell to his death down the hill lookin fer his true lady-love."

Paling, Orlena pressed her hand to her mouth. She lay back against the wall of the stables. McLintock went on, hacking out an ugly laugh.

"Mebbe if'n he picked his boots based on how useful they were rather than how slick they looked, he'd have made it back to town to git shot by us."

Everybody laughed.

Orlena's hand raised from her mouth t'her eyes, which shut against the stinging tears.

"Then I ain't reckon we needed to bust Felder here out," grunted one of the other men. "Yeh kin jes greet the coach with open arms, Wilt…or, should I say, 'Sheriff.'"

More howled laughter.

"Ain't gonna be that easy," said McLintock above it. "On accounta I ain't feel like payin."

"Whatchu mean?"

"I mean I ain't puttin up the money Lorenzo agreed to pay. Way I see it, if'n the Stone Hill Gang intercepts the delivery and the survivors show up empty-handed, I'm doublin my profits… Sh!"

The laughter stopped sharp.

Orlena strained through her sorrow, through the party, to hear what had stopped them.

Hooves.

Her heart seized in her chest. Was this it? Was it Lorenzo, her hero? Riding up the hill like a knight? Her Lohengrin—

"Boys? Boys—y'all up here? Somethin smells *damn* fine!"

"Ah, shit, it's Chrysler—"

The cheers that arose served to sharply deflate every hope Orlena had ever had.

There was no rescue coming.

She lay down upon the stable floor and shut her eyes, fighting back the soul-pain that came upon her to know what she now did.

Breath haggard, Orlena wrapped her arms around herself.

Seemed like if she was gonna get loose, she really would haveta do it herself.

But—maybe she'd think on it tomorra.

Once she'd cried herself out and into the deepest sleep she'd ever known.

Next mornin, she woke up to find her brother over her.

Dressed, shaved, his black hat low over his eyes, he regarded his sister a long while before telling her, "Today's the day. That big job I'ws tellin you bout."

She waited for him to elaborate.

"Ain't gonna wish me luck, huh…all right, well, I kain't blame yeh fer that. Yeh know, Orlena, I been thinkin…I don't know. Must be hard bein a woman, I reckon."

Surprised, disdainful, Orlena laughed. She made sure it was a cruel laugh, so he would know she was laughing at him and not with him.

All the same, he smirked.

"All's I'm sayin is…havin had a few days to think it over, I don't know if I kin entirely blame yeh fer whatche woulda done to me."

"I blame *you* fer everythin that's happened to me," she told him, staring defiantly into his face. "And if I ever see you again, Jimmy Felder, I'm gonna make damn sure you know."

His nostrils flared in substitute for a laugh.

Adjusting his hat, Jimmy rose. Looked at her like he thought about sayin somethin.

Didn't.

Left.

Orlena lay there an hour, sure it was all some kinda trick

and that they'd be back any minute. Soon as one of them clapped eyes on her it'd be bad news, and she wasn't sure how much more bad news the baby could take.

How much more she could take.

After an hour passed, though, she started getting the sense that maybe the coast really was clear.

Orlena stumbled up, navigating through the dim stables and out into the deserted presidio.

Her head hurt from dehydration and probably also from her brother punching her earlier in the week. That one really took her way the hell back when you got right down to it… kinda like the rape. Hardly felt a thing. Weather-watching.

Ain't matter. None of it really mattered on accounta she was gonna make it outta there alive and have Lorenzo's baby. This time, she would be a decent sorta mother.

This time, if a man came to her home in the middle of the night and shot her child right before her own two eyes, she wouldn't feel happy about it.

Not at all.

Though weak until she could get some food in her and get some rest outside of a pile of refuse, Orlena pumped water with all her strength. She gasped to feel it on her face and in her mouth. She drank it all up, lifting her head back for a sharp breath of air while letting the life-giving liquid run all down her front.

Alone as she was, she stripped off her clothes and washed herself in the middlea the presidio. Yes! Clean for the first time since at least a day prior to her captivity. Oh, Jesus, she cried.

More human, she replaced her clothes and limped into the covered kitchen.

Plentya food still here. They was countin on comin back. Orlena cooked up some beans, tearing apart a towel to fix around her waist like a belt into which she slipped a knife she had been allowed to cook with while under supervision.

Then she stood over the stove, staring emptily down at it. Could she make it out of the woods before a fire meant to burn down the presidio expanded into fire that raged through all the timber?

Hell…she wondered if she could even find her way out these goddamn woods without a forest fire at her back. McLintock, that bastard, had brought her to this hell at night. Where could she go to get her bearings?

Orlena was not sure, but she was sure she needed a few hours to recuperate before she could even think of such a thing.

She made herself a meal with all the fixins. Cornmeal porridge, beans, rice, and some salted venison that'd taken a slight turn but was such a relief to smell cookin and taste eatin that she couldn't dream of nothin better. Then, belly full, she took up a bottlea whiskey and sipped idly at it while meandering between rooms of the presidio.

These men lived like goddamn animals. She should not have been surprised. These were the sorta men that called Natives 'savages.' Trashy men, who developed a lotta trash around themselves.

Between the barracks and a patcha weeds that had probably once been a vegetable garden before the heat wave killed the crops there lay a dirty shovel. She picked it up with cold regard for its dirty spade, then went on to the shack. Her brother's demand for his services, no doubt.

Certainly was better than sharin a barracks with the other men, but it still left a lot to be desired. Orlena had the feelin it was once some kinda storage space fer grain; maybe munitions, or some such. Now it had a little cot, unmade from her brother's restless night. Bullets on a shelf. No gun. Some clothes on the nearby chair. She rifled through em, vaguely recognizin a paira trousers.

She faltered.

Orlena held the trousers up in both hands for a long moment.

Shame flooded her to think she hadn't recognized Bert's old clothes.

Whom had she insulted? Her dead husband? His clothes, the clothes she had washed herself hundreds of times?

Orlena stood, almost dizzy, his trousers in one hand and his shirt in the other.

She slowly lowered herself to the edge of the bed and marveled at how good she once had it. Bleedin into an outhouse and cookin in a kitchen that was well-stocked, all to feed a family that thought she loved them.

And now that they were gone, she recognized maybe she had loved them. She had, but she had never bothered showin em because she was too busy resentin the same life that was ultimately so systematic and routine. She had dishonored their memories by bein happy for their deaths.

And she was gonna have to live with herself, with that notion of herself and what it said about her, forever.

She didn't cry, but she did lay down in Jimmy's bed and close her eyes to think awhiles. Husband's clothes held in her arms.

She fell asleep.

When Orlena woke up it was gettin dark out. She answered nature's call and then, inside her brother's hut again, slipped off her tattered, bloodstained, profaned dress and dropped it on the floor.

Feeling as though there were somehow some religious significance of some kind in it, Orlena dressed in her dead husband's trousers and buttoned his shirt over her bosom. Tongue worrying over the split in her lip, she rolled her sleeves to her elbows and found his old belt. She had to cinch it so tight she ended up digging another hole with that dull carving knife. Kept the trousers up, though. Then, hair tied back from her face with a kerchief, Orlena slid the knife into her belt and slung the shovel over her shoulder.

When she stashed her whiskey bottle in Bert's trouser pocket, the glass clinked against something hard.

A sensation as cool and awesome as an angel's kiss slipped over Orlena Felder.

Her mouth opened slightly and, heart skipping a beat, she slid her hand into the pocket of her trousers. Orlena's fingers bushed the cool little object.

With a careful thumb and forefinger, she removed the valuable and held it before her fascinated eyes.

Not a pebble, or a coin.

No.

A gold tooth.

After staring at it in wonder for a few long seconds, Orlena gradually found her lips peeling back into a wide, happy smile.

She laughed; her eyes watered; she pressed the gold tooth to her lips and kissed it.

And, as she did, hooves clopped into the presidio.

Startled, Orlena dropped the tooth back into her pocket and pressed against the door. It cracked open beneath her hand, though she did not need to gaze out after all.

"Orlena?"

Her brother's frantic tone was unmistakable above the pacing horse that, navigating the woods at unnervingly fast speed, now had to loop around the presidio to stabilize itself.

"Orlena," he cried, "Orlena! You still here?"

His bird whistle followed. She said nothing; merely drew herself back into the corner of the hut along the same wall as the door. The shovel in her hands was ready for action. She held it high, ready to swing.

"Ah, shit," said Jimmy from the direction of the stables, raisin his voice to holler again. "Or-len-a! Please! I'm sorry for what happened before, Orlena, please, ah, shit—Rhodes made it back to town and he recognized me. You gotta talk t'him."

She mighta laughed if she didn't want to keep the elementa surprise. She did not laugh. She would never laugh about Jimmy again.

"Christ, Christ—ah, fuck, there's gotta be a gun around here somewheres—"

In a burst of movement, Jimmy slammed open the door of another structure in the presidio and could be heard rifling around through its contents. A minute or so passed before, swearing, he thundered out and tried another.

Another.

Orlena waited, the shovel at the ready.

Finally the sprinting feet came her way. Jimmy burst in through the doora the shack so quick Orlena didn't even have time to hit him.

Not until he'd rifled around the shelves for a few seconds, finding only bullets.

"I ain't find a gun neither," said Orlena, producing a satisfying, visceral leap of her brother outta his own skin.

He whirled around, falling back against the shelves.

Orlena sent the first swing of the shovel right across his ignorant bastard head.

With a noise like one of offense and astonishment, an "Ah!" so intense she almost felt bad, Jimmy looked blindly at his sister and staggered out of his shack. He got two steps before Orlena caught up with him, emerging to swing the spade at the back of one of his knees.

Her name on his lips, he went down face-first in the dirt and lay helpless while his sister beat the ever-loving shit out of him with the shovel.

Orlena's frantic, high-pitched panting filled the air between hard clangs of the metal down against Jimmy's body. For a few seconds he tried crawling away, but it exposed his spine so much he gradually took to curling into a tight ball with one hand over the back of his neck and the other folded around his side. She screamed and swore incoherently between smashes of the shovel. While the horse nervously looked on, she threw in a few kicks, too.

Eventually he stopped strugglin and just lay there cryin in the fetal position.

Outta breath, Orlena stood over him with hate in her eyes and the tastea blood in her mouth. Clenchin her teeth had resplit her lip. She spat the red mouthful into the dirt beside his head.

Her brother cried and cried. The quiet, soft tears of a man who had nowhere else to go and nothin left to do but experience the inevitable.

"I hope he makes it real slow," she told him, "but I ain't think he will. Likesta get things over with. You'll find out, I reckon."

"Orlena," Jimmy said weakly.

Ignoring him, Orlena dropped the shovel and mounted the horse he rode in on.

The trouble was gettin back to Sandspur. Night was falling. Clouds obscured the stars so that she could not garner the least sensea direction.

All the same, she rode out from between the palisades and did not look back.

For a little while the path seemed reasonably and regularly trod, and that was all well and good; soon enough, though, it was too clustered with overgrowth. Too many possible routes to decide.

The darkness grew dense.

Anxiety flooded Orlena's heart.

Would she have to spend another night here?

What if they came back and found her?

Despair.

Something light moved in the distance.

Deer? Owl?

Breathless with hope that this creature knew its way around even at night, Orlena urged her horse in its direction.

Whatever it was, it was huge—too thin for a bear, though.

It almost looked like a human woman from some angles, but the idea that a woman could be seven feet tall was outrageous.

Suddenly the creature moved with unnerving haste, darting into the trees and disappearing.

Frowning, Orlena kept her horse on at the same pace.

Ten yards later, she discovered a thin patch of trees that released them upon a vast ridge.

The great Texas landscape unfurled for her beneath.

23

THE BULLET BURNED in his back. Every time he moved his left side too much it burned worse; sent a little too much blood surging out. Consequently, Lorenzo limped to the doorway through which McLintock had departed rather than chasing after him. By the time the sheriff had his gun and wits situated to return fire, McLintock weren't nowhere to be seen.

"Give up now, McLintock!"

Where the hell was the other deputy? What in the hell had happened while he was with that strange woman? Everything had gone to pot. He had been right to come back.

Whatever it cost him.

His heart surged rapidly against a new wave of pain. Gritting his teeth, Lorenzo leaned around and scanned the street.

McLintock popped up from behind a barrel. Fired off a round half a second after Lorenzo had ducked back.

When Lorenzo sprang back out, McLintock was dartin down an alley. The gunfire in the distance was no longer so distant. Only a seconda hesitation. Then, with a half-skip to his step against the urge to limp but the need to be quick, Lorenzo dashed across the street and pressed to the corner of the pharmacy.

By now, the handful of people on the street had cried out. Most had got themselves gone, though one or two remained.

"Git outta here," Lorenzo called.

"We thought you was dead, sheriff," called back one of the gawkers.

"Not yet I ain't—and s'long as I'm alive I aim to keep yer ass safe. Now git the hell outta here."

With a quick twitch of his hand, the sheriff shot the whiskey bottle outta the itinerant's hand. Both onlookers leapt back, then turned tail and scrambled off while Lorenzo cleared the alley.

Another shot fired at him.

Cursing, Lorenzo glanced up to the roof of the pharmacy. Climbing was not an option right now. If he could just get inside the place without alerting McLintock to the sounda the door!

He drew back from the corner, heart pounding, back and side and hip all aching and wet with blood.

Tried to reason it out.

Got discouraged real quick.

But before he tried anything futile, the Good Lord proved He was jes a little better than Lorenzo had always reckoned.

That wild exchange of gunfire and shoutin and swearin and gallopin had officially careened over the bridge. Weren't but a few seconds afore here came the stagecoach with bandits in pursuit.

And who the hell should be drivin but that fella Jack Allen, wrestlin over a revolver with the one and only Jimmy Felder.

Ordinarily Lorenzo woulda shot off his gun fer joy, but instead he took advantage of the arrival to slip into the pharmacy and grab the bell once it had let off a single ding.

"You got roof access," asked Lorenzo of the frightened old man huddling behind the counter.

"Uh—uh—not as such, but y'kin climb out the bedroom winda—"

"Once I'm gone, find somewheres better t'hide till the shootin stops."

"Yessir, Sheriff. Sheriff—"

Lorenzo paused.

"I'm sure glad y'er back."

"Me too, Mr. Winston. Me, too."

Upstairs, loading his gun as he went, Lorenzo passed through and cleared a pair of small rooms over the shop. Found the bedroom and the winda recommended. Quiet as he could, Lorenzo opened it with a glance at the firefight on the street.

Damn! What a scene.

Allen had holed behind the stagecoach, havin shot the horses free to prevent a hijack. A ranchero the sheriff recognized lay dead in the street and another crouched just within the doorway of the sheriff's office, havin evidently gone down the street to find help but come up empty-handed.

Meanwhile, up the ways, what looked like five sonsabitches had set up their own camps with rifles behind any and all cover they could find.

The two groups exchanged a bursta fire round about the same time Lorenzo opened the winda, but after a useless report both sides seemed to perceive they was only wastin ammunition till an openin presented itself.

"Ain't no needta lose yer lives," called onea the robbers. Unseen and quiet as he could be, Lorenzo grit his teeth against the pain of leaning up outta the winda and gettin a grip on the edgea the perilously shabby wooden roof.

Ah, hell! The strain of dragging himself up made him feel like he was fixinta puke. Face red, breath hissing through his teeth, Lorenzo pulled through the pain and clambered atop the pharmacy with a gasp of relief once he fell flat upon it.

Beneath him, negotiations continued.

"McLintock to us Sheriff's already been gone near two weeks! Dead in the woods, prob'ly. He ain't even roundta pay yeh."

"I ain't in it fer money," Allen called back, quietly loading his gun where he crouched behind the coach. Wheezing against the pain and sparing only a quick glance down at the blood soaking the back of his white shirt, Lorenzo rolled back toward the edgea the roof. Made sure Allen would have it handled.

Now it was only four men crouchin up the street theres.

Nostrils flaring, Lorenzo scanned the street up and down.

After a brief whisper-consultation, the robbers called back through their mouthpiece, "Y'er Rhodes, aintcha?"

"That's onea the things they call me," answered the Man whom Lorenzo knew as Allen.

"Y'er the one what's fixinta bed down ol Jimmy. Ain't nonea us care none about him, neither!"

The three other robbers laughed just as Lorenzo caughta glancea somebody at the backa the sheriff's office.

Hands slick with sweat, Blaze unholstered his gun.

"What you thinkin, Rhodes? Say yeh lay down them arms and we let you kill Jimmy so's we don't hafta!"

"Sounds mighty fine," said Allen, studying the gun he clearly had no intentions of relinquishing. "What say yehs all step out here in the open. We kin shake on it."

Their laughter stopped. The four of them exchanged uncomfortable looks.

The one separated from the others, his sights set toward

where he knew Allen to be, sidled up to the moutha the alley with his gun at the ready.

Lorenzo shot him twice, heart and head, aborting a high scream. Gunfire caused Allen to whip his revolver toward the roof.

The Sheriff and the Man locked eyes.

Allen followed the aim of the Sheriff's gun while he leaned around the coach to note the dead body.

Onea the robbers took a shot that missed, but renewed the firefight.

With little more than a brief nod to the roof, the Man called Allen and Rhodes and what the hell ever else threw himself back into exchanging bullets.

Lorenzo leaned up and relaxed his gun hand for a few seconds.

Having figured his intent and made his own way up to the pharmacy's roof, McLintock cocked his revolver.

Lorenzo twisted at the sound, more blood surging from his side while he blind fired.

McLintock's head jerked back, his red eye socket looking as shocked as his open mouth.

He weren't shocked, though.

Never would be again.

Body fell to its knees, then face-down upon the roof.

Panting, his skin clammy and his kidney on fire, Lorenzo crawled to the edgea the roof. Thought he'd been shot again, maybe. Didn't want to see.

Gunfire continued beneath him.

It was all so strange.

A man could do anything—be anything, by God, if he had the will—and so many chose to be this.

Just this.

What in the hell.

24

BULLETS PINGED AROUND the coach while the Needless Man awaited a break. At least, an alternative to sittin and waitin fer another fella to get wise and sneak up on him while he was unawares.

Hadn't known what to makea the sheriff when leavin town. Good man after all. Reasonable shot, too.

Up the ways, the men whispered harshly to one another. From the doorway of the sheriff's station, the ranchero hissed, "What you think they're plannin?"

"Ain't sure. Prob'ly fixinta go four ways and box us in."

"What the hell do we do?"

"Kill em 'fore they kill us," the Man answered.

With their whispering, he took a chance to dart from the coach to the sheriff's station into which he pushed the ranchero. Another useless shot knocked a board off the swinging door that stayed open an extra few seconds before warily flapping shut.

"Wonder if it's true what they said about the sheriff bein gone," the ranchero pondered while the Man, striding by empty cells without a second look, shot off the padlock of a door on the far side of the room.

"If it was, he's back now."

The Man made short work of the rusted padlock's neglected remains and kicked open the door.

Would seem as though most of the munitions had been raided, if indeed the gang'd had control of the town or access to someone who did during the sheriff's absence. The Needless Man hurried in to pick through the ammunition and, while reloading his gun, spied a Colt that had gone unnoticed amid the favorable rifles—and, from the hiss that arose suddenly outside the station, something else undeniably worth the attention of any robber.

The Needless Man exhaled and loaded the second gun while stepping out of the munitions closet.

"What's that," asked the ranchero softly, crouched behind the desk.

"Sounds like dynamite."

"What!"

The ranchero's cry was drowned out by the explosion. While the Man ducked down beside the ranchero, rubble burst. The building rumbled open to the nearly night sky.

A few drops of rain started to fall.

Before the dust settled, the Man bolted upright and shot two men dead, one with each hand. Their silhouettes had just begun to appear through the cloud of dust; it was all he needed.

Them dead, he darted into the street and shot the first man he saw, havin anticipated any robbers would have their attention focused on the big-ass hole in the wall and not the front door.

While this fella screamed and fell to the ground, his remaining comrade made a choking noise not entirely due to the dust.

The Man stepped around the corner.

Eyes wild, the bandit scrambled away.

The Man shot him in the back of the head from fifteen yards.

He learned his lesson from the Comanche.

Slowly, the dust dissipated.

Thunder cracked across the landscape from the no-longer-so-distant genesis of the storm. A few more drops picked up a steady beat.

As he holstered his Schofield and slid the Colt into the backa his belt, a horse that had been runnin unheard amid the ringin in his ears stopped beside the coach at the behest of its rider.

The Man whistled low. Still bleeding from a scrape across the temple of his forehead, Roaring Bear dismounted the horse he had taken into town. His motions were hurried as he threw open the door of the stagecoach to stare inside with frightened eyes.

Only then did his posture relax.

"Yer little buddies all right in there, hoss?"

"A few loose," said the Brave, glancing up. "A damaged container. I am sorry I did not make it back to help you, my friend."

"Think nothin of it. Jes help me by dealin with all this and tellin what folks need tellin, so's I ain't gotta. There's somethin I need to see to."

"And when it is finished?"

"And when it's finished, I ain't comin back."

Nodding, Roaring Bear crossed to take the Needless Man's hand in Western fashion.

"I may stay here for some time longer than I once anticipated, myself. Safe travels, my friend."

"You, too, brother."

One of the stage horses had wound up in somebody's garden two streets over. The Man let it finish up its carrot and then, divesting it of the apparatus he had previously destroyed rather than remove, he mounted its back.

They had not ridden together two hours before crossin paths with another saddleless rider.

Thought it were a young fella at first. Thought it mighta been Jimmy; horse looked the same as the one he runnoft with. Hard to tell in the rain that sometimes slapped in sheets, occasionally flexed back down to a patter, and would then transform into a punishing gale that had made it tempting to stop for shelter in the hills.

He had pushed on, though.

And it had caused his path to cross with Orlena Felder, who recognized him before he recognized her.

She dismounted her horse while he was still twenty yards away.

"Stop right there," she told him, her hand at her hip on a handle of some kind. He couldn't make out what gun it was in the rain. Revolver, mebbe.

"Don't come no closer yet," she emphasized. "Ain't fixinta shoot less you are. Otherwise, I want to talk."

"Talk about why I ain't gotta kill Jimmy?"

"Hell no—hell no."

Now the Man was really listening. The disdain in Orlena's voice was real. Rich and withering.

Her hand dove down past the handle of her weapon and into the pocket of her trousers.

"I have it," she said. "And I aim to give it to yeh if you'll make me a promise right here on it."

"What kinda promise is that, Miss Orlena Felder?"

"That you'll make him suffer," she said, extending her fist and opening it to the lightening rain.

His eyes deceived.

The Man got down from his horse and made his slow, steady way over when he saw that the gun Orlena bluffed with had really been a dull old kitchen knife.

He stood before her, over a full foot taller than the woman who held his gold tooth in her palm.

Well, hell.

Sure enough.

The Needless Man opened his hand.

Orlena set the tooth into it.

He raised it higher than his face and inspected it with one shadow fewer.

Even in the dark and driving rain, it seemed to shine.

"I ain't the typea fella what likesta torture a man less he earned it."

"There's a lotta different typesa sufferin in the world," Orlena told him.

His lip lifted past the top row of his teeth.

Orlena's expression tightened with fear to see him smile.

"Reckon that's jes about the only universal truth there is," he said, closing the tooth in his fist and sliding that fist into the pocket of his duster. "I'll see what I kin do."

"Thank you."

Looking fully intent on saying not a word more, Orlena remounted her horse sideways, then carefully negotiated her leg over its back. Pregnant.

"Never did say whose boy that was, Orlena."

She glanced over her shoulder at him.

"Ain't never gonna see yeh agin, am I?"

"If'n yeh do," said the Man, "I reckon it'll mean you didn't learn anythin the first time."

Her snort of derision also seemed to be one of agreement. Her face turned away.

"Mind yeh don't let Jimmy get too far, now. He's in the presidio up there in that timber."

Beneath the slam of her heels, the horse tore off into the night.

Hand running over his jaw, the Man watched her go until she was a shadow in the blurry dark.

By the time the Man and his horse reached the presidio she'd described, Jimmy weren't nowhere to be found.

Not at first.

The wagon caught his eye on accounta the divots in the dirt that indicated it was moved back and forth quite a lot. Then there was all them boulders piled up to the side, and the one halfway cross the moutha the little limestone mine bored into the rising hill.

The Needless Man stood under cover to roll and light a cigarette.

Smoked the whole thing. Waitin fer Jimmy to launch an ill-advised sneak attacka somekind.

He never did emerge.

Gun in his hand, the Man squeezed past the boulder and down into the dark mine.

Didn't haveta look fer him. His haggard breathing gave him away.

The Man shot through the dark, eliciting a cry as the bullet impacted beside Jimmy's head.

"Now yeh know I ain't need light to shootcha. Come on out."

Without turning his back, the Man stepped out of the mine again. Once more waited under cover.

After a long minute, Jim contorted between the boulder and the mouth of the mine.

Half-fell into the open.

He did not long stay in the mud but forced himself to his feet. His eyes glowed through the night with that same hate that imbued his sister's gaze.

"Go on then. Put me down; this leg ain't never healin right after the whoopin Orlena gave me."

"I reckon you earned it."

Observing his prey was unarmed, the Man slid his Schofield back into its holster.

Jimmy looked at him with scorn.

"Come all this way jes t'have a changea heart?"

"Ain't gotta heart," said the man, "and kain't change, neither."

"Then best git out yer gun and shoot afore I find a way to git one over on you."

The Man shook his head, stepping out from his cover and into the rain to make his way to Jim.

"Nah, Jimmy…ain't fixinta do that, neither. Ain't right killin a man in such sorry shape. And, anyway, I aimta do a favor fer yer sister on accounta she gave me back what you took."

"And what favor is that?"

"I reckon you'll find out after you've had a few weeks t'git patched up," said the Man.

Jimmy's face screwed up while the Needless Man stood a foot before him.

"What do yeh mean?"

"I mean we already spent quite a whiles livin together in close quarters. Compared t'our cell, this place is downright spacious."

The smaller man's face fell, his emotional affectations disappearing into silence.

In that second, Jimmy understood.

The month was long. Waves of rain were not infrequent for the first two weeks, but even once they had passed, Jimmy was a difficult patient. Tried to escape six different times. Each time, the Needless Man caught him before he got two miles. Each time, brought him back to the presidio. Only one time, the last time, about halfway into his recuperation, Jimmy made it all the way through the timber to the banks of the Pecos.

That time, the Man dragged Jimmy up through the timber while tied to the back of a saddle found in the presidio. All through the mud and the bugs and the violent rain.

Jimmy ain't tried runnin from his fate no more. Not after that.

Way the Man saw it, the month was twofold. Gave him a chance to fulfill his promise to Orlena, and gave Jimmy a chance to save his own skin.

He'd done a reasonable enough job escapin prison and survivin through now. Ain't right to throw away a man's life if it weren't in the heata the moment; not unless he had a way to defend himself.

Crippled by Orlena's attack, Jimmy ain't had no way to do that. He mighta managed to fire a gun even with his hand, but his eye had swollen with the impact of whatever she'd used to pummel him. As a result, his aim wasn't worth a shit.

Slowly, though. Slowly but surely, with the passagea time and the food generously hunted by the Needless Man, Jimmy recovered. His eye healed and remained bloodshot another couple weeks before it mended; his walk was acceptable when he limped out of his shack to sit across from the Man at the firepit on rain-free nights, though the Man reckoned Jimmy was right. Never would heal all the way, that knee. Never did feel the need to tell the Man what Orlena beat him with, neither, though he reckoned it didn't really matter.

The Man knew it was time when one afternoon, after the rain had finally ended fer the season, he heard some kinda pingin round back behind that shack.

He stuck his head round the corner.

Sure enough, there was Jimmy with a buncha pebbles in his hand.

Aimin at some target he'd stuck to the backa the shack.

Ping.

Ping.

Ping.

Yes, sir.

It was time.

The next day he woke Jimmy a few hours after dawn.

"Today's the day," was all he said.

Jimmy ain't say nothin.

The Man, poised outside, let him get out and get some water from the pump.

"What say we walk," suggested Jimmy, glancing up at the sky once he'd wiped clean his face. "Seems like a mighty fine day."

So, they walked. The two men made a silent hike down the hillside, through the timber, and down to the plains of Texas.

A rich wind gusted toward Sandspur as they emerged from the timber.

Jimmy turned his face toward it, his chest expanding.

"You got a belt fer me?"

The man unslung it from his shoulder.

Jimmy nodded, affixing it to his waist.

When Jim was ready, the Man set his hand upon his Schofield and slowly reached behind him.

Jimmy's eyes lit to see the Colt.

"If you pick it up afore I'm at least fifty paces back, I'll shoot early."

Jimmy ain't say nothin in response.

The Needless Man stooped to set the Colt on the ground.

Hand still on his Schofield, he made his way back fifty long paces.

Jimmy waited.

"Okay. Go on."

Eyes remaining on the Needless Man for a few long seconds, Jimmy genuflected. Slowly, carefully picked the weapon from the turf. His movements were small and tight, as though he anticipated the Man to go back on his word and take a cheap shot.

He did not.

Eyes lifting to the Man again, Jimmy slowly rose. Slid the gun into the holster.

The Needless Man jerked his chin up toward the distance.

One step at a time, Jimmy backed fifty paces.

The Needless Man lifted his hand from his Schofield.

Jimmy stopped, the wind raising to an intense bluster between them.

"You ready, Jim?"

Jimmy's hand hung low beside his gun.

"I'm ready."

The Man watched him, tongue set against his bottom rowa teeth.

Jimmy watched him back. His eyes narrowed with focus.

The Needless Man's nostrils flared, sweet oxygen blooming in his chest. Filling his brain with a crispness.

A bird in the timber sang to indicate the humans walking through the woods had left.

The Man's palm had slickened with the first drops of sweat.

Jimmy's hand, still hovering by his side, crept slowly in.

His heart beating in his throat, the Needless Man grew aware of the shape and location of his Schofield like he felt his own limbs.

He waited for the slightest twitch from Jimmy.

A white cloud sweetened the horizon.

Jimmy's hand jerked to the gun.

The Schofield fired two rounds: three total cracked in the air.

Gunsmoke curled into the Needless Man's sinuses.

Jimmy stood across the way, the Colt in his hand.

A small smile cracked across his lips.

He made a sound like a laugh.

Blood bloomed in a profane rose across his chest.

Jimmy Felder fell to the ground.

Didn't try to get back up.

The Needless Man holstered his gun.

Closed the distance.

Mouth open, eyes already sliding off into space.

Jimmy stared at God.

He took a last breath in.

The Needless Man breathed in with him.

When the Needless Man breathed out, Jimmy didn't.

Stood there for a few moments.

Buried him.

Ain't put no marker.

When it was done, the Needless Man returned to the presidio.

The horse waited there.

He got on its back.

They left.

OTHER WORKS
FROM PAINTED BLIND PUBLISHING

REGINA WATTS

INDUSTRIAL DIVINITY (2020)

WILD GIRL RUNNING (2020)

DOTTIE FOR YOU SEASON 1 (2021)

THE BURNINGSOUL SAGA (2021-)

I WAS AN OP DEMON LORD (2021-)

BE MY BULLY (2021)

SEDUCED BY SABINE (2021)

MAYHEM AT THE MUSEUM (2021)

IDOL (2022)

M. F. SULLIVAN

DELILAH, MY WOMAN (2015)

THE LIGHTNING STENOGRAPHY DEVICE (2017)

THE DISGRACED MARTYR TRILOGY (2019-2020)

CLEAR LIGHT (2023)

ADA DART

THE RIFT BRIDE (2022-)

FINN VANDERGRIFT

SKINSLUT (2023)

ABOUT THE AUTHOR

Regina Watts is the penname of M. F. Sullivan, founder and flagship author of Painted Blind Publishing. From her cozy home a few universes away from this one, Watts transmits Sullivan stories that are then transcribed and published. Her available titles range from transgressive erotica to psychedelic fiction to horror to romance. Be sure to sign up for her mailing list at hrhdegenetrix.com!

ABOUT THE PUBLISHER

Painted Blind Publishing and its erotic imprint, Painted Blue Publishing, are the brainchild of author and devoted editor to Regina Watts, M. F. Sullivan. Founded in 2015 while Sullivan resided in Tucson, PBP is a house dedicated to bringing readers the finest in consciousness-expanding fiction. Be sure to check out the wide variety of essays available for free at paintedblindpublishing.com to learn more about the company, Watts, and Sullivan.

www.ingramcontent.com/pod-product-compliance
Lightning Source LLC
Chambersburg PA
CBHW051256210726
48287CB00002B/528